'What are you doing here? This is our place! Mine and Kenny's!' he barked at her like an angry terrier.

Jess was a bit scared but the boys did both look younger than her, she was pretty sure of that. So she spoke up with more firmness than she really felt.

'*Your* place? But it's *my* place! I come here every Sunday. I've come for months and months now.'

'Oh, Sundays!' said the white-haired boy beside her with relief. 'That's all right then. Gen'rally, we don't come on Sundays. We come all the other days. Straight after school. And Saturdays. It *is* our place, you know.'

'Nonsense!' said Jess sharply in her bossy, Girl-Guide voice. 'It's *my* place just as much as yours.' She glared back at the boy.

'We'll just have to share it then,' said the other boy up on the bank rather grumpily.

JUDITH O'NEILL

Jess and the River Kids

MAMMOTH

First published by Hamish Hamilton 1985
Published 1990 by Mammoth Books
an imprint of Mandarin Paperbacks
Michelin House, 81 Fulham Road, London SW3 6RB
Reprinted 1990 (three times), 1991

Mandarin is an imprint of the Octopus Publishing Group

Text copyright © 1985 Judith O'Neill

ISBN 0 7497 0047 5

A CIP catalogue record for this title
is available from the British Library

Printed in Great Britain
by Cox & Wyman Ltd, Reading, Berkshire

Contents

In memory of
my mother and father

1
Sunday

It was the last Sunday in January – hot and dry. The minister's sad, Scottish voice droned on and on in the heat. He was praying for all the people in the world and Jess knew it was going to take him a very long time. She had glanced at her new birthday-watch as he'd begun. Twenty past eleven. His record was seventeen minutes and Jess liked to keep a check from week to week to see if he would ever beat it. Mr Adam was a youngish minister – or so everyone said when he first arrived from Scotland just the year before. Jess thought he looked quite old. Almost as old as her father. While Mr Adam patiently told God about the many troubles in the world, Jess opened her eyes and looked up at the window over his head. All the people in the church had their heads well down. All their eyes were closed. Even the minister had his eyes shut tight so nobody noticed that one thirteen-year-old girl was sitting bolt upright in her uncomfortable pew, her eyes fixed on the high stained-glass window.

Her lips moved silently now and then but not in prayer. Jess was counting the tiny, bright panes of red and blue, green and gold, each carefully fenced around with thin strips of black lead. 'Fifty-eight, fifty-nine, sixty, sixty-one . . .' She half heard the minister's familiar plea for 'the sick, the sad and the suffering'. 'Seventy-three, seventy-four . . .' Now it was 'those who fight on the land, those who fight on the sea, those who fight in the air . . .' The war seemed a long way off to Jess as she reached the hundred mark. That would do for today. She was tired of counting and of shifting her eyes slowly and carefully from one little coloured pane of glass to the next. In any case, the minister was getting round to 'our homes and our loved ones' so she knew he was near the end. He always moved from distant problems to those close at hand. Jess stared at the window and, half closing her eyes, wondered for the very first time what all those glinting shapes were really about. Bearded men pulling on the oars of a long brown boat. A green sea. A torn net teeming with fish. Red fish. Gold fish. A beach of yellow sand in the distance and a shining man in long white robes who waved from the shore. 'Amen' said the minister. The end had come at last. Jess looked down at her watch. Eleven thirty-one.

Everyone in the church straightened up and there was a shuffle of coughs and hymn books. Further along the pew Jess could see her mother fossicking about in her handbag, bringing out an old envelope and a stub of pencil. Mum was writing something. As the children's hymn began, Mum passed her note along the row. Everyone in the family read it on its way to Jess. First Nico read it, then Laura, then Dad. Dad passed it on to Jess. 'Dear Jess,' she read, 'Please throw potatoes round roast and set table, love Mum.' Jess nodded and smiled along the row to her mother who now joined heartily, though rather tunelessly, in *All things bright and beautiful*. Escape was near at hand for Jess. The hymn ended and as the congregation sang the long, slow 'Amen' all the children moved out of their pews, squeezing past parents and older brothers and sisters who had to stay in for the sermon. Jess dreaded the day when she would have to stay too. Only a year to go. Now she was quickly up the aisle, out of the door, on to her bicycle and down the road in the blazing heat, white gloves (grey at the finger-ends) flung in her front basket and one hand clamping her white straw hat firmly on her head.

The straggling, untidy palm trees seemed to scream in the midday sun. Up in their stringy leaves and all down their brown, scaly trunks, hundreds of cicadas kept up their endless, raucous noise. Jess pedalled past the red, dusty side-streets, each with its beautiful cool-sounding name. Lime, Pine and Olive lay behind her already as she flashed past Orange and Lemon and, coolest of all, Magnolia. In winter these streets were thick with red mud that clogged up Jess's bicycle wheels until she could no longer turn them. Now, in the breathless heat of January, the dust lay quiet and still, waiting for wind or rain. Jess turned into her own street and into her own front gate. She propped her bicycle against the back wall of the house. The wire door banged behind her and then the back door. A shock of cool, dark air met her in the kitchen. Jess went to the ice-chest first, feeling her way in the dim light. Lifting the lid, she chipped off a bit of ice with an old screw-driver. Sucking the ice, she remembered the potatoes. They lay, pale and peeled, in a blue bowl of water. Jess deftly opened the oven door with her foot and listened to the satisfying, sizzling sound of the roasting leg of mutton. She dried each potato on a tea-towel and threw it neatly into the oven, standing well back so as not to get splashed as it landed in the hot fat around the cooking meat.

A warm and marvellous smell flowed out of the oven. Jess shut the door, again with her foot, and had a look into the fire-box. The fire had burned rather low. She pushed in a couple of splintery pieces of yellow wood and a smallish knob of mallee-root; she slammed the fire-door shut and edged open the ash-pan to set up a good draught. All was now well and when the table in the dining room was set ('*Knives* and forks and *spoons* and forks and *cruet* and glasses and *water*' she chanted mechanically to herself as she did the job) Jess lay on the cool lino on her bedroom floor to read *Tom Sawyer* until the rest of the family came in from church. For Jess this was the most peaceful half-hour in the whole week.

'Well Jess,' said Dad as he carved the Sunday leg of mutton, 'what are you going to do this afternoon? Is it the river again?'

Mr McCallum was a big man, tall and broad-shouldered. He had the deliberate walk and the healthy red cheeks of a Scottish farmer, though any real Scottish farmers were a good two generations back in his family.

'Yes,' said Jess, 'I'm off to the river. If Rona can come, that is.'

'What on earth do you *do* there?' asked Nico. 'It seems very boring to me.' Nico was seventeen, the eldest in the family. He never took Jess very seriously.

'It's *not* boring!' said Jess indignantly. 'We paint and we talk and we swim and we eat and we read. There's *lots* to do.'

'But why go to the river to do it?' put in Laura who was two years older than Jess. 'Apart from the swimming, you could do it all here, right in your own front garden. Why ride all that way in this blazing heat?'

Jess was silent. If they didn't understand about the river, how could she ever explain?

The pudding that day was trifle. It was always trifle on Sundays just as it was always roast mutton and mint sauce. No sherry in this trifle though. Mum didn't hold with sherry. Just good plain sponge cake, red jelly, sliced banana, egg custard and 'lashings of cream' as Mum herself said proudly.

Jess was off and on to her bike as soon as the usual squabble about the dishes broke out between Nico and Laura. It was their turn on Sundays but they always made so much fuss about who would wash and who would dry that often Mum and Dad ended up doing the dishes themselves, just to get some peace and quiet. Rona's house was only round the corner. Jess pedalled quickly there to call for her. Calling really did mean *calling* in that river town. You propped yourself, still seated on your bike, against your friend's front gate. Then you called out her name or even sang it, loudly and clearly, over and over again until at last she heard you and came out to talk with you at the gate. You never walked up the path or knocked at the front door. That was just for grown-ups.

'Ro-na! Ro-na!' called Jess, balancing carefully against the green gate-post. There was no answer.

'Ro-na!' she called again, still more loudly.

The front door was eased open and Rona's young brother came out on to the verandah. His name was James – James Fraser. Never did anyone call him Jim or Jimmy or even Jamie but always James. He was eight. Neat and well-scrubbed was the impression he generally made on Jess. His hair was carefully parted and neatly smoothed down on each side with water; his white shirt was clean and fresh; his khaki shorts still had their sharp crease on each leg; his long socks were kept up with garters and never sagged around his ankles. All James's four older sisters were equally neat. Their long, smooth plaits were rubber-banded firmly at the ends. Rona, Iona, Eriskay and Sandray were their names. 'We're all called after islands,' Rona had once explained to Jess. 'It was Gran's idea.' Jess envied the Fraser girls those long, smooth plaits. Her own hair was short and untidy. Golden, her mother lovingly called it, holding her bright wedding ring against it to prove her point, but everyone else called it ginger and Jess was afraid they were right.

James stood on the verandah in the full glare of the sun, shading his eyes with his hand to see Jess better out at the gate. One foot against the metal letter-box kept her firm.

'Rona can't come!' he shouted to Jess with a note of triumph in his voice.

'Why not?' shouted back Jess.

'Mum says she can't go to the river any more. She says it's far too dangerous. She says Dad wouldn't like it if he knew!'

Jess was stunned. Rona had gone with her down to the river almost every Sunday for months, ever since September when the yellow wattle was out. Rona's Mum had never seemed to mind. What could be the matter?

'*Why* is it dangerous?' she called out to the boy.

'Mum says there might be funny people about.

There might be pickers. So Rona isn't coming any more.'

'Where *is* Rona then?' called Jess.

'She's on her bed, howling and howling,' James bellowed back, 'cos she wants to go to the stupid old river!'

Jess rode slowly home. All the pleasure seemed to have drained out of Sunday. Suddenly the heat was unbearable.

'Back already?' asked Mum, surprised, as Jess stumped in through the back door.

'Rona's not allowed to go. Her mother says it's too dangerous. Funny people about, she says. Pickers!' Jess muttered indignantly. 'And now I suppose you won't let me go either!'

'Why ever not?' asked Mum calmly.

'All by myself?' Jess was amazed. 'What about the funny people?'

'Do you ever see any funny people?'

'No. We never see anyone at all. Except just a few boys fishing now and then.'

'I think you can go by yourself, Jess. You're a sensible girl. Just use your sense, that's all. Draw us a quick map so we'll know exactly where you are.'

Jess grabbed a pencil from the kitchen drawer and an old brown paper bag. She smoothed out its creases with her hand and drew the wide sweep of the river, the dirt track through the bush, the sandy bend and then, marked with a cross, the special place she and Rona had found back in the spring, all shaded by red-gums and right by the water's edge.

'There's the spot!' said Jess, pointing to her bold, black cross. 'It's only about a mile past the sandy bend.'

'Right. Off you go then, Jess, and be sure to leave the river at five o'clock. Not a minute later, mind!'

Jess gathered up *Tom Sawyer*, her apples and biscuits, her paint brushes and little tubes of paint in a toffee-tin, her drawing block, her brown sun-hat with elastic to go under the chin and a tattered, green fly-net hanging from the brim.

'Thanks Mum,' Jess said with a grateful smile, 'see you later!' and she shot out of the door, dumped her things in her bike basket and set off on the long, hot ride to the river.

'Mad!' muttered Nico from where he lay in the front garden under the almond tree.

Jess didn't hear him. She was alone! How lovely to be alone. Rona was good fun and it was a pity she couldn't come but how much better to be going down to the river all alone!

Jess's long ride took her first through the sleepy, Sunday streets of Glencarra, the northern river town where she had lived all her life. Blinds were half down that afternoon to keep out the glare of the sun; no one stirred. Jess rode past all the churches, quiet and deserted now after their brief burst of morning activity. The Anglican church was dark and mysterious, hidden away behind tall yew hedges and gloomy pine-trees. Jess's own church, the Presbyterian, was bold and self-confident, its high steeple dominating the whole town with an air of importance; the Methodist church was ugly, round rather than square, and built in bright yellow brick; the Catholic church stood a block or two away from the rest and always had more confetti scattered untidily over its wide bluestone steps than any of the others. Either they had more weddings in there, thought Jess, or

14

their caretaker was too slap-dash. Jess had never even looked inside that church. She knew no one who belonged there. 'Our friends up the road,' her minister would call them in his kind, Scottish voice when he wanted to disagree with them.

Once out of the town, the smooth road turned to a dusty track patterned with the intertwining marks of bicycle tyres and ridged with hard corrugations. Jess's bike rattled and shook its way along. On both sides of her now lay the wide, green blocks. Jess's mother still liked to call them vineyards but no one ever knew what she was talking about. Blocks was their proper name and blockies were the men who owned and farmed them. The rows and rows of grapevines, held up by an orderly network of posts and wires, were heavy now with grapes, green and purple, waiting for the pickers to descend. Beside each block stood the drying racks, gaunt and empty till the picking began. Behind the racks was the blockie's shady homestead with its wide verandah. And far beyond the furthest row of vines ran the broad irrigation channel, brimming with water from the river, bringing life to the dry red earth.

As Jess thrust down hard on her pedals, standing up on them to heave her bike over the steep rise of the channel bridge, she left all that orderly greenness behind her and rode on into parched, brown scrubland and down towards the Murray River. At the sandy bend she saw a few families picnicking and swimming. The river swept out in a great wide arc here, leaving a beach of smooth white sand, well-shaded by giant red-gums. The track became still rougher now. Jess dodged about to avoid potholes but she could not escape the shuddering corrugations.

Beyond the sandy bend the scrub grew thicker and the trees taller. Jess was out of the burning sunlight now and under the cool grey-green leaves of the gums. The cicadas screeched on and on all around her. There was a sharp turn of the main track to the left and Jess swung her bike down a narrow side-track to the right and past a thick clump of wattles with dust on their feathery leaves. This little track dipped down to the river itself. A semi-circle, about five paces across, had been gouged out of the river bank by some violent flood years ago. Guarded by two great red-gums, whose roots held up the sides of the bank, the floor of the secret place was covered with clean white sand, gritty and rough to the touch. Jess propped her bike against one of the trees and jumped down into her secret alcove, spreading herself out at full length and gathering up huge handfuls of sand.

Jess wasn't going to swim today. If Rona had been here it might have been different but on her own she felt a bit scared of the quiet, powerful river rolling past her. She was no great swimmer anyway, unlike almost all her friends. While they streaked along in the pool or muddy billabong or out across the river itself, clad in shining black 'speedos' and hardly even rolling from side to side, Jess usually just splashed about on the water's edge, doing a few unimpressive strokes and puffing in slight alarm. She never liked to be out of her depth and wanted to be able to feel the soft, squelchy mud under her feet. So today she was content to take off her sandals and dangle her feet in the cool water while she tipped out her store of paint-tubes on to the sand.

Jess was no great artist either. Her passion for painting was a strange one since she could barely draw an apple or a chair, let alone a tree. But painting, she had found to her surprise, was not quite the same thing as drawing. Although she wasn't very good at it, she found it curiously satisfying. She loved the thick worms of bright colours that oozed out of the little lead tubes. She loved their names – crimson lake, burnt sienna, viridian, cobalt blue, ultramarine, chrome yellow. They sounded exactly like the colours they were.

Today Jess squeezed a little dollop of each paint into the round cups on her palette, dipping her brush in the river and paddling it about in each cup. 'Not too much water, Jess,' Mr Sefton, her art teacher at school, used to warn her in lessons. Jess was afraid she'd overdone the water yet again. The blue looked particularly wishy-washy. She sat with her back against the curved bank, a hard root pressing into her shoulder. With the sketch-pad balanced on her drawn-up knees, she set to work. It was the vast trunk of the taller red-gum that she wanted to catch – mottled with white, brown, red and green; rough here and smooth there; patterned with sunlight that strained through the drooping leaves. Dipping in and out of her little wells of paint, plunging the brush into clear river-water between colours, stroking the thick white paper with one full brushful after another, slowly she saw a weird, patterned trunk beginning to emerge. This was Jess's idea of Sunday happiness – alone by the river with a toffee-tin full of paints.

2
The River Kids

A flock of galahs, pink and grey against the brilliant
blue of the sky, flew screeching overhead. The river
was no barrier to them. They swirled noisily
together, high above the quiet brown water, and
filled the branches of an old gum on the far bank.
Silence fell again. Jess put down her brush and sat
just looking at the river. She never tired of looking
at it. Sometimes she and Rona spent half an hour
simply sitting and looking. The water slid past,
smooth and unbroken except for an occasional stick
or a tangle of floating river weed. Brown and green in
the shade of the trees, whiter and almost blue out in
the full sunlight, on and on it rolled. Never ending.
Almost silent but not quite. Jess could just faintly
catch its even, pulsing murmur.

A new sound broke in on her now, carried along
the water from well up river, beyond the sandy bend.
It was the first faint noise of the Sunday paddle-
steamer. For ten long minutes the peace of the afternoon was shattered as the great, lumbering boat
churned its way along that stretch of river. As the
steamer passed Jess, snug in her secret place, she
could see the decks crowded with happy families on
some birthday outing; soldiers in khaki, home on
leave, lounging against the rail; laughing, sky-
larking teenagers; and the sober white-clad figures of
a visiting bowls-team. The enormous paddles swung

round, beating up the frothing water in their path. The old steam-engine chugged and snorted. A tinkling piano or perhaps a pianola played brightly in the lounge and some half-hearted community-singing drifted across the water. The galahs shrieked again and moved on. Slowly the steamer drew further and further away, down the river, until Jess could hear it no more. Now there would be peace for an hour longer until the paddler's return voyage to Glencarra broke the stillness of the bush again. Then it would be almost time for Jess to think of going home.

Her tree-trunk was almost finished and she held the wet painting out at arm's length to look at it, half closing her eyes to make the picture seem a bit better than it really was.

'Not bad,' she said to herself.

Suddenly she heard voices. Then, quite close, she heard feet crunching over the dried sticks and leaves on the little track above her head. Jess was about to jump up to see who it was but then decided it might be better to stay still, not to move at all. Perhaps they'd pass by and not even see her. No such luck. A boy's voice gave a shout as he flew through the air and landed on the sand right beside her. At the very same moment another voice wailed out from the bank by her head.

'Oh look, Snowy, look! There's someone here! Someone's gone and pinched our place!'

The boy on the sand picked himself up and glared at Jess. His hair was so fair it was almost white.

'What are *you* doing here? This is *our* place! Mine and Kenny's!' he barked at her like an angry terrier.

Jess was a bit scared but the boys did both look younger than her, she was pretty sure of that. So she spoke up with more firmness than she really felt.

'*Your* place? But it's *my* place! I come here every Sunday. I've come for months and months now.'

'Oh, Sundays!' said the white-haired boy beside her with relief. 'That's all right then. Gen'rally, we don't come on Sundays. We come all the other days. Straight after school. And Saturdays. It *is* our place, you know.'

'Nonsense!' said Jess sharply in her bossy, Girl-Guide voice. 'It's *my* place just as much as yours. And my friend Rona's too. She comes with me most Sundays.' Jess thought that two sounded much stronger than one so she didn't mention the fact that Rona wasn't allowed to come to the river any more. She glared back at the boy.

'We'll just have to share it then,' said the other boy up on the bank rather grumpily. With that, he jumped down on to the sand beside Snowy.

'This is Snowy,' he said bluntly, 'and I'm Kenny. Who are you?'

'I'm Jess and I'm thirteen. How old are you?'

'Snowy's ten and I'm eleven – nearly twelve,' said Kenny, a bit crestfallen.

'Good,' said Jess with a satisfied smile, 'then I'm the eldest. You can share this place with me if you promise to leave it all clean and tidy. I don't want to find lolly papers left about on the sand when I come on Sundays.' Jess sounded fierce though she still felt scared and half wanted to run away.

'All right,' said Kenny, grudgingly, 'and the same goes for you too. We never knew anyone else came here. It always looks the same.'

'Yes, that's true,' admitted Jess, 'I've never seen any signs that *you've* been here.'

The boys looked at Jess and she looked at them. There was still some suspicion on both sides, a wariness, an uncertainty, a sense of disappointment. The secret place wasn't quite so secret any more. Snowy's white hair, short and untidy, stuck up around his freckled face in a series of wisps and points. Kenny was altogether darker – brown eyes, brown hair and a smooth olive skin.

'Can they really be brothers?' Jess wondered, 'they're nothing like each other.' Only their voices seemed somehow the same, sharp and clear like the yelps of cheerful pups. Their bare legs and feet were so brown, Jess couldn't tell if it was suntan or dirt.

Then Snowy saw the painting.

'That's real good,' he said in surprise. 'Look at it, Kenny. It's our tree.'

'Yep. It's *quite* good,' admitted Kenny. 'Look at the way she's done that rough bit of bark. Are you some kind of artist then, Jess?'

'Well, I'm not much good at it really,' said Jess with unusual modesty, 'but I just like doing it.'

'Did your teacher say you'd got to?' Kenny asked.

'No. I just felt like it.'

Kenny and Snowy looked rather puzzled at this but they let it pass.

'When will you be fourteen?' Kenny asked suddenly.

'Not till next January. I only turned thirteen three weeks ago. I got this watch.' Jess held out her arm so they could see.

'Mm. Next January.' Kenny went on without

more than a glance at the watch. 'Then you'll be able to leave school, won't you? Lucky thing!'

Jess was shocked.

'Leave school? Goodness, no! I'll be at school till I'm seventeen – nearly eighteen,' she said primly.

'Whatever for? Don't you know you can leave when you're fourteen? Everyone does,' said Snowy.

'No, they don't. Everyone *I* know stays on.' Jess sounded smug.

'Whatever for?' It was Kenny asking this time.

'Well,' Jess began patiently, not quite sure what she could say, 'they stay at school because they want to go on to university. Down in Melbourne. That's a sort of school too. Only much harder. You can learn to be a doctor down there. Or a lawyer. Or a dentist. Things like that.' Her cocky speech had rather fizzled out.

'And are you going to be a dentist?' asked Snowy suspiciously, staring at Jess.

'Oh no!' Jess laughed, 'not a dentist. I'm going to be something famous.'

'Like what?'

'Well, Prime Minister, probably,' admitted Jess. There was a long pause.

'But you *can't* be Prime Minister,' Kenny said at last. 'You're a girl.'

'So what?' said Jess.

'Ladies are never Prime Ministers! Never! Have you ever heard of one?' Kenny asked.

'No,' Jess said reluctantly, 'there hasn't been one yet. Most likely I'll be the first.' Her tone was quite matter-of-fact.

Snowy gave a yelp of laughter and grinned at Jess in disbelief.

'What if you're not Prime Minister?' put in Kenny. 'What else will you be?'

'Well, I might be a famous scientist like Madame Curie or a famous singer like Madame Melba.'

'I suppose you'll be Madame Jess,' said Snowy, still half laughing but beginning to be impressed.

'Oh, no! I'll use my full name when I'm famous. Not just Jess. That's only a kid's name. I'll be Jessica Margaret McCallum!' The name rolled off her tongue as if she'd practised it often. There was another pause.

'Heck!' exclaimed Kenny suddenly. 'D'you know what I think, Jessica Margaret McCallum? I think you're a bit stuck-up! A bit too pleased with yourself!'

Jess knew that he was right really. Stuck-up, bossy and hot-tempered. It was her ginger hair that did it, Jess was sure. But she wasn't going to admit all that to a couple of kids. So she quickly changed the subject.

'What will you do, Kenny, when you leave school?'

'The day I'm fourteen, I'm going to leave,' he said emphatically. 'That'll be in the July but I'm not waiting on at school till the end of the year. No fear! I'm getting a job up on Mr Reardon's block. He's promised me. That's where Dad does the pruning every year.'

'What'll you do there?' asked Jess.

'Everything!' said Kenny. 'I'll do the lot! Pruning. Rolling on. Picking. Dipping. Packing. Then there's all the citrus. Everything! It's a real good job.'

'What about you, Snowy?'

Snowy looked glum.

'I dunno,' he said. 'I want to be a grocer but Kenny says that's silly.'

'No, it's not silly,' said Jess. 'My friend Rona's

23

Dad's a grocer. Or he was. Before the war. Just now he's a prisoner-of-war in Burma. When he comes back he'll just put on his white coat and be a grocer again. You could work in his shop, Snowy. It's up in Orange Avenue.'

Snowy looked pleased.

'See!' he said to Kennny.

'Do you ride your bikes out here every day after school?' Jess suddenly asked. 'It's a terribly long way from the town.'

'We don't live in the town,' said Kenny. 'We live just near here. Round the next bend.' He waved a hand vaguely down the river.

'I didn't know there were any houses near here. I thought it was bush for miles,' said Jess.

'So it is. But we don't live in a house. We live on the river. In a boat,' said Kenny.

Jess stared.

'In a boat? Like Noah's ark?'

'Sort of. But there's no animals. Just me and Snowy. And Dad when he's home. And Mum'll be back soon. With Annie.' Kenny's information came out in jerks.

'Are they both away? Your Mum and Dad?' Jess sounded worried. 'Who looks after you?'

'Old Lizzie does,' said Kenny. 'She lives next door. In a funny old paddle-boat tied up next to us. The paddles don't work, of course. Our boat is bigger than hers. It's a barge, really.'

'Why don't you come and see?' asked Snowy, who hadn't been able to get a word in till now.

'Yep,' added Kenny. 'Old Lizzie'd like to meet someone who's going to be famous. *She* was going to be famous once only it didn't work out.'

'I'd like to come,' said Jess, 'but I can't. I promised Mum I'd only go to this spot. But I could ask her about next week. Probably she'd let me come and see your boat then.'

'She'd never even know if you came today.' This was Snowy. He grinned at Jess but she only looked worried. Kenny gave Snowy a kick with his bare foot.

'OK Jess,' he said. 'You ask your Mum. We'll come here next Sunday. You come here too. Then we'll take you to the boats. Old Lizzie'll be real pleased, won't she Snowy?'

Snowy nodded.

'What's your proper name, Snowy?' asked Jess. Snowy didn't answer. His face went very red.

'Go on, Snow! You might as well tell her,' said Kenny, laughing.

'It's Leo,' mumbled Snowy, turning still redder and pushing his heels through the sand, 'but don't you ever call me that! I hate it!'

'All right. I won't. What about you, Kenny? Is it short for Kenneth?'

Now Kenny looked awkward and even annoyed.

'No. It isn't,' he said. 'It's Kenelm.'

'Kenelm?' Jess repeated slowly. 'Is that a made-up name? Did your Mum make it up?'

'No! Of course she didn't make it up,' Kenny was indignant. 'It's a saint's name. Saint Kenelm.'

'Is it in the Bible?' asked Jess doubtfully, 'like David and Goliath? I don't remember it.' She looked at him suspiciously.

'I don't know about the Bible,' said Kenny, 'but it's a proper saint all right.'

'Probably it's Moses' second name. Moses Kenelm,' said Jess in a kindly voice. 'That's probably why I haven't heard of it. I don't know everyone's second name in the Bible.'

Kenny didn't look at all convinced but he said cheerfully, 'prob'ly is.'

The churning, chugging, tinkling paddle-steamer was on its way back from its Sunday jaunt down the river. Jess and the two boys could hear it coming long before they could see it.

'There's the boat,' said Jess rather sadly. 'I've got to go now. Five o'clock.'

She stood up and put on her sandals. The boys helped her pack up her paints and her paper block. They shoved everything higgledy-piggledy into her bike-basket.

'See you next week then,' she said as she wheeled her bike from the big tree.

'Yep. See you later, Jess,' said Kenny.

'Madame Jess,' added Snowy, half under his breath. Jess wasn't sure if she'd heard him right. She decided to let it pass. She rode off down the dry track, perched uncomfortably on a bike saddle that was still hot from the blazing afternoon sun.

3
Old Lizzie

It wasn't as easy as Jess had expected to ask her mother about next Sunday. She tried to raise the subject casually a couple of times but then lost her courage at the last minute.

'Mum?' she began on Monday at tea time as the family sat round the kitchen table.

'Yes dear.' Mum was clearing away the dirty plates and the pot of Irish stew.

'You know when I was down at the river yesterday?'

'Mmm.' Mum was busy dishing up the apple crumble.

And then, somehow, Jess couldn't go on. She had the feeling that her mother might not like the idea of her visiting two grubby boys and an old woman who lived on the river in broken-down boats. So she quickly changed to, 'I saw that paddle-steamer go down the river. Full of people, it was.'

'Yes, of course, dear. It goes every Sunday.' Mum paused with the serving spoon in the air and looked at Jess in a puzzled way. Then she went on dishing up the apple crumble.

On Wednesday, Jess had a chance to try again. On that day Jess had double art at school – the best lesson of the week. The art teacher, Mr Sefton, was kind and gentle. Rowdy classes of children splashing paint about were almost more than he could bear but he never lost his patience.

'Jess McCallum!' he said wearily on Wednesday afternoon, 'there you are talking again. Can't you *possibly* paint without talking?'

'I don't really think I can,' said Jess honestly.

'Don't you realize that if you talk for just one minute out of three, by the end of this year you'll have talked for one whole term out of the three? By the end of six years in this school, you'll have talked your way through two of them! That's far too much time to waste.'

Jess was impressed by these unexpected figures.

'I'll really try to keep quiet,' she said meekly.

She did try but it wasn't easy. Rona was just beside her and the temptation to keep up a constant, running conversation was hard to resist. They were doing posters that day in thick, bold colours. 'Dig for Victory', 'Travel by train', 'Save petrol and save lives'. Jess had produced her usual picture of a Pacific Island – one ragged palm tree with bright green leaves, one sailing ship, one brilliant yellow sunset streaked across the sky. Underneath this scene, drawn partly from what she imagined a Pacific Island must look like and partly from faded brown photographs on her Sunday School wall, she printed her poster's message.

Come to the New Hebrides for your Honeymoon

Mr Sefton came and looked over her shoulder. He was smiling at her palm tree, sailing ship and sunset.

'Jess, you always do that sort of picture! Can't you do any other tree but a palm tree?' he asked.

'Oh yes,' said Jess, 'I do gum-trees when I'm down by the river but I didn't think they'd look any good on a poster. As a matter of fact, I brought one to show you. I did it last Sunday.'

Jess delved into her bag on the back of the chair and pulled out a cardboard roll. Inside the roll was her gum-tree picture. Mr Sefton shook it out and unrolled it. He held it well out in front of him, leaning back and looking at it carefully. He was surprised.

'Jess, that's *very* good! Miles better than your usual

28

old palm trees and yellow sunsets. I do like the way you've got the texture of the trunk. And the way that branch comes in there. It's really splendid! You must do some more.'

Jess went pink with pleasure. It was nice to be praised. Perhaps she could be a famous artist as well as Prime Minister.

Telling her mother all about Mr Sefton and the gum-tree picture that night, Jess seized the chance to mention the boys.

'By the way, Mum. I met a couple of boys down at the river on Sunday.' The words tumbled out quickly, one on top of the other.

'Boys?' Mum sounded suspicious. 'I thought you never saw anyone.'

'Usually I don't. But these two little kids came along. Snowy and Kenny, they're called. They're only ten and eleven. Much younger than me.'

Then all the rest came out in a rush.

'They live in a boat. And their mother and father are away so Old Lizzie looks after them. She lives in the paddle-boat next door. And they asked me if I could go and see their boat next Sunday. Can I go, *please* Mum?'

Mum looked doubtful.

'I don't know about that. It's very lonely down there on the river. And we don't know these people, do we? It sounds a bit odd to me. The father and the mother both away. Where are they?'

'I don't know. The boys said they'd be back soon.'

'Well, I'll think about it. I'll see what Dad says. But I don't think he'll like the idea.'

Mum was right. Dad didn't like the idea at all.

'We can't have you traipsing about on the river

29

bank with people we don't even know, Jess,' he said firmly.

Jess saw there was no hope. Then Laura had a good idea. Generally she poured scorn on Jess's schemes but this time she was helpful.

'Mum, why don't you and Dad drive down there and have a look? The boat must be only a couple of miles past the sandy bend. It's a rough track but not too bad. Then you could see this Old Lizzie person for yourself. You must admit it's more peaceful here if Jess goes to the river on Sundays.'

'Oh yes. Go on Mum!' put in Jess.

'I suppose we could,' said Mum uncertainly. 'But I wouldn't like this Old Lizzie, whoever she is, to think we'd come to look her over. We'd have to make up some excuse. What do you think, dear?' She turned to Dad.

'Righto,' said Dad suddenly, very much to Jess's surprise. 'We'll go down after work tomorrow and just see what the set-up is. But mind you, Jess, I'm not promising you can go on Sunday. It depends what we find. I want to give you plenty of freedom but there are limits you know.'

So when Dad got in from the office on Thursday, soon after five o'clock, he backed the old Ford V8 down the drive and Mum got in beside him. The day had been hot and sticky but the cool of the evening was just setting in with a bit of a breeze from the south. Jess waved from the front verandah as they set off on what Laura called their 'tour of inspection'. Then she wandered slowly inside to listen to the Children's Session from the big, square wireless in the corner of the front room. Spread out on the carpet, with her head on a cushion that was jammed up close to the set, Jess half escaped into a world of Greek heroes where valiant argonauts tossed about on the wine-dark seas, rowing on and on towards the land of the Golden Fleece. The other half of her mind was with Mum and Dad as they rattled down the red, sandy track to two old boats tied up on the Murray River.

Mum and Dad were away for ages. The Children's Session came to an end with a gripping serial called 'Bill of Yarrawonga'. Laura peeled the potatoes. Jess shelled the peas, scattering a good few over the kitchen floor in the process and eating a good few more; Nico stoked up the fire stove at last after Laura had asked him three times. When seven o'clock came and still no sign of Mum and Dad, Laura decided they'd better eat. The meal was already an hour later than usual and no one could wait a minute longer. Nico sliced up the cold meat. It used to be called 'German Sausage' once, as Jess could just remember, but in these days of war patriotic shopkeepers had renamed it 'Victory Sausage'. The taste was exactly the same. The pudding, made by Laura, was Jess's favourite. This recipe had come down from Grandma, and was called Hole-in-the-centre. A plain, domed cake was cooked on a white enamel plate. Laura cut off the top of the dome and filled up the hole with raspberry jam, squashing the cap back on again so rivers of jam trickled down the sides. With creamy top from a bottle of milk in the ice-chest, the hot pudding was delicious.

The meal was over and still Mum and Dad had not come back from the river. It was all very odd. Nico and Jess actually did the washing up without argument or fuss. Laura kept going out to the front gate to see if the familiar car was coming. By nine o'clock the sun had set and the street was quite dark. Jess began to think of terrible, crazy possibilities. Perhaps her father had missed a turning in the track and driven straight into the river. Perhaps a gang of wicked robbers had sprung out at them from the shadow of the boats. Perhaps Old Lizzie had turned out to be a witch and had spirited them away or changed them into trees. Laura thought these ideas of Jess's were ridiculous.

'Go and have your shower, Jess, and get into your pyjamas for pity's sake. You know you're supposed to be in bed by nine o'clock.'

Laura was unbearably bossy tonight but for once Jess didn't argue. She did exactly as she was told. All clean and fresh from her hot shower and clad in her ancient pink pyjamas that had been Laura's before they were hers and came only halfway down her legs, she jumped into bed and lay there, stiff and still, waiting for Mum and Dad to come back.

Jess's bed was in the sleep-out. Everyone else in the family slept inside in a proper bedroom with four solid walls and a carpet on the floor but her bedroom was more like a birdcage than a room. On two sides the walls went only three feet up from the ground. The top half of these walls was a screen of fine-mesh wire-netting to keep out the flies and mosquitoes and to let in the fresh air. It was supposed to be very good for the health to sleep bathed in waves of fresh air and, as Jess was a prey to colds and coughs, the general feeling was that this sleep-out was the only sensible cure. In summertime, Jess loved to lie in her airy cage, looking up through the wire-netting at the stars that winked brightly through the mesh and enjoying the cool breeze that often sprang up at the end of a scorching hot day. With only a white sheet to cover her, she felt she was camping in space. But in winter, when the nights were cold and frosty and Jess huddled down under a pile of blankets with nothing but her nose sticking out, she found it hard to believe that all this fresh air was doing her any good. On the floor was a square of cold, green lino; the high and old-fashioned bedstead of white-painted ironwork had been bought second-hand from a hospital; there were no curtains to muffle the breezes as they flowed freely through the wire screen.

There was not a breath of a breeze tonight as Jess lay there waiting and wondering. Why were Mum and Dad taking so long? What had they found at the river? What did they think of Old Lizzie? And of Snowy and Kenny? Would they let her go there on Sunday?

Jess drifted off to sleep but woke up suddenly when the lights of the car lit up her sleep-out. She lay and listened. The car doors slammed and she could hear her mother and father laughing and talking together as they came out of the garage and walked round to the front of the house.

'Shshsh!' she heard her mother say softly, 'you'll wake Jess,' but Jess's father just went on laughing his loud, hearty laugh that seemed to shatter the quiet darkness of the sleeping street. Jess leapt out of bed, pulled on her red dressing-gown, and ran in bare feet to the hall just as her parents opened the front door. Laura appeared from her room at the very same minute, looking rather stern, like a mother when her teenage children have been out far too late.

'Where *have* you two been?' she began in her

severest voice. 'We've all been very worried about you.'

Nico came dripping from the shower with a towel wrapped round him. Dad was still laughing.

'Well, Jess,' said her mother with a smile, 'we've had a lovely evening! Snowy and Kenny are the sweetest little boys I've seen since Nico was that age.'

Nico gave a snort and hitched his towel tighter.

'I was never *sweet*,' he said indignantly. 'But what about this Old Lizzie? Is she sweet too?'

Mum and Dad looked at each other and smiled. Dad spoke first.

'No, I wouldn't say she was sweet exactly. It's not the right word. But she's a remarkable old lady all right. I haven't enjoyed myself so much for years! The stories she told us, Jess! You're going to have a grand friend there in Old Lizzie!'

'Yes, Jess, you can certainly go down and see her on Sunday,' put in Mum. 'You're in for a surprise or two. She's nothing like the kind of person I imagined. In fact she's nothing like anyone I've ever met before.'

'What *is* she like then?' squealed Jess, hopping from one pink-pyjamaed leg to the other. 'Tell me! Tell me! You've said nothing yet! Nothing at all!'

Dad just began to laugh again and went off to the kitchen to make everyone a cup of tea.

'Wait till you meet her, Jess,' said Mum. 'I couldn't begin to describe her. You'll see her for yourself on Sunday. But I'll tell you just one thing.'

'What is it?' asked Jess.

'Old Lizzie is deaf! Stone deaf! She hasn't heard a thing for forty years!'

4
Dust!

Never had two days taken so long to pass – or so it seemed to Jess. Friday was weighted down with lead and moved with slow and heavy steps. School, of course, was quite enjoyable. It usually was. But Jess's mind was not on school. She sat through every hot lesson, half turning towards the open windows, thinking about the river, the two old boats and next Sunday. She and Rona spent their lunch-time in a far distant corner of the playground where no one else ever came. They lay in the long grass under a drooping peppercorn tree with its bunches of dusty pink berries. Jess told Rona what little she had been able to glean from Mum and Dad about their visit to Old Lizzie. Rona's eyes widened. She was half envious and half horrified. She wished she could be going with Jess next Sunday to meet this deaf old lady and the two boys who lived on the river but at the same time she thought it all sounded very odd.

'I told Mum you'd met those boys,' Rona said, a trifle smugly, 'and she said she was very glad she hadn't let me go with you. Worse than pickers, she said they were.'

'Nonsense!' said Jess sharply.

Rona changed her tone and began to excuse her mother.

'Well, you know what it's like for her with Dad

away all this time. She thinks she's got to be very strict with us. If only Dad could come home, things would be different.'

'When will he come home, do you think?' asked Jess, feeling rather guilty that her own father wasn't a soldier too.

'Not till the war's over. It could be years, Mum says. She writes to him every week but he's not allowed to write back. We don't even know if he gets Mum's letters. We all write a bit at the bottom. Just stuff about school, you know.'

'Haven't you heard *anything* from him?'

'We get a post-card through the Red Cross every six months. It just says he's alive and well. Nothing else. It's a sort of grey-coloured card with printing on it. Mum keeps them on the mantelpiece.'

Jess picked a long grass stem and used it to wave the flies away.

'What's he like really, Rona?' she asked.

'I'm not sure,' said Rona. 'It's three years since he went off. I can't really remember what he looks like. Mum's got a photo in her room but when I look at it I can't seem to remember him. I *do* remember how he used to play the drum in the Highland Pipe Band. He could twirl the sticks right up over his head and let them go and catch them again. The whole Pipe Band joined the army together. They marched right through the town and played all the way down to the station.'

'Yes, I remember that too. I saw them go.'

'Now they're all prisoners. Building a railway in Burma, that's all we've heard.'

'It's hard for your mother,' said Jess.

'Mmm. Every day she's waiting for a letter from

Dad. She listens for the postie's whistle and runs out to the box. But the letter never comes.'

The school siren wailed out across the playground. Time to go back inside. Jess and Rona dragged themselves up to their feet and tried to smooth out the creases in their checked green dresses.

The next day was Saturday. Jess had to do the usual messages. A long wait in the butcher's first to buy the leg of mutton, with her mother's black purse and the ration books all ready. Then a quick dash to the fruit-and-vegie shop around the corner. Then into the centre of town for a few odds and ends from Woolworths. The blockies were all in town for their Saturday shopping and the wide streets were lined with their dusty utility trucks.

At the corner bookshop with its narrow stairs up to the first floor, Jess spent her usual hour sitting on the second step from the top, reading the books of poetry that nobody ever bought. The shop was as good as a library to Jess. She loved the feel of soft leather bindings in her hands, the crinkle of thin, thin, rice paper, the shine of gold-edged pages, the magic sound of the words inside:

> Break, break, break,
> On thy cold grey stones, O Sea!
> And I would that my tongue could utter
> The thoughts that arise in me.

The shop-keeper didn't seem to mind Jess sitting up there on the stairs every Saturday and never buying a book. He was far too busy selling ink and newspapers in the crowded shop below. Perhaps he didn't even notice her.

Jess frittered away the whole afternoon. It was too hot to do much. Rona had gone swimming at the baths but Jess couldn't be bothered riding down there in all that heat. She did a bit of gardening with Dad, trundling the wooden wheelbarrow full of weeds to the incinerator out the back; she did a bit of cooking with Mum, making oatmeal biscuits and chocolate cake in the kitchen. But her heart wasn't in any of the usual Saturday pleasures. She kept thinking of Sunday.

She decided to go to bed very early in the hope that the night would pass more quickly. On one chair she set out all her church clothes neatly – white socks, white gloves, white hat, best dress, clean underclothes, best shoes; on the other chair she arranged her river-clothes just as carefully – red shorts, blue shirt, sandals, old hat with the green fly-net. Jess had her shower and got into bed but sleep wouldn't come. The night was tense and breathless. With only a cool sheet over her, Jess still felt the dry heat prickle and burn along her legs and arms. She tossed this way and that, trying to find a comfortable position in the hard bed. She got up and padded into the kitchen for a drink of water. She tried reading for a while. She sang a few Guide songs, rocking rhythmically from side to side in her bed. At last she fell asleep, dreaming of old boats riding on the quiet river.

When Jess opened her eyes early the next morning, she sensed at once that something was wrong. The sky through her wire screen looked ominously dark. A hot, restless wind was lashing at the verbena bushes outside. Already there was grit between her teeth.

'Dust!' groaned Jess out loud. 'Dust! And on my river day!'

No one else was stirring yet but, with the dust-storm coming, Jess rushed in and woke up the whole family.

'Dust's coming, Mum!' she called as she started on the windows. Everyone hurried out of bed and ran around in cotton nightdresses or pyjamas, not pausing for dressing-gown or slippers. First they slammed down the windows that had been wide open all night to catch the slightest breath of wind. Dad went outside and unrolled the thick canvas blinds around the verandah and the sleep-out, tying them firmly down so they couldn't flap or bang in the wind. Laura drew down the brown blinds inside the house, one for each window, and stuffed a wad of newspaper under the front door. That was where the north wind always blew the dust straight in. An old sheet went over the piano, another over Grandma's antique table, another over the good sofa.

'That'll be enough,' said Mum with a resigned sigh. 'There's nothing much more we can do. The dust always gets in somehow. Let's have breakfast anyway. That might cheer us up.'

Outside the house, the wind was blowing harder and stronger now. Jess lifted the blind in the kitchen and looked out. Pink dust was whirling through the air, beating in thousands of gritty grains on the window-pane, darkening the sky with strange, unearthly clouds.

'Perhaps we needn't go to church today,' she said hopefully, turning to the rest of the family where they sat around the breakfast table. The light was on now that all the blinds were down.

'Of *course* we'll go to church!' said her mother indignantly. 'It takes more than a dust storm to keep the McCallums away from church on the Sabbath. But we might have to take the car, don't you think, dear?' She turned to Jess's father with an uncertain frown wrinkling her forehead. Driving to church was felt by Mum to be almost a sin.

'We *could* stay home, Mary,' he suggested mildly.

'You're as bad as Jess, Arthur!' said Mrs McCallum with a laugh as she began stacking up the dishes. Then she suddenly stopped, a plate in each hand.

'But Jess,' she said, 'I really don't think you'll be able to go down to the river today. Not in a wind like this. You'd be blown right off your bike. You couldn't even see where you were going.'

'Aw Mum! Please, please, please let me go! I'll go to church. I'll do anything. I've been looking forward to it so much. And the boys, Kenny and Snowy. They'll be expecting me. And Old Lizzie. I've got to go, Mum! You know I've got to go!'

'I don't think Old Lizzie, as you call her, would expect you on a day like this, Jess,' said her father. 'Better wait till next week.'

'I can't wait! I can't wait! You know I can never wait!' wailed Jess.

'That's true enough,' put in Nico, 'she never can wait for anything, that girl.'

'Now Nico, you keep out of this,' said Dad sternly.

'Well,' said Mum, 'we'll see. Let's decide after dinner. The storm might be over then. Now all of you get ready for church while I put this roast on.'

'Roast! On a day like this! It's crazy, Mum!' exploded Jess.

'I know dear,' said Mum patiently, 'but I do like to have a proper dinner on a Sunday. It wouldn't seem

40

like Sunday at all without roast mutton, now would it?'

'Some people don't have roast mutton! Some people don't even have to go to church!' muttered Nico.

'Really?' asked Mum, genuinely surprised. 'Don't they, dear? Well *I've* never met them, I'm sure. Now hurry up and get ready, all of you.'

Soon the whole family was ready for church. Mum had on her best navy-blue dress with the white dots and her broad-brimmed navy-blue hat. The girls' hats were white. All three had white gloves and white leather shoes. Dad and Nico were in their neat grey suits and sober ties. Hot and dusty it might be but Mum always insisted that there was a proper way of dressing for church. Dad had agreed to get the car out and Jess had a sense of something delightfully wicked as she climbed into the back seat with the others. It was only half a mile to St Cuthbert's church but today they would arrive there in style. The tall palm trees were being slashed about in the hot wind. Red dust blew in angry clouds around the car making it hard to see more than a few yards in front so Dad crawled carefully along Eleventh Street at ten miles an hour. No one else was about. The streets were deserted. In every house the blinds were down.

A very thin congregation had assembled in church that morning. Most people had decided to stay at home and the few who had braved the dust looked rather pleased with themselves as they settled into their places. Jess thought it would be sensible if such a small gathering moved up to sit together in the front two pews. But no. Everyone went to his usual seat, carefully dusting the gritty bench before he sat down. So there were people dotted about here and there in the vast church with long empty pews between them. All the lights were on, yellow and dim; the singing was ragged and half-hearted. *From Greenland's icy mountain* seemed to Jess an odd choice for a day like this but at least it gave her a cool picture to think about as she sang. The minister was brief. He must have felt grateful to the faithful little flock who had come to church at the height of a dust-storm and he prayed the shortest prayers Jess had ever heard him utter. She sat through the sermon rather than walk home alone in the swirling dust but she didn't pay much attention to it. She listened anxiously instead to the wind outside and wondered if it was beginning to drop.

Over dinner, the family argued about whether Jess could go to the river or not on a day like this. All except Jess were agreed that it would be madness to go. The windy ride could actually be dangerous. The boys would surely not be expecting her. Everyone at home would be worried about her. Jess kept insisting that she'd be perfectly all right. She had almost given up hope when a slight lull in the dry, raging wind outside made her father think the storm was ending.

'It sounds as if it might be easing up, Mary,' he said to Jess's mother. 'We might as well let the girl go. She'll drive us mad if we keep her cooped up here all afternoon. I'd like some Sunday peace.'

Mum agreed reluctantly.

'You'd better take this jar of marmalade to Lizzie then. She was so kind to us the other night. Ride carefully so it doesn't break. And Jess, you *must* leave the river at five o'clock. Not a minute later.'

42

'All right, Mum,' said Jess meekly.

'There'll be no pleasure-steamer on the river today,' added her mother, 'not in a dust-storm like this, so you'll have to rely on your watch.'

Jess was a model of helpfulness for once, clearing the table, drying the dishes though it wasn't her turn, sweeping the floor, all with great speed and efficiency. Then off with her church clothes, on with her river clothes and out the back door to her bike. She rode off into the dust with the jar of grapefruit marmalade bouncing about in her front basket.

'Cheerio,' she called as she disappeared into the tumbling, pink haze. 'See you later.'

Within ten minutes, as Jess pushed desperately against the wind, sometimes standing up on her pedals and sometimes leaning right down low over the handle-bars, she realized that the ride was going to be far worse than she'd imagined. The wind had not dropped at all. It buffeted her in bursts and gusts so she could hardly steer straight; the dust was stinging her face, her arms, her bare legs, as it blew against her in fiery waves; the grit was under her eyelids, between her teeth and along her tongue. She heaved her body against the wind and lurched from one pedal to the other, blinking her eyes furiously to protect them. At one point, just beyond the channel, Jess almost turned back. Tears were burning in her eyes and her whole body ached. But she was well out of the town now and closer to the rough bush by the river. Perhaps the trees would give her some shelter from the wind. They did. Here there was more noise as the dust-storm tore at the leaves and tossed the branches wildly about above her head, but at least there was less force in the wind down below, broken

43

and weakened as it was by the mesh of tree trunks and saplings. Jess felt much more cheerful now. Past the deserted sandy bend she rode with a new burst of speed and on along the blowing track to her old, secret place at the river's edge. Flopping down on the sand, she leant out over the water and scooped up cool, dripping handfuls to splash her face and wash the dust from her eyes. She pushed her wet hands through her untidy hair and tried to smooth it down. Then, with her back against the tree roots, she looked out over the river. It was whipped up into angry froth by the wind and darkened by the red, dusty sky. There she sat and waited for the boys to come.

At first her feelings were those of triumph. She'd made it! The windy journey was behind her. How silly they all were at home to think she'd give up or fall off. Ten minutes passed. Then twenty. Jess began to wonder why the boys hadn't come yet. Slowly her feelings of triumph began to ebb away. Now she felt quite uncertain. Perhaps her family had been right to suggest that the boys would never turn up on a day like this. Perhaps they'd never expect her to come to the meeting place in such a storm.

Doubts went backwards and forwards in her head. Several times she jumped up, thinking she heard the boys coming but always it was only a dry stick or a leafy branch blown down from the trees. She felt very sorry for herself and close to tears. Then, suddenly, she felt angry. How dare those little river kids let her down like this! When she'd come all this way, battled against that wind, expecting to be met! Propelled by this burst of anger, Jess climbed up the bank to her bike and set off again towards the main track.

'I'll find those blinking boats by myself!' she

muttered. 'They can't be far. They must be easy to find.'

They *were* easy to find. Far easier than she'd expected. Only half a mile along the track, which narrowed a bit as the bush grew thicker, Jess came to a wide river-bend she'd never seen before. It was further on than she'd ever been. The bend was quite sandless but sheltered with gum saplings growing close together and surrounding a small clearing at the water's edge. There, through the trees, just past the furthest outward swing of the river, were the two old boats. They were tied up to trees on the bank by rusty chains fore and aft and tied to each other by a thick, tarred rope. In the fierce wind, the boats pulled restlessly against their moorings.

Jess propped her bike against a tree and came closer. The cabin blinds were all down. The doors and hatches were shut tight. Not a sign of anyone. The boats looked completely deserted. Which one was which, she wondered, looking from one to the other. Where did Kenny and Snowy live? Which boat was Old Lizzie's? Jess decided to try the one at the back first. She could see its name, 'Lucky Strike', painted boldly on its bows. This boat was certainly the bigger of the two. The paint was brighter and cleaner. It was long and flat, like a barge, and lay low in the water with a house-shaped cabin built on top and stretching almost from one end of the boat to the other. The wide gang-plank rose and fell with the movement of the boat on the water. Jess balanced her way carefully up the plank and knocked hard on the cabin door that faced the bank.

'Kenny!' she called loudly, 'Snowy! It's me! Jess! I'm here! Let me in! Please!'

45

There was no reply. No sound at all but the harsh scream of a crow, whirled from one tree-top to another, and the constant roar of the wind.

Down the gang-plank Jess marched and along the bank to the other boat. Here the paint was peeling and the iron rails were rusty. The blades of the old paddle had broken off and the gilt decoration on its round wooden casing had faded to brown. Jess could only just make out the name: 'Sally Jane'. Altogether, this boat looked rather a wreck. No engine. No funnel. No water-tank. All these must have been ripped out years ago and left to rust on some un-known bend of the river. Only a tatty canvas, stretched across the wide, ugly gap amidships to form a makeshift roof, showed where once they had been. Just above water-level, a narrow walk-way ran all the way round the hull, a corroding brown rail still guarding its edge. At the only gap in this rail, halfway between bow and stern, the gang-plank was tied to its place. One cabin lay to the left of the plank, one to the right. Between them, high above, stretched the billowing canvas. The plank was narrow. Jess had to edge herself carefully along it, turning sideways so as not to slip off.

Once under the canvas, she banged on the cabin door to the left.

'Snowy! Kenny! I'm here! It's Jess! You said I could come!' she called desperately.

At once there was a rush of feet and a shout from within.

'It's Jess!' she heard a boy's voice call. 'Let her in! Let her in!'

The door swung suddenly inwards and there were the two boys.

'Jess!' squealed Kenny in excitement, 'we never thought you'd come! We thought your Mum would never let you! Quick! Before the dust gets in!'

They pulled her into the cabin, so pleased to see her, so amazed that she was there at all. They slammed the door shut behind her. Jess looked around her with a sharp pang of disappointment. It wasn't at all what she'd imagined. The cabin was poky and dark. An odd-smelling kerosene lantern hung from the centre beam of the low ceiling and sent out a shaky yellow light. But there under this lantern and seated in a painted wicker chair was Old Lizzie herself. Who else could it be? Jess stared.

The boys pulled her forwards, one on each hand. Jess saw that Snowy was moving his mouth, opening and closing it in a strange, exaggerated way like a clown at the circus, but no sound came out at all. Now Kenny was doing the same thing. The old lady fixed her eyes first on one boy, then on the other. Then she spoke in a funny high-pitched voice.

'Yes, boys. I know it's Jess. I'm so glad you've come, dear. What a ride you must have had through this wind! Now sit down here by me.' She crooked her yellow forefinger into a beckon of welcome, almost like the kind witch in an old fairy-tale, and smiled at Jess.

Jess kept on staring as she stood there. What a strange-looking woman Old Lizzie was! Her hair was straight and grey, not tidied back into a neat roll or a smooth round bun like the hair of other old ladies but cut square and short like a schoolgirl's. Her face wrinkled and brown with smiling creases by her eyes and her lips. Her loose print dress looked to Jess like the sort that missionaries issued to grass-skirted

47

islanders in the Pacific, so well known from old pictures on the Sunday School walls at St Cuthbert's. The dress hung awkwardly on her as if it were too big. The bright floral pattern looked almost childish. Lizzie's freckled, blue-veined arms stuck out boldly from the short sleeves, looking not quite right to Jess. But Lizzie's eyes were kind and her mouth was still smiling.

Jess sat down in the chair beside her, suddenly feeling quite at home.

5
The Gold-Nugget Brooch

Jess looked around her. The kerosene lamp swung backwards and forwards as the boat moved on the river, lighting up first one corner of the cabin and then another. Jess's eyes followed the pool of light. The little room was stuffed full, too full, of heavy old-fashioned furniture – a high cedar chest of drawers that had a reddish glow in the moving lamplight, a round polished table, an oak sideboard crowded with photographs, a bookcase stuffed with books, two wicker armchairs and two upright chairs of cedar. No sign of a bed and certainly no room for one at all. Lizzie must sleep in some other part of the boat. No stove or sink or cups or plates. Wherever did she cook her meals? Jess saw a low door opposite the one she had come in by. Perhaps Lizzie's kitchen lay through there – or was it called a galley? Jess wasn't sure about the names of things on a boat.

Above the low bookcase and reaching almost to the ceiling of the cabin hung a huge picture in a square gilt frame. Jess stared at it. An enormous grim castle reared up on a rocky seashore and great frothing waves broke almost on its very walls. Only a thin strip of sand cut off the castle from the sea. The picture seemed to Jess to belong to another world, a world very remote from the familiar bush, the wide Murray River, the low verandahed houses of Glencarra.

Jess pulled her attention back to the two boys. There was Kenny's mouth opening and closing in slow, silent grimaces just as it had done before. Old Lizzie's eyes were on him and she was smiling and nodding.

'What's the matter with him?' whispered Jess to Snowy anxiously.

'He's talking to Lizzie. He's telling her all about how you're going to be famous when you grow up.'

'But I can't hear a word and I'm not deaf! How can *she* hear him?'

'Look at her! Can't you see? She's reading his lips. He doesn't need to make any sound. She just hears with her eyes.'

Jess looked. In fact she stared. Lizzie's eyes were folowing every peculiar contortion of Kenny's mouth. Suddenly Lizzie laughed – but in a nice way, not in scorn.

'So you're going to be famous, Jess?' Her voice still sounded odd and loud and high-pitched. 'I'm not at all surprised. As soon as I saw your ginger hair I knew what kind of a girl you were. My hair used to be exactly that colour, you know.' And she chuckled a strange, high chuckle.

49

Jess looked with some disbelief at Lizzie's short, grey hair. What does the colour of anyone's hair have to do with being famous anyway, she wondered. But Lizzie was going on.

'Will you be a poet, do you think, or a pianist?' she asked seriously with no trace now of a laugh.

Jess didn't know how to reply. It was useless to speak. Lizzie couldn't hear. It was impossible to try to make her mouth talk silently like Kenny's. That looked far too difficult, almost like a foreign language. It must take years of practice. Jess felt desperate and very foolish. How could she ever break through this barrier of silence that hung down like a thick wall between them? She looked around the cabin with worried eyes. On the sideboard was a pile of old letters. Jess reached out and took a blue envelope from the top of the pile and a pencil from beside it. Leaning the envelope on the table, she wrote a quick message to Lizzie on the back.

'No. I can't write poems and I'm no good on the piano though I've been learning for six years so I'm going to be Prime Minister.'

Jess passed the message across to Lizzie and waited, feeling awkward. Lizzie read it, smiled, and then nodded vigorously.

'Prime Minister! Very good idea! What this country needs is a sensible woman in charge of things. I'll be sure to vote for you, Jess – if I'm still here, that is.' And she laughed her squeaky laugh again.

The boys looked surprised. This was not quite what they'd expected. They gazed at Jess now with puzzled but respectful eyes. Kenny's mouth began to move again. Jess looked hard at him, trying to follow, but she still could not make head nor tail of what he was saying.

Lizzie spoke. 'Oh – Kenny says you might be a famous scientist or a famous singer. Well – they're all good ideas, Jess.'

Jess suddenly remembered that Lizzie was once going to be something famous – or so the boys had said. She ripped the old blue envelope open and this time wrote on the inside.

'Did you want to be famous too? Why aren't you?'

Jess pushed the paper across to Lizzie, turning rather red as she realized that the questions sounded a bit abrupt and rude. She did hope Lizzie wouldn't get annoyed. All was well.

'Yes dear, I did,' said Lizzie in a matter-of-fact voice. 'I was going to be a concert pianist. In fact, I really *was* a concert pianist for a year or two. You know, Jess, I used to practise the piano for six hours every day from the time I was about your age. Winter and summer. Nothing else mattered to me then except music. I gave some good concerts too, though I say it myself. That was in Newcastle in the Old Country. Right back before the Great War. Years ago now.'

Jess wanted to know more. She reached out for another envelope. The first one was full up, covered with Jess's untidy writing on both sides. This time she paused to look at the name and address.

> Miss Elizabeth Forrester,
> P.O. Box 175,
> Glencarra,
> Victoria,
> Australia.

So *that's* her proper name, thought Jess, who had never heard anything more than 'Old Lizzie' from the two boys. She wondered if perhaps it would be more polite to use it. So she dashed down her next message:

'Dear Miss Forrester,' Jess wrote, 'Where did you live in the Old Country? Why do you call it the Old Country? When did you come to Australia? Why did you come? Are you going back?' Jess looked at her message. It looked very bald so she added, 'Yours sincerely, Jess' – and passed the envelope to Lizzie.

'My word! What a girl you are for asking questions, Jess,' said Lizzie comfortably. 'Still, it's a very good sign. That's the only way to get at the root of things. Well now, let me see. You needn't call me Miss Forrester by the way. I like Lizzie better. We'll start on the first question first of all. Where did I live in the Old Country? The boys know that. I've told them about it many a time. I came from Northumberland. That's right at the very top of England, just before you get to Scotland. Do you know where I mean?'

Jess shook her head. She knew her Australian geography pretty well and she knew about Eskimos who lived in icy igloos but she'd never so much as heard of Northumberland.

Lizzie levered herself up on to her feet by pushing down on the narrow arms of the wicker chair. She walked on stiff legs around the polished table and over to the bookcase beneath the strange picture. Bending down to the bottom shelf, she pulled out an old school atlas that had certainly seen better days. The covers were dog-eared and the printing on the front had faded.

'Here we are,' said Lizzie as she limped back to her chair. She opened up the atlas on her knees and turned the pages until she came to a map of the British Isles, coloured in pale pink and surrounded by pale blue oceans.

'Here's England,' she said, tracing around its coastline with one finger. 'The Old Country. I still call it that after all these years, I'm afraid. And there's London down there, see? Now right up here in the north is Scotland.' Again her finger traced the coastline. 'And here's Edinburgh on the east, look, and Glasgow over there to the west.' Lizzie's finger ran down the map below Edinburgh and she jabbed at the page. 'There's Northumberland, Jess! A huge county it is! See those miles and miles of coastline. And over here are the Cheviots. A grand range of hills! I've climbed them many a time with my father in the old days.'

Lizzie lifted her finger again and then pounced on the page once more.

'And here's Bamburgh. That's the place I come from. It's just a village with about three hundred people. Right on the edge of the sea and right under the shadow of the castle. Look up at that picture on my wall there, Jess, and you'll see Bamburgh Castle. I used to see that castle every day of my life when I was a girl. It seems all black in the picture, I know, but really the stone is pink and grey. Just like the rest of the village. Pink stone and grey stone in huge square blocks.'

Jess and Kenny and Snowy lifted their eyes to gaze at the picture.

'Did you live in the castle?' wrote Jess.

Lizzie laughed her peculiar, cracked laugh.

'Goodness, no!' she said. 'It used to be a school for girls when I was very young and then for a while it was a hospital for shipwrecked sailors.'

'Where *did* you live?' wrote Jess.

'In a stone house in the village, just near the school. My father was the schoolmaster,' said Lizzie. 'I can just remember the stonemasons building his new school in a big green field. I went to school there myself when I was six. There were only two rooms – one for the younger children and my father's room for the big children. The chimneys smoked on and off all winter, I remember that. Whenever the wind blew from the west we'd know the chimneys would be sure to smoke.' Lizzie laughed to herself as she remembered, her eyes on the picture of the castle one minute and back to Jess and the boys the next. She was in full flow now and no one could stop the flood of memories.

'There were about a hundred children at the school but it wasn't often that my father saw them all there together. If it snowed or stormed or even if it poured with rain, half the children stayed home. Then they'd be away with scarlet fever and sometimes my father would have to close the school down to stop the fever spreading. Then they'd be away for the Sunday School picnics and away for potato picking and harvest and away for the Belford Hirings and the May Flittings and away whenever a wreck was washed up on to the sand. The children loved to go down to the wrecks to see what they could find – firewood and bottles and sailors' clothes. What a time my father had trying to keep them all in school when news of a wreck ran round the classroom! I'd try to sneak out too but he never let me go far. 'Back to your books, Elizabeth!' he'd call and back I'd have to come. The other children felt sorry for me, having a schoolmaster for a father!' Lizzie paused for a minute and then went on. 'But he was a good teacher, I will say that. I learned almost all I know from him. From my very first day in his room I always kept one ear cocked for what he was teaching the oldest ones. That's how I got ahead fast. He made me a monitor when I was twelve and then I helped teach the little ones.'

Jess opened her eyes in astonishment. She was more than twelve herself but she couldn't imagine herself teaching anyone anything.

Kenny had his nose down close to the atlas, examining the sea near Bamburgh. He looked up to ask Lizzie something with his silent mouth.

'Those little black dots?' said Lizzie. 'They're the Farne Islands, Kenny. Very wild and rocky, they are. Look! This one is Longstone where the light-house is. You've heard of Grace Darling, haven't you?'

Kenny and Snowy both shook their heads.

'Goodness gracious!' exclaimed Lizzie. 'Well, Grace Darling was the daughter of the lighthouse keeper here on Longstone. In one terrible storm a ship was wrecked there on the rocks. Grace and her father rowed out through the huge waves and managed to rescue nine people. All the rest were drowned. She became a national heroine. People came from miles around just to see her. But all that was long before my time – more than thirty years before I was born. My mother had a little bit of Grace's lace cap. She kept it under a glass dome in the front parlour.' Lizzie laughed.

Jess *had* heard of Grace Darling. The story had been in her Sixth Grade Reader. She clearly remembered the picture of a young woman with flowing hair and anxious face, heaving on the oars of her father's little boat. For some strange reason, Jess had always imagined the famous rescue taking place on the rocky coast of Western Australia. That was about the most remote and dangerous place she could imagine so in her mind she had placed it all there. How astonishing to find it had happened off the *English* coast – and such a very long time ago. Before this Old Lizzie was even born!

Now Lizzie was scanning the atlas once again and picking out another island with the pencil.

'And this black dot, Jess, is Lindisfarne. Do you see it? Just a bit to the north. Holy Island is its other name. That's where Aidan lived – and Cuthbert.'

Jess thought Lizzie must have been talking about her brothers until she added, 'All that was twelve hundred years ago, of course.'

'Can't be her brothers,' thought Jess to herself, looking carefully at Lizzie. 'She *is* old but she can't be as old as all that!'

Now Lizzie had brought her pencil back to Bamburgh.

'My father taught me to swim just there. In the sea by Bamburgh Castle. The waves are calm and gentle near the sands but when you wade out further you can feel the pull of the undertow. It's very strong and very treacherous. My father used to take us out in a fisherman's boat and make us swim against the tide. He was always there to pull us out if we began to go under, of course. He kept very close all the time. Bit by bit we became confident. I was a good

56

swimmer in those days, Snowy. Just as good as you are now.'

Kenny and Snowy looked at Old Lizzie with some disbelief in their eyes. Jess was thinking to herself 'She does talk an awful lot. More than Mum even. But I quite like it.'

Just then Lizzie's paddle-boat gave a violent lurch as a sudden gust of wind struck it side-on. The little cabin was hot and stuffy with every window closed. The swaying of the boat and the acrid smell of the swinging lantern had begun to make Jess feel dizzy and sick. She stood up unsteadily and held on to the table, her brown freckles standing out starkly in her pale, pale face.

'What's up, Jess?' asked Kenny.

'I feel sick,' she muttered. 'I'll have to go outside.'

Kenny helped her to the door and she staggered down the gang-plank and threw herself full-length on the twiggy, gritty, leafy bank of the river, gasping in huge mouthfuls of air. The dust-storm was beginning to ease now, the wind was dropping, but the air was still hot and dry and full of dust. To Jess it seemed quite fresh after the close and breathless fug of the cabin. She let it fill her lungs and the queasiness started to ebb away. Kenny and Snowy and Old Lizzie had all followed her out of the boat and they stood around her now, looking worried.

'It's nothing much,' said Jess. 'I'll be all right in a minute. I just need some fresh air.' And she drew in another lungful.

Lizzie went back to the cabin to get Jess a drink of water. Jess could see her pulling back the curtains, flinging open the windows and blowing out the lantern.

'The worst of the storm is over now,' Lizzie called through the window. 'We'll let the air blow through the cabin for a while.' She brought the cool water out to Jess.

Jess sat up carefully on the bank and sipped slowly at the water. Her giddiness and sickness were passing now. She felt more her old self again.

'I'll make a cup of tea,' said Lizzie, 'and we'll all have it out here on the bank. Boys, why don't you take Jess to see your boat?'

The boys jumped up quickly.

'No thanks!' said Jess firmly. 'No more boats today. I'd love to see it next time but I'd sooner stay on the firm land for now. I still feel a bit funny.'

Snowy looked decidedly put out.

'We would've shown you our Mum's brooch,' he said sulkily.

'Can't you bring it out here?' asked Jess. 'I'd really like to see it.'

'I s'pose we could,' said Kenny, rather reluctantly, and he went up the plank of the 'Lucky Strike' and disappeared into the cabin.

A few minutes later Lizzie came through the door of the 'Sally Jane' with a laden tray in her hands and Kenny appeared from his boat with a small, black, padlocked box held close to his chest. Jess watched Lizzie as she walked easily down the gang-plank, in spite of her stiff legs, balancing herself and the tray in complete confidence born of long practice. For the very first time, Jess actually noticed Lizzie's legs. They were encased in thick, brown, lisle stockings, all wrinkled in folds around the ankles, and her feet were shuffling along in old pink slippers, one with a round fuzzy pom-pom and the other without.

'If I saw her in the street,' thought Jess to herself, 'I'd think she was some old tramp.' Then remembering her manners, she jumped up to help Lizzie with the tray. It was heavy. There was a big brown teapot at one end and a round sponge-cake on a plate at the other. In between were four cups and saucers, striped blue and white, a milk jug and a sugar basin, a breadknife and a spoon. Jess was glad she felt so much better. It would have been a pity to miss a feast like this. She put the tray down carefully on the ground and Lizzie spread a rug where all four of them could sit in comfort, away from ants and twigs. Then Lizzie took up the teapot and poured out four steaming cupfuls. With the breadknife she cut the sponge-cake into eight thick wedges, red jam oozing out of the middle of every slice.

'Two bits each,' said Snowy approvingly.

'Mmmm. This is lovely,' said Jess as she sipped her tea.

'It really is true that tea survives you, isn't it Ken?' Snowy remarked seriously, a little frown on his forehead.

'*Re*vives, silly! Not *sur*vives!' laughed Kenny. Jess tried hard not to smile.

'Much the same!' mumbled Snowy crossly through a mouthful of cake.

Jess wondered why boiling hot tea could be so refreshing on a boiling hot day. She'd often watched the pickers downing great enamel mugfuls of it, black and steaming, straight from the billy. They would lean back under the leaves of the vines, their feet sticking out in the dust and their heads in the shade, gathering strength from the tea to go on down the row, filling still more dip-tins with grapes. Now she felt just as much in need as any picker and she gulped down the hot tea gratefully.

Jess wanted to talk to Lizzie again and to ask her all the questions still left unanswered. The pile of old envelopes was back inside the boat. So was the pencil. However could she say to Lizzie what she wanted to say? 'I suppose I could ask through the boys,' she thought to herself.

'Kenny,' she said out loud, 'would you please ask Lizzie to go on telling us why she wasn't famous?'

'Ask her yourself!' said Kenny, taking his second piece of cake.

'I can't! I don't know how to,' said Jess indignantly.

Lizzie seemed to sense what the trouble was.

'Jess,' she croaked in her loud voice, 'we can't always have pencils and paper. That's far too slow. You'll just have to learn to talk to me the way the boys do. Now, just look me straight in the face. Speak very, very slowly. Use your lips and tongue to make each word carefully so I can read what you are saying. It doesn't matter if any sound comes out or not. The main thing is to shape each word clearly with your lips.'

Jess felt awkward. She'd forgotten now what she wanted to say. The two boys were watching her.

'Go on, Jess,' said Snowy kindly, 'it's not so hard! If we can do it, you can.'

'Yes. Go on, Jess,' said Kenny.

So Jess began. She gazed into Lizzie's old blue eyes and slowly formed each word with her lips, stretching them further than they'd ever been stretched before.

'Wh-y were-n't y-ou fam-ous?'

'Well done, Jess! I could read that easily. Why wasn't I famous?' Lizzie gave a short, sharp laugh. 'Well, surely you can guess for yourself. My musical career was just getting under way and then, when I was about twenty-five, I began to go deaf. At first, I didn't worry. I thought it was just a passing thing. It would soon wear off, I thought. But it didn't wear off. Bit by bit, it got worse. By the time I was twenty-eight, I was stone deaf. I went to doctors in Newcastle and doctors down in London. They all said the same. There was nothing to be done. You can be a good pianist if you're blind, Jess, but not if you're deaf. I know Beethoven went on composing – but I was no Beethoven.'

'What a terrible thing!' Jess burst out. 'How could you bear it?'

'Slower, slower, Jess! I can't read you if you gabble.'

Jess had forgotten. Slowly she repeated what she had said, though the words seemed rather flat and empty when she had to mouth them so carefully. Lizzie watched her.

'I didn't bear it very well,' admitted Lizzie. 'That was the worst year of my life. I spent most of it crying. Then I pulled myself together. I'd had one very good friend at music school in London. Brendan Meath. He was an Australian singer – he'd gone back to Australia and he kept on writing to me, even when I told him I was going deafer and deafer. He kept asking me to go out to Australia and marry him. In the end I agreed. So I worked in a library in Newcastle for a year till I'd saved the fare and then I sailed for Australia in 1903. That's forty years ago, Jess. Forty years ago next month.' Lizzie paused and looked across the river to the far bank as if she'd forgotten Jess and Kenny and Snowy. Then suddenly she added, 'He was a good singer, Brendan Meath, and a good man too.'

Jess tried to peer at Lizzie's left hand to see if there was a wedding ring on her fourth finger. She couldn't quite see. There was nothing for it but to ask. Slowly Jess began, looking straight at Lizzie.

'D-id y-ou marr-y h-im?'

'No, I didn't,' said Lizzie more quietly than before. 'By the time I arrived in Melbourne it was almost four years since I'd seen him last. And in that time, of course, I'd gone deaf. We'd both changed. We couldn't talk easily anymore. My deafness was like a wall of cotton-wool between us. So we decided not to marry and we parted good friends. And there I was, stranded in Melbourne. I'd come so far and I couldn't face the thought of going back again all that way to England. So I just stayed on. And here I am still, forty years later.' Lizzie broke off, 'But look, Jess! The boys are going to show you the brooch.'

Jess turned towards Kenny. He had unlocked the tiny padlock on the black box and was lifting the lid. Inside Jess saw a mass of screwed-up white tissue paper, ball upon ball of it, packed tightly together. Kenny carefully took out one white ball of paper after another, piling them up on the rug beside him. Halfway down, he came to the brooch and lifted it out. He held it in the flat, open palm of his hand. Jess stared hard. It was the oddest-looking brooch she had ever seen. It was a dull gold colour; its shape was bumpy, uneven, knobbly, with edges like the coast of a desert island. Behind it was a kind of safety-pin, firmly fixed in place, and attached to this pin was a tiny chain with a much smaller pin at the end. Jess didn't quite know what to say. She felt puzzled and disappointed. She wasn't even sure she *liked* the brooch – such a funny shape, such a funny colour. It wasn't really pretty. The boys were looking at her expectantly so she knew she ought to try to say something.

'How unusual!' she said at last, politely.

'Don't you like it?' asked Snowy suspiciously.

'I'm not quite sure what it is,' said Jess, who'd decided it was best to be honest.

'Don't you *really* know what it is?' asked Kenny in amazement. 'It's a gold nugget. A real, true gold nugget. Dad found it down at Eaglehawk ten years ago. He saw it, just lying in a dried-up old river bed. And he got one of his mates to solder this pin on the back so Mum could have it for a brooch. And this little chain and this tiny pin is to keep it safe in case the big pin comes undone. It's worth lots and lots of money, isn't it Snow?' Snowy nodded solemnly.

'I always thought gold was much brighter and shinier than that,' said Jess, 'but I do love its knobbly shape.' She took the brooch in her hand and felt its heavy weight on her palm. She rubbed her fingers over all its strange bumps.

'What was he doing in a dry river-bed?' she asked suddenly.

'Who?' said Kenny.

'Your father.'

'Looking for gold, of course. That's what he's doing now. He's a prospector half the year. The other half, he's here with us, working up on Mr Reardon's block.'

'A prospector? I thought there was no gold left to find these days. Does he really find any?'

'Not much,' Kenny admitted, 'but he gets a few grains every month. It all mounts up. He likes the life, you see. That's really why he does it. He doesn't want to settle down. He likes to keep on the move. We don't worry about him. He always turns up every April.'

'But where's your mother, Kenny? Why didn't she take the brooch with her?'

'She's down in Melbourne with Auntie Vi. She had to take Annie down there. Annie's terribly sick but there's a good lady doctor down there who's making her better.'

'Kenny and Jess!' put in Lizzie rather sharply, 'I do wish you two would turn this way. I can't see a word you're saying to each other.'

Kenny turned towards Lizzie and spoke slowly again.

'I w-as j-ust tell-ing Jess ab-out Ann-ie.'

'Oh yes. Annie,' said Lizzie. 'She's got infantile paralysis, Jess. Polio's its other name. Can't move her legs – or rather, she couldn't. The boys' mother wrote to me last week and said there's a marvellous improvement already. Annie is getting round on crutches quite well now and she'll be able to come back home again.'

'Does your Dad know about Annie being sick?' Jess asked Kenny in a worried voice, forgetting to speak so Lizzie could understand. She was puzzled by this scattered family and wondered how on earth they kept in touch with each other.

'Oh yes. He knows now. He's down in Melbourne with them at Auntie Vi's,' said Kenny cheerfully, 'but Mum had to get the police to find him. She didn't know where he was herself. All she knew was he was somewhere up the Ovens River. The police tracked him down all right. It took them a few weeks though.' Kenny laughed. 'I bet old Dad got a fright when he saw the police coming for him!'

'Your poor mother!' Jess burst out. 'All that trouble with Annie, and your father away.'

'She's very tough, Mum is. She's used to him being away, you see. She had a real good little job, helping Mrs Reardon in the house. Used to ride up there on her bicycle twice a week. Had to stop, though, when Annie got sick. Mrs Reardon's a good sort. She gave Mum the fare to Melbourne, didn't she Snow?'

Snowy nodded. Then he added, 'They had to travel in the guard's van, Jess. Annie was on a stretcher and it wouldn't fit anywhere else. Mum sat up in a chair beside her all night. I wish I could've gone too.'

Lizzie hadn't followed much of this. She looked quickly from one to another, a slight frown on her forehead as her eyes grasped an odd word here and there. She seemed to have picked up just enough to have a fair idea what Kenny and Snowy were telling Jess.

'Your mother is a saint!' she said emphatically to the two boys. 'A saint! I won't say what I think about your father!'

'H-e al-ways c-omes b-ack i-n Ap-ril,' said Snowy, slowly and loyally, staring hard at Lizzie.

Lizzie looked across at Jess and Jess looked back at her. They nodded at each other as if they were agreed about something. Jess smiled.

'Your mother is a saint,' Lizzie said again to the boys, 'and don't you forget it. Now, lock up her brooch, Kenny, and put it back under her bunk. We

65

want it all safe and sound for her when she brings Annie back.'

'Yep,' said Kenny and he wrapped up the brooch carefully in all its layers of tissue, put it back in its box, and carried it off to his boat.

Jess looked at her watch.

'Goodness! It's five o'clock. I must go.' Then she remembered Lizzie and pointed to her watch. Lizzie nodded. Jess jumped up and held out her hand politely to Lizzie. She knew that's what grown-ups did at the end of a visit and she was feeling rather grown-up all of a sudden.

'Th-ank y-ou for hav-ing m-e. C-an I c-ome b-ack n-ext Sun-day?' She mouthed carefully.

'Yes Jess, please do. I like you,' and Lizzie gave her old cracked laugh.

Jess climbed on to her bike and pushed against her pedals. Slowly it got under way. She waved to the boys and to Lizzie as she wobbled towards the broad track, the sound of that strange, friendly laugh still ringing in her ears. The north wind had dropped now and the bush along the river-bank lay dry and exhausted after the storm.

6
A Visitor

The ride home was easy. The dust-storm had really blown itself out. The whole world seemed stunned and quiet after its long battle with the wind. At home, the furniture and floors were thick with fine red dust in spite of all the family's careful pre-cautions. Mum was standing looking at it in despair when Jess got in.

'What a mess!' she sighed. 'When will I ever get it clean again?'

'Leave it till tomorrow, Mary,' said Dad. 'Don't go and ruin your Sunday with housework. You know what Grandma would have said about that! We'll all lend you a hand in the morning.'

Laura and Nico did not look at all pleased with this kind offer which their father had made on their behalf. They began making excuses but Dad was firm.

'It won't hurt us to get up an hour earlier for once. If we all work together we'll have the whole place clean again in no time.' He changed the subject to ask Jess about her visit to Old Lizzie and the boys. Now Jess was able to solve one puzzle that had been bothering her.

'Dad, however did you and Mum talk to Old Lizzie? Can you do that funny silent talking the boys do?'

'No. We certainly couldn't,' said Dad laughing. 'We just talked to her through the boys. We told them what we wanted to say and they passed it on to her. In fact, we didn't need to *say* much at all. Lizzie did most of the talking. How did you manage, Jess?'

'Well, first I wrote things on paper but then I began to get the hang of that slow talking. The funny thing is, I can't stop doing it now. I keep stretching my mouth with every word.'

Jess told them all about the boys' parents, about Annie's paralysis, about the gold-nugget brooch locked up in the black box.

'If I had a gold nugget, I don't think I'd leave it with a couple of kids in a river boat,' remarked Nico.

'No one knows it's there so I suppose it's safe enough,' put in Laura.

'Poor little kids!' said Mum.

'It's lucky Lizzie's there to keep a good eye on them – and to feed them,' said Dad.

'Will you go down there again next Sunday, Jess?' asked Laura, half envious, and half amused at her sister's adventure.

'Yes. Next Sunday and every Sunday – that's if you'll let me, Mum,' Jess added quickly, turning to her mother and trying to read her face.

'Yes, Jess. You can go. We liked Lizzie – Miss Forrester, I mean. You really must stop saying *old* Lizzie, Jess. It's terribly rude. Even *Lizzie* doesn't seem very polite to me. Anyway, you can go so long as you don't wander away from those two boats and so long as you leave the river at five o'clock sharp. *And* so long as you don't talk too much when you're there.'

'Not much danger of that,' laughed Dad, 'once Old Lizzie gets going – oh, sorry, Miss Forrester, I mean, dear.'

The next morning, Monday, began at six o'clock instead of the usual seven. In a whirl of dusters, mops and brooms and to the constant drone of the vacuum cleaner, the house was soon transformed. Nico had bagged the best job – or so Jess thought. With an iron bucket full of water and a red rubber Squeejee mop, he swished down the floor of the front verandah until its tiles sparkled in the early morning sunlight. From up and down the street came the sounds of similar activities in all the other houses. Two or three of the women had started on washing their dirty lace curtains and already had them flapping on the lines out the back. There was a noisy banging of mats, a shaking of bedspreads in front gardens, a brushing of sofas, a dusting of shelves, a sweeping of floors. Blinds were pulled up and windows flung open again.

Then Mum made a good breakfast for all the family – bacon and eggs, tea and toast, golden cumquat marmalade that tasted deliciously sweet and bitter at the same time. Jess practised the piano for her usual reluctant fifteen minutes. By half-past eight, Nico, Laura and Jess were riding off to school on their bikes with lunch in their front baskets. Dad was walking into his office in town. Mum was left alone in peace at last to read *The Age* and make herself a fresh pot of tea. The best time of the day, she always said it was.

Jess's life now began to fall into a regular pattern through these hot February days. There was home, there was school, there were the messages to do on Saturdays, and on Sundays there was the river with Old Lizzie and the boys. The minute Sunday dinner was over, Jess was out of the house and on her way, riding past the green blocks and their long rows of drying racks, thickly hung now with grapes in the hot sunshine, and along the winding bush track to the river. Lizzie was always there on the bank waiting for her, sitting erect in her wicker armchair with an old brown rug spread out beside her on the ground where Jess could flop down the minute she arrived.

The summer weather eased up a bit now. No rain

yet but at least no more dust storms. The steady, dry heat was enjoyable rather than exhausting. Jess lay on the rug in the mottled shade of a giant red-gum, patches of sunlight breaking through the leaves, falling here and there on her bare legs. Blue sky, brown river, and Old Lizzie talking on and on. Jess loved her Sundays. She didn't need to say much or even to ask much. Just the occasional slowly-spoken question, or, if it all became too complicated, the occasional quickly-scribbled message in a notebook that Jess kept now for talking to Lizzie. Lizzie needed little prompting. She had a whole life-time to talk about and she'd never had such a good listener. Jess was happy to listen. Kenny and Snowy came and went between the 'Lucky Strike' and the river-bank where Lizzie sat. They had games of their own to play and Jess looked on with half an eye, sometimes jumping up to join in or to sort out a quarrel but generally just lying on the rug, listening to Lizzie.

The distant landscape of Lizzie's childhood in Northumberland became clearer and clearer in Jess's head until it seemed almost more real than the river-bank where she lay now. In her mind's eye, she saw the heavy draught-horses in their high pointed collars, standing patiently ready for the ploughing or the mowing. She saw the women in their bright scarves and broad-brimmed straw bonnets, hoeing a field full of turnips. She saw the fishergirls, gutting and barrelling the herring catch at one little fishing port after another. She saw the farm-workers 'flitting' to their new jobs on the twelfth of May with all their goods and chattels piled up on a ricketty cart. She saw the wrestling matches at the country show, the annual visit of the gipsies with their dancing bears and monkeys, the lifeboat surging out over the breakers in a storm, twelve strong men pulling on the oars, the pit-lads with their blackened faces at West Bank colliery, the barefooted expeditions to Holy Island over the wet sands at low tide. Behind it all rose the Cheviots, purple with heather in summer. To Lizzie these scenes were still as vivid now as they had been when she last set eyes on them, forty or fifty or even sixty years ago. To Jess they slowly became as vivid as her own familiar world where the wide River Murray slid quietly past her.

At four o'clock sharp, every Sunday, Old Lizzie paused in her flow of memories and made a pot of tea, boiling up a kettleful of river-water on her Primus stove in the cramped galley beyond the main cabin. The boys came to join Jess on the rug and the four of them feasted on flat oatcakes, thick shortbread and large hunks of gingerbread.

One Sunday, the very last day of February, they were all sitting as usual on the bank, sipping strong tea and munching their shortbread. Suddenly Jess noticed Kenny looking past her and towards the track, a puzzled frown between his eyes. She turned her head to see what he was looking at. There, only a stone's throw away, a stranger was bent over, easing a blue swag down off his shoulder and then slowly straightening up again. Jess just heard his soft groan of relief as the weight fell to the ground but she had certainly not heard him coming. He was simply there, with his bushy grey beard and his faded brown jacket. His neatly-rolled swag, now on the ground beside him, was topped by a black billy

71

carefully wrapped round with pink newspaper and tied with string. String tied his shoes, too, instead of laces. He was a harmless-looking old swaggie but somehow Jess felt alarmed by his sudden and silent appearance.

'Who's that?' she whispered urgently to Kenny.

'Never seen him before,' muttered Kenny, still frowning.

'What's that, Jess? What did you say?' asked Lizzie, leaning towards her. Jess pointed at the man and Lizzie looked up and saw him.

'Oh. Good-afternoon,' she said pleasantly with her odd, crooked smile and no trace of alarm. 'Nice day.'

The swaggie came closer.

'Nice day. Very nice,' he said slowly. 'Pretty warm though. And so *these* are the boys! Now which one is Kenny and which is Snowy?' he asked, looking carefully from one astonished boy to the other and smiling at them both. Jess noticed his teeth, yellow, almost green, from years of pipe-smoking.

'I'm Snowy,' said Snowy bluntly. 'And who are you?'

'Aw, I'm just an old mate of your father's.' Jess seemed to have heard that somewhere before but she couldn't think where. The swaggie went on. 'Met up with him in the Ovens valley. Must have been a good six months back now. Any time you're passing down the big river, he says, any time, just you call in and see them boys and the little girl and the missus. They'll always be glad to give you a cuppa and a bite to eat. That's what he said to me, your Dad, so here I am. Seems to be just the right time for a cuppa too,' he added, looking at the brown teapot.

Kenny and Snowy glanced at each other doubtfully.

'Where's your Mum now, boys? P'raps you'd give her a shout and tell her I'm here. She'll be real glad to know her old man was hale and hearty when I seen him last.'

'Mum's not here,' blurted out Snowy. 'She's down in Melbourne with Annie. Dad's there too. Old Lizzie's looking after us.'

Kenny frowned. He didn't like Snowy telling all the family business.

Now the swaggie was staring at Lizzie for the first time. He hadn't taken any notice of her up till now.

'Aw yeah! Old Lizzie. Your Dad told me all about the poor old girl. Deaf as a post, he said she was. Can't hear a thing.' The stranger leant down towards the boys, almost as if she *might* hear if he spoke too loudly. 'A bit potty, too, I expect. Looks a bit potty, anyway. Poor old girl!' and he winked at the boys.

Jess leapt up. Her face was scarlet with rage.

'She is *not* potty! And you just clear off! We don't want you round here. Now *scram!*' Jess was shouting at the man. The words fell out of her mouth before she could stop them. Lizzie put out her hand to Jess's arm.

'Jess, Jess. What's the matter? Just give the old chap a cup of tea and he'll be on his way.' Lizzie's voice was quieter than usual.

Jess swung round, her eyes still blazing.

'B-ut h-e s-aid y-ou w-ere p-ott-y,' she yelled slowly at Lizzie.

'Well, well. Never mind, Jess. It's not the first time people have called me potty. I suppose I do look a little odd.' And she gave her high cracked laugh. 'What does the old codger want, Jess?'

'H-e s-ays h-e's a m-ate of the b-oys' f-ath-er,' mouthed Jess silently.

'Oh, yes! We've had them before,' said Lizzie cheerfully. 'Jim is always sending his mates along. He has lots of mates, that father of theirs. Well, give him some tea, Jess, and don't let him worry you.'

Jess didn't want to give him a thing but she stumped up the plank into Lizzie's boat and brought out an extra mug. Lizzie put in the milk and sugar and filled it up with tea.

'Here you are,' said Lizzie, holding out the tea to the swaggie. 'This'll set you up again. And have some biscuits too.'

The swaggie looked embarrassed at her kindness and more embarrassed that she talked quite like a normal person. He took the tea from her, avoiding her eyes, and drank it down in one long gulp, as if he had a throat of cast-iron.

'Thanks, Missus,' he mumbled. 'That was real good. Well, I'll be pushing off now.' And as he shoved the shortbread biscuit into his pocket, he heaved the swag up on his back again. The neatly-tied billy bounced up and down on top. Without another word he was gone, trudging down the track, little puffs of red dust rising behind his heels.

'Thank goodness he's gone,' said Kenny. 'I didn't like him at all. Do you think he really knows Dad, Jess?'

'He must,' said Jess. 'He knew your names and everything. He knew about Lizzie being deaf.'

'Yeah. Well, I don't like him. We've had a few other mates of Dad's along this track before. They were decent blokes. But this old geezer crept up on us, somehow.' Kenny sounded worried.

'I wish Mum was here,' said Snowy.

'Come on now boys,' squawked Lizzie loudly and briskly, getting up and stretching out her stiff old legs, one after the other. 'It's getting cool. Jess'll be going home soon so let's take the things inside. Kenny, you take my chair. Snowy, you take the rug.'

Everyone felt better with Lizzie firmly in charge again. The boys set to work, shaking the rug between them and sending crumbs flying.

'You *did* get wild with him, Jess,' said Kenny over his shoulder as he staggered up the gang-plank with the wicker chair.

'Yes, Jess. You went all red,' added Snowy, half laughing at her.

'I know I did,' said Jess quietly, picking up the brown teapot.

Time to go home. Jess was glad, as she pedalled down the track towards town, that the swaggie had gone off in the other direction. She didn't want to see him again.

7
An Awkward Week

That Sunday marked the beginning of a difficult week for Jess. Her troubles had nothing at all to do with Lizzie or the two boys. The real problem was Linda Betts. Or perhaps Jess herself was the source of the problem and Linda Betts had simply triggered it all off.

Linda Betts had always been the centre of interest in Jess's class. It had been that way since their very first day in the High School, now just over a year ago. Until that day Jess had never even heard of Linda Betts but within a week Linda was the accepted leader of the class.

Jess was not quite sure what gave Linda her position. Certainly she seemed rather older than all the rest although she was really much the same age. Linda's face had a serious, grown-up look and she lived a little apart from the other girls, who all felt rather like young children when they were with her. Everyone, of course, wanted to be Linda's friend. Everyone jostled to sit next to her in class, to have lunch with her out in the long grass beyond the oval, to ride home with her past the olive-oil factory that reeked of crushed olives on these hot afternoons.

Linda arranged her best friends neatly on lists. She was not the only one who did this. Everyone in Jess's class was obsessed with listing friends, with changing the lists every day, with passing the lists secretly from hand to hand under the desks during lessons. Everyone that is, except the boys. They did make up half the class but Jess had no idea what they were doing or thinking. They did not seem to go in for list-making as far as she could tell. They took up all the desks on the window side of every classroom but, as far as the girls were concerned, they lived in another world.

Linda would number her best friends in their proper order from 1 down to 10. Anyone below 10 did not really count. Jess seldom appeared in a better position than 8th or 9th. Sometimes she dropped right off the list altogether for weeks at a time. This didn't worry Jess very much. She liked to be on Linda's list but she was really far more concerned with Rona's list. Ever since that amazing day, in January 1942, when Rona had asked her to be her best friend, Jess was anxious, above all else, to stay in that happy position. On the whole she succeeded in staying there but every now and then some brief but tempestuous quarrel would send her tumbling down to position 2 or 3 or even 4. These episodes were devastating for Jess. She told no one, not even Mum, and retreated into a glum silence until, miraculously, Rona would pass her a new list only a few days later with J McG firmly at the top once again.

The lists themselves, drawn up on long strips of lined paper torn from exercise books, each girl's name shown only by her initials, were an endless source of intense pain and pleasure to everyone in the class. Round and round they went, under the girls' desks, surreptitiously passed when Miss Stevens or Miss Wilcox was writing on the blackboard, to be studied furtively with smiles of satisfaction, or with frowns, giggles, sighs. Linda's list was always the most important of all. To be Linda's best friend, even if for only a week or two, was to reach the heights of fame and happiness in Form IIA that year. Jill, Franny and Eileen all jockeyed for the coveted position but, in the end, they had to be content to take it in turns. Linda had mastered the tactful art of giving each one of her three closest friends a brief and blissful turn at the top before moving her down again to place 2 or 3. Even the teachers seemed somehow aware of Linda's powerful position in the class and often Jess felt that the entire lesson was being directed at the quiet, grave, self-contained figure of Linda in the second row from the back.

On the first Tuesday in March, Linda was away from school. This, in itself, was most unusual. Linda was never away. But there was her empty seat and it seemed to catch the eye of every teacher who came into the room.

'Where's Linda?' they asked in surprise, one after the other, all day.

'Away,' chorused the class.

Everyone felt odd without Linda in the room. Not that she ever said a great deal in class; not that her work was particularly good. It was just average. But she was always *there*, calm and powerful, holding the whole class together. Without her, the girls felt uncomfortable and restless.

On Wednesday Linda was still away. Now the rumour began to go round the room that Linda's father had died. No one believed it, of course. Mr Betts was a strong, healthy man. Everyone knew him by sight. Jess, herself, had seen him only last Saturday, buying his paper in the bookshop when she was up on the stairs above. He'd looked just his normal, cheerful self. He owned a thriving hardware shop and was helped on Saturdays by his two eldest sons. 'No,' thought Jess to herself. 'He couldn't possibly have died.'

But, strangely enough, the news was true. The headmaster, Mr Simmonds, came in just before lunch-time and spoke to the whole class. Linda's father had died of a sudden heart attack. The funeral was to be at the Methodist Church on Friday after-noon. Everyone was to bring threepence tomorrow for a wreath. Linda would be back at school sometime next week. Everyone must be very kind to her. It was a terrible blow for the whole family. And then Mr Simmonds looked vaguely around the classroom and hurried out again.

There was a stunned silence after Mr Simmonds had gone. How could this have happened to Linda, of all people? Miss Stevens called everyone's attention back to the blackboard and the lesson dragged on.

Straight after school that same afternoon, Jess rode into town to change her books at the children's library. She generally went there two or three times a week. Biggles was her present craze. Before that it had been Dimsey; before that, Pollyanna; before that, William. There seemed, luckily for Jess, to be an endless stream of these satisfying heroes and heroines, all much braver or much wickeder or much funnier than she was herself. There was still a whole shelf full of Biggles' adventures just waiting to be read and it never took Jess long to hand two books in and take two more out.

The library was cool and quiet, almost dark after the glaring, bright heat outside. Jess could hardly make out the shapes of the shelves at first. The place seemed quite deserted apart from the nice library-lady at her counter with her rubber stamp and a pile of new books. Jess put her two books down on the counter and went across to the Biggles shelf to find her next two. Her eyes had still not quite adjusted to the dim light and she could barely read the titles on the spines. She was peering at one called *Biggles Flies Again* when suddenly she noticed someone sitting very still at the far end of the library, half in shadow.

Jess's heart gave a lurch. Without turning her head at all, she slid her eyes sideways to get a proper look. Yes. It was Linda! Linda Betts, just sitting there, alone, in the library.

Jess felt cold all over. What on earth should she do? Should she go up and speak to Linda? What could she possibly find to say? She began trying to form a suitable sentence in her head while pretending to study *Biggles Flies Again* very closely. 'I was sorry to hear the dreadful news . . .' or 'Hullo Linda . . .' or 'It's very sad about your father . . .' But everything she tried out sounded awkward and clumsy. She couldn't possibly say any of them.

Perhaps, Jess thought hopefully, perhaps Linda hadn't even seen her. The library *was* terribly dark. She snatched at another Biggles book, not even pausing to read its title, and held it hard against her chest with *Biggles Flies Again*. Without turning at all to right or left, Jess edged her way slowly and carefully along the shelves, her eyes on the rows of books, always getting further and further from Linda. She reached the counter and slid her two books silently across to be stamped. Keeping her head well down, she tiptoed across the shiny brown linoleum to the door. She stepped outside into the white, blazing sunlight. Jess stood still. What *had* she done? Surely she should have said something to Linda. She half turned to go back, one hand on the library door, but it was impossible. She was too frightened. There was nothing she could say.

Jess rode home and buried herself almost at once in the adventures of Biggles. She lay on her bed in the sleep-out with the book propped sideways across her face. It was, she knew, supposed to be bad for her eyes to read like that, but she always did it just the same. In the world of Biggles, death seemed an altogether simpler affair than in Glencarra. Everyone knew just what to do and what to say. Biggles never found himself tongue-tied and embarrassed, scuttling sideways out of libraries. Jess pushed all thought of Linda out of her mind.

On Thursday, Miss Stevens collected the three-pences for the wreath. On Friday morning the wreath itself was brought into the classroom for everyone to see. It lay on Miss Stevens's desk, a perfect round of white chrysanthemums, and its strange, sad scent filled the classroom. Mr Simmonds himself was to take the wreath to Linda's house and Jill, Franny and Eileen were allowed to go with him. Back at school an hour later, they were the centre of buzzing attention. They had been right inside Linda's house, right into the front room, and there were lots and lots of white wreaths piled on the table and on the floor, and they'd even talked to Linda who didn't cry at all. Jill looked hard at Jess.

'I've got a bone to pick with you, Jess McCallum,' she said sharply.

Jess followed her outside to the quadrangle where no one could overhear them.

'What is it?' asked Jess, her heart pounding because she knew very well what it was.

'Linda says you saw her in the library. On Wednesday. And you wouldn't even *speak* to her.'

Jess was silent. Then she said nervously, 'I didn't think she saw me.'

'Well she did. And she wants to know why you didn't even speak to her. You knew her father was dead. We all knew.'

'I didn't know what to say to her,' said Jess truthfully. She was uncomfortably red in the face now and near to tears. Jill was joined by Franny and Eileen who stood around Jess staring at her with shocked and hostile eyes.

'Come on, you two,' Jill commanded suddenly, turning on her heel. Franny and Eileen walked off after her and Jess was left by herself.

In the English lesson that afternoon, Jess saw more than one girl in the class giving her an odd, accusing look and she could half hear the whispered mutters passing from desk to desk.

'She wouldn't even *speak* to her!'

'It wasn't exactly that I *wouldn't*,' thought Jess miserably to herself as she blindly turned the pages of *Kidnapped*, 'it was more that I *couldn't*.' But she didn't try to explain herself to the others, not even to Rona. It could only make things worse. The minute the last siren of the day had gone, Jess ran to the bike-shed, lifted down her bike from the hook where it hung by its front wheel to the rafters, and pedalled furiously home to escape from them all. At home, Biggles was waiting to help her forget Linda all over again.

Next Sunday when Jess rode down to the river, she had a question already written out for Old Lizzie. Lizzie was in her chair on the bank as usual and she put on her glasses with the round tortoise-shell rims to read Jess's untidy writing.

'Dear Lizzie,' she read out loud as Jess stood awkwardly beside her, 'What do you say when you meet someone whose father has just died?'

'Mmmm,' said Lizzie and for a while she said nothing more but just looked out across the river.

Jess began to wonder if her question wasn't clear enough but then Lizzie looked up at her.

'Yes, Jess,' she said, 'that's very difficult. Has it happened to you already?'

Jess nodded.

'Well what *did* you say?' asked Lizzie.

'Noth-ing,' mouthed Jess slowly, feeling her eyes pricking and burning.

'Yes, it happened to me too, Jess. When I was about your age. No, I was a bit older. I must have been fourteen. Twice it happened. Twice in the one year. And I was no better at it the second time than I was the first.'

Jess flopped down on the rug beside Lizzie's chair feeling better already. If Lizzie herself hadn't known what to say then it wasn't so bad after all. Lizzie was talking again.

'It's much easier when you're grown-up, Jess. Then you can write a letter. The minute you hear your friend's father has died – or her mother, or whoever it may be – you sit down and you write her a letter. You need good paper, mind. White unlined paper. And none of those dreadful little condolence cards with black printing on them. You simply say how sorry you are to hear of the death and you offer your sympathy. You can generally say something kind and truthful about the person who has died. If you can't, of course, say nothing. It's hard to write the letter, of course, but not as hard as trying to say something on the spur of the moment when you see your friend unexpectedly. You must post the letter at once so it gets to her quickly. When you do see her – at the funeral or at church or in the street, wherever it is – she'll begin by thanking you for your kind letter and everything goes on more easily from there.'

Jess wasn't at all convinced. She couldn't imagine herself writing that kind of letter to anyone, let alone Linda, on any kind of paper, lined or unlined.

'Of course,' Lizzie broke in on Jess's worried thoughts, 'if it's a really *close* friend whose father's died, a letter won't do at all. You must go straight round to see her. Take some flowers from the garden. You won't need to say anything at all. Just put your arms round her. The right words will come in time.'

Jess was thankful that Linda couldn't really be called a very *close* friend of hers. After all, she was only 9th on Linda's present list and she'd been there only a couple of weeks. She certainly couldn't imagine herself knocking on Linda's front door or putting her arms round her or giving her a bunch of flowers. All that belonged to the grown-ups' world, perhaps, but not to hers. Suddenly she remembered Rona's father, a prisoner in Burma.

'Oh dear,' she thought desperately, 'I do hope he doesn't die.'

Lizzie went at once to make the pot of tea, although it was still early. She could see that Jess could do with it now and with the comfort of gingerbread.

Jess felt a lot better. She had another question for Lizzie and she wanted to forget about Linda.

'Why do you live in a boat?' she scribbled on the back of her piece of paper and held it up for Lizzie to read.

'I haven't always lived in a boat, you know,' laughed Lizzie; 'only for about the last six years. Before that I lived in a house just like anybody else.'

'Wh-ere?' asked Jess slowly, looking up at her.

Lizzie settled herself comfortably back in her wicker chair, her third cup of tea in her hands.

'Well, Jess. I told you all about Brendan Meath and how we didn't get married after all. That must have been in 1904. Yes it was March. Just this time of year. It seemed so odd to me then to have an autumn in March. Now I've seen it come and go almost forty times and it seems quite natural. I'd been in Melbourne about five weeks. I knew no one else at all except Brendan and his family and I couldn't hear anyone. I was staying in a place they used to call the Coffee Palace, just a small family guest house in Little Collins Street. I only had enough money for a couple more weeks so I knew I'd have to get a job. There aren't many jobs you can do if you're deaf but there are some and I was determined to find one. I wanted to get out of Melbourne, too. It's a fine city but far too big for me. I wanted to live in some little place. Somewhere near water. On the sea or by a river, I didn't care which. So I went out and bought myself two things – a newspaper and a map of Victoria. I came back to my room in the Coffee Palace and spread out my map on the bed. Then I searched through all the advertisements for jobs that were listed at the back of the paper. The only ones I could see were jobs for fencers and shearers and drovers. Then, just as I was about to give up, I saw an advertisement headed 'Echuca'. I'd never heard of Echuca but the job sounded promising. A widower wanted a housekeeper. He offered two rooms and a fair wage and one day off a week. I started at the bottom of the map of Victoria, searching and searching for Echuca, slowly working my way up to the top.

There was no index. I just had to go backwards and forwards, reading the name of every little township. It took me ages. Then suddenly I saw it plain and clear, right up on the Murray River. I remember how I put my finger on the blue line that marked the river and traced its whole course from the mountains to the sea. 'That's the place for me!' I thought to myself; 'right by that river.'

'So I wrote off the very same day to the gentleman in Echuca and I got the job. I told him I was deaf but he didn't care a jot. Said he didn't want to have to talk anyway. I caught the horse-coach up to Echuca and my boxes came after me in the wagon the next week.

'I liked the place as soon as I saw it. It was only a little town, just as I'd hoped, and the gentleman was kind. I had a bedroom and a proper housekeeper's sitting room. I kept the whole house clean for him and did the cooking. I did the shopping too and even that was easy once I knew the shopkeepers. They just nodded or shook their heads or wrote down prices on a brown paper bag for me.' Lizzie laughed as she remembered.

'And I had the river, Jess. That was the best part of all. This same Murray River that we're looking at this very minute but it's not quite so wide up at Echuca and it seemed to move a bit faster – or I thought it did in those days.

'Two things kept me sane in Echuca: books and birds. I didn't have any real friends. I just walked along the river on my weekly day off or in the evenings before the dark came down. That's where I saw the birds. They were nothing like all my English birds that I knew so well in Bamburgh. I had to start from scratch to learn their names from a book. The magpies, the currawongs, the butcher birds, the willie wagtails, the miners, the honey-eaters, the tree-creepers, the galahs, the cockatoos, the lorikeets, the blue wrens, the water hens, the kookaburras . . .'

'Jess!' bellowed Kenny from the gang-plank of the 'Lucky Strike'. Jess looked across at him suddenly and Lizzie had to break off her unending list of birds in mid-stream. Jess felt annoyed at the interruption.

'What is it?' she bellowed rudely back.

'When are you coming to play with us? We're going to our secret place to swim.'

'I'm not coming! I'm listening to Lizzie!'

'Lizzie! Lizzie! You're *always* listening to Lizzie!' roared Kenny angrily. He went inside for a minute to get his bathers and towel. He and Snowy set off for their swim at the secret place without another word or even a glance at Jess and Lizzie.

Lizzie hardly seemed to have noticed the interruption. She went on as Jess turned back to her.

'And the books, Jess. They were just as good as the birds. I'd brought a few with me from home, Shakespeare, of course, and Jane Austen. But in Echuca I began to buy more from a funny little shop that sold all sorts of second hand junk. In among the broken pictures and cracked plates I'd often find a pile of old books. Bit by bit I built up my collection. All of Dickens I got and all of George Eliot and all of Hardy. I just read my books over and over again all through the winter months by the wood fire in my little sitting-room . . .'

Lizzie trailed off, thinking and remembering. Jess had to tap her on the knee to get her attention back again.

'H-ow l-ong d-id y-ou st-ay?' asked Jess, carefully, looking up at Lizzie.

'I'd meant to stay there only a year or two. In the end it turned into ten years. I didn't move on till the year the war broke out – 1914. Mr Clissold, my old gentleman, died that year and I decided to pull up my roots and make a move.'

'Wh-ere to?' asked Jess.

'I wanted to stick to the river, Jess, so I found a new job in Swan Hill. I did the book-keeping for Burns and Halliday. They're a firm of grain merchants – chaff and grain. I think I only got the job because they couldn't get anyone else. All the men had gone off to the war – and most of them never came back. I had to learn the job first. I'd never done anything like it before but I soon got the hang of it. Swan Hill was like Echuca in a lot of ways. I felt at home there. Just a quiet little place it was in those days. A one-horse town. That's just what I liked about it.'

'Wh-ere d-id y-ou l-ive?' asked Jess.

'In a house! A proper house of my own in Nettle Street. I didn't own it, of course. I rented it unfurnished from Burns and Halliday. Just four rooms and a front verandah but that was more than enough for me. I had to set about buying some bits of furniture. Nettle Street's down near the river. Only a stone's throw away. That's where I first met Christine.'

Jess looked puzzled. She'd never heard Lizzie mention anyone called Christine before.

'Christine,' explained Lizzie, 'Kenny's and Snowy's mother. She was only a little girl herself then. About five she must have been when I moved into the house in Nettle Street. She lived next door at number seven. She was the youngest of the four Gilroy children. Her parents, Tom and Jean, were my first real friends in Australia. In Echuca I'd kept to myself. I was a real loner. But Tom and Jean cured me of all that. They kept popping in and out to borrow things or to ask me in for the children's birthdays and bit by bit I became almost part of their family. Christine spent as much time in my house as her own — playing with my bowl of shells and stones when she was little and then reading my books when she was older.'

Lizzie stopped. She was looking across the river and seemed to have lost her train of thought altogether. Jess waited. She looked across the river to see what had caught Lizzie's eye but there was nothing there except the red-gums on the far bank and the clear blue sky of early autumn.

At last Lizzie came out of her dream and went on.

'Yes. Well, Christine got married. That was in the depression. Her mother and father didn't think much of Jim Drury. Neither did I, to be honest. He never seemed good enough for our little Christine. Still, that's what she wanted and there was nothing we could do to stop her. She and Jim moved down the river here near Glencarra and bought their barge. Christine's mother never got used to the idea of her daughter living in a river-boat. She said it wasn't at all respectable.' Lizzie gave a short laugh. 'I must admit I felt much the same. And I missed her such a lot when she'd gone.' Lizzie went off into another dream and Jess had to prod her foot with a twig to make her go on.

'So in 1937 I decided to retire. I was sixty-four by

then and I'd been with Burns and Halliday for twenty-three years. Christine and Jim were living down here on their barge and they wrote a card to tell me about a little paddle-boat for sale. I could buy it cheap, they said, and tie it up next-door to them. At first I thought the whole idea was ridiculous. But Christine kept on at me. She was lonely down here on the river when Jim was away on his prospecting trips. So I came. Jim arranged everything for me. I will say that for him. He was a good friend to me. As good as a son. He repaired the paddler and had her towed up river to this spot and made sure she was all safe and water-tight. He was going to paint her too but he's never got round to it. I sold off some of my furniture and brought the good stuff here with all my books. I came in the furniture van myself, sitting right up in the cab beside the driver. The best journey of my whole life, that was. We travelled at night, I remember. It was just six years ago – the year of the terrible mice plague. As we drove along in the moonlight, the whole road was alive with mice! They flowed across in front of us like a river. Yes, six years ago. So I've stuck to the Murray for forty years. Never been down to Melbourne since the day I left it. Never wanted to either.'

Jess fished out her notebook. Her questions were getting too complicated for easy lip-reading.

'Don't you wish you lived right in Glencarra? Isn't it lonely and scary out here so far from town?'

Lizzie shook her head and smiled so that her brown old face was all wrinkled round her eyes.

'No,' she laughed, 'I'm never lonely. There's always the river. And there's Christine next door – or there was till she had to go down to Melbourne. And there's Annie and the two boys. And there's Jim for half the year. Christine does my shopping for me in the town – the boys have to do it just now – and I help her with the washing. We hang it out on the line between the two saplings there. And I keep an eye on the kids for her when she goes up to Mrs Reardon's place or into town. And the boys collect any letters from the Post Office now and then – not that I get many these days. I've only one sister left in Bamburgh now and she's over eighty. So, all in all, it works out well, Jess. I don't like lots of people around. When you're deaf it's nice to be alone most of the time so you don't have to worry what people are trying to say to you. I can always understand Christine. She learnt to talk to me slowly when she was just a little girl and she's made sure the boys can do it too. Jim never got the knack – but he writes down what he wants to say. Terrible speller, Jim is! Still, I know what he means all right.'

'When will Christine be back?' wrote Jess.

'I wish I knew,' said Lizzie. Her voice sounded worried. 'I'll be glad to see her, I can tell you that. It's quite a responsibility looking after those two boys on my own. Annie's much better now. I think they might all be back in a couple of weeks but it could be longer.'

Jess stretched out her legs on the rug and picked off a bull-ant that was approaching too near. With shattering whoops and calls, Kenny and Snowy came running back from the river after their swim.

'Jess, make some more tea, dear, would you? I'm sure you and the boys could do with another cup and so could I.'

Jess jumped up and walked across to the 'Sally

Jane'. Lizzie settled back comfortably into her chair, pulled a pale grey shawl around her shoulders and opened up yesterday's newspaper that had been lying unread on her lap all afternoon. Kenny and Snowy sprawled out on the rug and lay there half in the sun, half in the shade, waiting for the new pot of tea.

Making the tea in the galley, Jess suddenly remembered Linda and the library. It was still an uncomfortable thought but nothing like as bad as it had been. Lizzie's long story of forty years by the river seemed to make Jess's blunder seem less disastrous. For the first time since Wednesday, she felt almost happy.

8
Silver-Bike

Jess loved Lizzie's little kitchen – the galley, as the boys told her she ought to call it. Jim had built it right into the very bow of the paddle-boat with a long, narrow window running lengthways on the bank side and another overlooking the river. Jess liked to peer through this window and over the broad stretch of moving water to the opposite bank, thick with saplings and fully-grown red-gums. Grass and trees all looked greener over there.

Jim had fitted a little old fire-stove under the bank-side window, with a round, shiny metal chimney going up through the ceiling and out into the fresh air. Under the river-window was a scrubbed wooden bench, a tin washing-up dish and a wire soap-saver with a square of Velvet soap in its cage for frothing the washing-up water. There were no taps. Lizzie simply took a bucket out to the river and dipped it in whenever she needed water. Below the bench, she had a cupboard for cups and saucers, mugs and plates, saucepans and frying pan. She kept her food in another cupboard set in beside the stove – flour and sugar in white metal bins, salt and oatmeal in earthenware crocks, biscuits in a round tin. Kenny and Snowy gathered wood for Lizzie along the bank, twigs for kindling the fire, larger bits for keeping it going. They stacked it in a wooden box in front of the stove. A Primus for quick cooking when the fire-stove was not alight stood at the far end of the bench.

Today the stove was burning brightly and the heavy black kettle hissing gently, just on the boil. Jess took the brown teapot, heated it carefully with water from the kettle, put in the tea and filled it up with boiling water. While it was drawing at one side of the stove, Jess put out the blue and white cups, the milk and sugar and a plate of shortbread on a large Coronation tin tray. She carried the teapot out first, through the main cabin, up two steps to the narrow deck, down the springy gang-plank and put it on the ground beside Lizzie. Then back for the tray, balancing its heavy load carefully and picking her way slowly down the plank.

'Snowy! Kenny!' she called, 'it's cup-of-tea time.'

'Coming!' called the boys together from their boat and scuttled out to join Jess and Lizzie on the bank.

'Jess,' muttered Kenny softly after she had poured tea for everyone and passed around the shortbread, 'we want to have a serious talk to you.'

'Who does?' asked Jess in surprise.

'Me and Snowy. We've been discussing things. We need to talk to you.'

'All right. Why not now?'

'No. We want you by yourself. Come over into our boat after the cup of tea.' Kenny talked as if to the rug and the twigs.

'All right. I'll come. But what's it all about?'

'Can't tell you now. Lizzie'd want to know all about it. Wait and see.'

Kenny and Snowy gave each other a secret glance full of importance. They finished their tea off quickly and, one after the other, wandered casually towards their boat again. Snowy was whistling his rather tuneless whistle.

Jess felt very curious. She gulped down her tea faster than usual and then made signs to Lizzie that she was going over to the boys' boat for a while. Lizzie nodded, helped herself to another cup and picked up her paper again.

Jess ran to the 'Lucky Strike' and bounded up the gang-plank and into the day cabin. This boat was built to be lived in and was altogether more roomy, more comfortable than Lizzie's crowded cabins. Here the day cabin lay aft in the long barge-like boat and stretched right across its full width, lit by two round port-holes on each side. To the left of the gang-plank, running up into the bows, was a narrow central passage-way with two little sleeping cabins overlooking the bank and a larger cabin and a poky galley on the river side. Hidden away among trees on the bank was a square brown canvas tent sheltering the latrine, nothing more than a long deep trench in the ground. Every few weeks Jim (or the boys them-

94

selves when Jim was away) moved the brown tent along to a new section of the trench and filled in the old section. Jess didn't think much of this arrangement but she had to put up with it as best she could.

Now as she bounced into the cabin she found Kenny and Snowy sitting solemnly side by side on a sofa.

'Well? What's up?' she asked them.

'Please sit down,' said Kenny politely. 'It's just that we want to talk to you.'

Jess curled her legs under her in a broad comfortable armchair opposite the boys. She waited. Kenny and Snowy looked awkwardly at each other.

'*You* say it,' muttered Kenny.

'No. *You* say it. You're older,' replied Snowy.

'All right.' Kenny turned to Jess. 'Jess, the trouble is this. Me and Snowy asked you down to the river to play with us, to share that special place we've got on the bank. And what's happened? The last three Sundays you've spent all your time with Lizzie, making her cups of tea, writing messages to her in your little book, getting her to talk on and on all afternoon. We're sick and tired of her talking. And we don't think it's fair. You're meant to be *our* friend, not Lizzie's. We found you first.'

'Yes,' Snowy broke in here. 'So we want you to stop sitting all Sunday afternoon with Old Lizzie. We want you to play with us.'

Jess was silent. She did not know what to say. The boys were right really. But how could she stop sitting with Lizzie and listening to her talking on and on. That's really what she came for now. The boys' chatter seemed empty compared with Lizzie's vivid tales.

95

'But I *like* Lizzie,' she said at last, rather weakly.

'Yes, we like her too. But we don't spend all our time sitting around with her, do we? Sitting around is just for old ladies, not for kids.' Kenny's voice was scornful.

Jess didn't like being thought an old lady. She was only thirteen, after all.

'Well, what do you want me to do then?' she asked huffily.

'We want you to help us with our hut. We're building a very secret hut with branches and bracken and grass and stuff like that,' said Snowy.

'Where is it?'

'Just past Lizzie's boat. It's so well hidden, I bet you've never seen it.'

'No, I haven't. Come and show me.' Jess had jumped up and was all ready to go. The boys led the way down the plank, past Lizzie reading in her wicker chair and then another twenty yards further on among the slender saplings. Behind a huge red-gum with its broad, rough trunk forming a solid wall, the boys had their half-built humpy. It wasn't much more than one long branch propped against the side of the tree, with lots of leafy boughs sloping up to it on either side.

Jess peered inside.

'Oh, it's really lovely! Can I go in?'

'I'll go first,' said Kenny and he crawled around the side of the tree trunk and into the opening of the green, leafy tent. Jess crawled in after him and Snowy came last. All three squatted on the prickly ground and looked up at the sunlight filtering in through the gaps in the roof.

'All it needs is some more bracken,' said Jess. 'We

could weave it in and out. And we really need a rug to make it more comfy. And a few old cups and plates for our meals.' Already she was imagining how they could all sit hunched up on the rug inside the hut, sipping their tea and peering out around the tree-trunk to the river.

'Yeah, we know that's all it needs. But are you going to help us? You can't come into the hut if you're not going to help us.' Kenny sounded stern.

'And you can't help if you're going to spend all your time sitting around with Lizzie,' added Snowy.

Jess hesitated. How could she choose. She'd love to finish building the hut with the boys and then to play in it. But she wanted to sit with Lizzie on the bank to find out more about the other world that Lizzie still called the 'Old Country'.

'I know,' said Jess suddenly. 'I'll spend the first half of the afternoon with you and then at four o'clock I'll make a pot of tea and sit with Lizzie.'

The boys didn't look very pleased. They wanted more of Jess than just half an afternoon but she was firm so they made the best they could of it.

'You'll have to tell Lizzie, Jess,' said Kenny. 'We're not going to be the ones that tell her.'

'All right,' said Jess reluctantly, 'but not just now. Let's get started on the hut.'

'You could sweep the inside all smooth and clean if you like,' said Snowy to Jess. 'I'll go with Kenny to get some more branches for the sides.'

'No thanks,' said Jess sharply. 'I'm not going to be stuck inside sweeping while you two boys do all the interesting bits. I'll get branches too. You could do the sweeping yourself, Snowy.'

'Me! Sweep!' shouted Snowy indignantly.

No one did the sweeping. They all searched for small branches and supple sticks and fronds of bracken and handfuls of dry, wiry grass. All three of them carried great armloads back to the hut. Together they set to work, weaving the new branches and bracken in and out of the framework the boys had already built. Bit by bit, they filled up all the holes between the boughs, pulling fronds in and out, over and under, tucking in the loose ends, plaiting bracken and dry grass together to pad out an empty corner here or a slack space there. Inside the hut, almost no light trickled through at all now. It was cool and dark. Each time Jess and Kenny and Snowy peered inside they were more and more pleased. It was more than just any old humpy; it was a proper hut with a roof that was almost rain-proof. Not that any rain was likely to fall!

'I'll do a bit of sweeping now,' said Jess after an hour of weaving when her arms ached and her legs were stiff from standing up for so long.

'I'll help,' offered Kenny unexpectedly, 'and Snowy can go and get Lizzie to come and look.'

Snowy scampered off to the boats while Jess and Kenny, each with a long bracken frond as a broom, carefully swept over the floor of the hut, pushing every little twig and gum-nut and stone firmly to the walls and leaving a smooth, sandy surface. They finished only just in time. As Jess and Kenny crawled out the 'front door' one after the other, dusty and hot, with the limp bracken still in their hands, Lizzie and Snowy came towards them through the trees.

'What a marvellous green tent!' exclaimed Lizzie as soon as she set eyes on it. She was delighted and astonished by it all.

'Can I go right inside?' she asked.

The three children nodded and Lizzie dropped down on to her stockinged knees and crawled into the shady tent of leaves. Jess, Kenny and Snowy crawled in after her and the four of them crouched on the freshly-swept floor and admired it all.

'Really beautiful!' said Lizzie. 'You boys could even sleep out here on a warm night, couldn't you?'

Jess felt a sudden stab of envy. She'd have to be back in her boring old sleep-out while Kenny and Snowy had all the fun of camping in the hut the three of them had made together. The two boys began talking excitedly to each other about the idea.

'Let's come outside again,' said Lizzie. 'I'll never be able to see a word you say if we stay in here. It's so lovely and dark!'

So out they all crawled again, skirting the broad tree-trunk by the entrance, blinking in the strong sunlight and brushing leaves out of their hair. The Sunday paddle-steamer was already grinding its way back along the river, getting closer and closer every minute.

'Five o'clock,' sighed Jess, brushing the dust off her watch. 'Time to be going home.' She was desperately trying to work out how to tell Lizzie in these last five minutes about the new plan for Sundays – about playing with the boys before after-noon tea and talking with Lizzie afterwards. It seemed too long and complicated a sentence to say in that slow, careful speech but there wasn't really time now to sit down and write it all out.

'Go on Jess,' whispered Snowy, poking her sharply in the arm as she bent down near the boats to put on her sandals. 'Go on! Tell her!'

'All right. All right. I'm just going to say it. Don't be such a fuss-pot,' Jess muttered back at Snowy. As she straightened up, there was Old Lizzie packing up the cups and saucers on to the tray.

'Jess,' said Lizzie smiling her crooked smile at her, 'why don't you ask your mother if you could come out and see us on Saturdays as well as Sundays? You'll be wanting to play with the boys in that splendid hut you've all made. And the boys really do need someone sensible like you to be with them. You could play with them on Saturdays, and then on Sundays you and I could have our nice comfortable chat on the bank – or inside my boat when the weather gets colder. What do you think?'

A wave of relief flowed through Jess. Lizzie understood already. She didn't need to explain it at all. And Lizzie's plan was so much better – a whole afternoon with the boys and a whole afternoon with Lizzie. But would Mum agree? *Two* afternoons at the river might be a bit too much to ask. Still, it was worth a try.

'I-ll a-sk M-u-m,' she said slowly back to Lizzie. And smiled.

Jess wheeled her bike out to the track and with a quick wave to Lizzie and the boys she was off on her bumpy way home again. Uncomfortable thoughts about Linda Betts pushed their way into her mind again. Linda might be back at school tomorrow. Jess would have to say something. She'd have to try to say she was sorry about not speaking in the library. She'd do it first thing. No use putting it off and waiting for the right minute.

'Oh dear! It will be terrible!' groaned Jess to herself out loud.

Her mind was so full of Linda Betts that she didn't see the crowd of boys until they were almost on top of her, careering wildly along the track towards her, swooping, calling, laughing, shouting in voices that broke suddenly from low to high and back again. They were all around her now, ringing their bells in a loud, jangling chorus, grinning in a way that was threatening, not friendly. She was forced to get off suddenly and to stand there hedged around by seven bikes and seven boys much older than herself. They looked about sixteen or even seventeen and seemed to tower above her.

With a commanding wave of his hand, the tallest boy stopped the ringing of the bells.

'Where d'you think you're off to, Sheila?' he asked Jess. His black hair was sleeked down with oil. So much oil that Jess could see round drops of it on his neck. His bike was painted bright silver. His voice was hard and sneering.

'I'm just going home,' said Jess nervously, holding tighter to her handle-grips.

'Where've you been then?' asked another boy. He had red hair and half-shut blue eyes.

'Just down the river.' Jess was cagey.

'I bet your Mum don't know you're down here all on your own,' said Silver-Bike, smiling slyly.

'She does so! She *said* I could come!' Jess was indignant and sounded braver than she felt.

'She's off her rocker then!' Silver-Bike said rudely. 'Don't she even know it's dangerous down here. There's a queer old girl lives just along here in a boat. And a couple of real wild boys. You'd better look out, kid, or you'll be in trouble.'

Jess kept quiet. She couldn't tell if he was warning her or threatening her.

'And there's the tramp too! Have you seen that old swaggie with a scruffy grey beard?' put in Red Hair.

'Yes. I saw him last week. Not this week though. He's gone. Must've left the district.' Jess's words tumbled out on top of each other.

'He's still around somewhere. We seen him Wednesday. Not far from here.' This was Silver-Bike speaking again. 'We're looking for him. Going to give him a fright. Chase him along the track. You oughter keep right off of this bit of the river, Sheila. Anything happens down here.'

Again, Jess said nothing. She was scared. There was an awkward silence. Suddenly a smaller boy with round glasses leaned forward and peered hard at Jess.

'Aren't you Nick McCallum's sister?' he asked, frowning.

'Yes,' said Jess.

'Nick McCallum should have more sense than to let his little sister come down here on her own!'

'But it's quite safe really,' said Jess. She felt on firmer ground now they'd mentioned Nico. 'I just come to see some friends and then I go home again. There's nothing dangerous by the river.'

'Friends?' cried Round-Glasses. 'What friends?'

Jess felt caught. She hadn't meant to let on that she knew Lizzie and the boys.

'Just some friends. They live in boats.'

'Not that mad old girl and them cheeky little river kids!' exclaimed Silver-Bike.

'I'll have to talk to Nick about you,' said Round-

Glasses in a maddeningly superior voice. 'He'll have to keep his eye on you, I reckon.'

Jess was furious. She kept thinking of all the things she wanted to shout back at these great hulking boys with their sneers and their threats. But, in fact, she said nothing at all. Her face went redder and her eyes felt hot and tired. She looked around at the seven bikes, hemming her in with a metal fence. Only the one was painted silver. All the rest were black.

'Let her go!' said Silver-Bike suddenly, pulling away from the others. 'We'll never catch up with the old swaggie if we mess around here all day. Let her do what she wants. If she gets into trouble, it won't be our fault, will it? We've told you, kid, haven't we, to keep right off of this bit of river?'

'Yes,' said Jess.

'Well, mind you do! *We* run this bit of river! See! Come on you lot!' And with that he was away, speeding down the track again with the other six tearing after him, bike bells ringing, heads bent down over the handlebars, loud voices laughing and shouting.

'Ta ta, Sheila!' one of them called insolently over his shoulder.

Jess rode slowly home. The river didn't seem quite so safe and happy a place any more. She knew there was no danger really, but this gang acted as if they owned whole miles of the river bank. They'd never hurt her, she was pretty sure of that. Their threats were all empty talk. But she never wanted to have to see them again. They scared her with their pushing and their shoving all around her, their rude questions, their cross-examinations. They made her feel small and stupid. Well, she'd see what Nico said, she thought to herself.

9
Uncle Norval

Jess burst through the wire door at the back of the house. It banged noisily behind her.

'Nico!' she called.

No answer. The whole house seemed oddly quiet. No one in the kitchen. Then she heard soft voices from the front room but the door was shut. Jess crept into the hall and put her ear to the front-room door and listened.

'Visitors,' she thought to herself, 'but who?'

She could hear a man's gentle voice going on and on but she didn't recognize it at all. Not the doctor. Not Mr Philips from over the road who sometimes came to borrow the lawnmower. Jess heard Nico's voice, laughing politely. Then Laura saying something and Dad asking a question. Then the man's voice again, on and on. She couldn't catch any words. It did now seem vaguely familiar, but who? 'I'll have to go in,' thought Jess, 'No use staying out here trying to guess who it is.'

Turning the handle firmly, Jess opened the door and walked in.

'Hullo Mum, I'm back,' she announced. She looked round the room. All the family was there. They sat ranged in a circle – two on the sofa, two on hard, upright, dining-room chairs, and there by the fire-place, spread out comfortably in the best arm-chair, sat the large figure of Uncle Norval.

'Oh no!' groaned Jess silently to herself, 'not Uncle Norval!' He usually came once a year, every October, and this was only March! While unkind thoughts were racing madly through Jess's head, she was smiling politely and holding out her hand to the figure in the best armchair.

'Oh, Uncle Norval! I didn't know you were here. How nice to see you.'

Mum looked particularly relieved that Jess had managed to conceal her true feelings. Only two years back she had embarrassed them all by groaning out loud when she had set eyes on Uncle Norval. And a year or two earlier she'd even called him Uncle Awful to his face but this wasn't really intentional. The words had just slipped out before she could stop them. Now Nico and Laura gave each other quick looks full of amusement as they watched Jess's polite, grown-up performance. 'The little hypocrite!' their looks seemed to say. But plainly, they were relieved too.

'Had a good afternoon, dear?' murmured Mum, not really expecting an answer.

'Yes thanks.' Jess gave her a desperate look. There was so much she wanted to say but with Uncle Norval sitting there it was impossible even to begin. It would all have to wait.

Uncle Norval was not, in fact, an uncle at all. Not their uncle. Not anyone's uncle. He'd been at school with Dad, ages ago in Gippsland. Jess always found this hard to believe even though she'd seen a photograph of the school cricket team in 1915 that proved it. Their names were neatly printed underneath the row of faded white and sepia figures, sitting so solemnly with bat and wickets in the centre front.

'Arthur B. McCallum' and 'Norval A. Johnson'. So it must be true that they'd been at school together but, when Jess looked at the two men, she noticed a world of difference. Dad, of course, was very old. Over forty. But he didn't look so very old. He walked along with a bouncing, springing step and planted each foot firmly on the ground. His hair was still thick and black, not thinning on top yet, not receding in front. Uncle Norval looked an old man. Not a haggard, worn-out old man but a plump and well-fed one. His skin was pale and smooth, almost grey; his hair was white; he moved very slowly when he moved at all, almost in a shuffle; he sat solidly, heavily, his broad, well-dressed bulk filling the whole span of the best leather armchair, from one wide brown arm to the other.

Jess took her place on the one empty chair in the family circle. Uncle Norval gave her a brief, kindly nod and went on talking as if he'd never been interrupted. He was talking about his house at Byron's Creek, about the dahlias, the phlox and the lupins; about the new tank he'd had put in around the east side; about the crazy footpath he'd laid himself, up the slope at the back of the block; about the wallabies that came to be fed at the fence; about the rabbits that were such a dratted nuisance. On and on, he went in a voice that seldom changed its mournful note. Then there was a sudden pause. Dad waited a moment and asked:

'And how is your mother, Norval?'

Mother was quite well it seemed. Still living in Leongatha on her own. He got in to see her most Saturdays. He'd taken her up to Sydney for a short holiday just before Christmas. The short holiday took, Jess thought, a long time to tell. And so did Christmas itself. Uncle Norval and his mother had spent it at her sister's place in Drouin. There were just the three of them. They'd had a quiet time. Another pause.

'And how's your health been lately, Norval?' asked Mum. 'You hadn't been at all well when we saw you last.'

Uncle Norval still wasn't at all well, it seemed. His circulation was the chief trouble but then there were the headaches.

'Right down the back they go, Mary. Right down the back,' he sighed.

Nico glanced at Jess but Jess was studying the pattern in the carpet, trying not to listen to the details of the headache in the back. Uncle Norval had tried this remedy and that, he said. He'd been to a herbal doctor who had given him different kinds of herb tea to drink.

'Health is a precious gift, you know, Arthur. A precious gift.' Dad nodded seriously and Jess kept frowning at the carpet.

Jess knew that Dad was just about to ask Uncle Norval if he'd seen any of their old school friends lately. That was always the next question. Dad himself never saw any of them nowadays, stuck up here as he was by the river in the north but Uncle Norval moved around Gippsland a good deal, selling insurance to farmers, and he often ran into Ted or Dick or poor old Larry. Before Dad could open his mouth to ask his question, Jess herself rushed in to fill the gap.

'Uncle Norval,' she said rather too brightly, 'I've been down to the river today.'

107

Uncle Norval was silent for a few seconds and then he said, 'Have you now, young lady?' Jess smiled weakly but could think of nothing more to say. There was another pause and then Uncle Norval turned his gaze slowly, very slowly, round to Dad.

'I saw poor old Larry a couple of months back, Arthur,' he said; 'he's going downhill fast, I'm afraid.' Uncle Norval was off on the long list of old school friends from Leongatha days. Some were doing better. Some were doing worse. Most were much the same. Jess gave another of her silent groans and went back to gazing at the carpet and its purple flowers.

Mum asked Uncle Norval to stay to tea but he had to be off. He'd be glad to come to tea tomorrow. Uncle Norval pushed himself slowly to his feet, one large, white, smooth hand spread out on each arm of the chair.

'Well children,' he said, beaming blandly round at Nico, Laura and Jess, 'it *has* been nice to see you all again and to hear all your news.'

Jess wanted to shout out, 'But you *haven't* heard our news, you silly old bandicoot! You never listen! You just go on and on about your mother and the dahlias and your headaches and poor old Larry!' But Jess could feel her mother's firm restraining eye on her so she said nothing at all except 'Goodbye, Uncle Norval,' very meekly.

Dad walked back with Uncle Norval to his hotel. Mum and the girls threw some tea together in the kitchen and Nico put all the bicycles away in the woodshed.

'Aw, Mum!' wailed Jess, 'why does Uncle Norval have to come at this time of year? He's gone and ruined our whole Sunday!'

'Don't be silly, Jess,' said Mum, rather sharply. 'He's a poor, lonely old chap and he's a friend of your father's. The least we can do is listen to him when he comes.'

'But it's so boring! And it's all about himself!'

'Well, *you* might be like that if you lived alone.' Mum was annoyed and was banging the plates around noisily. Jess knew her mother was just as bored by Uncle Norval as everyone else but didn't like the children to criticize him.

'Come on now, Jess,' Mum's voice was firm and crisp. 'Get the table set quickly and call Nico. We won't wait for Dad.'

Jess fell silent. She could see it wasn't the right moment to ask Mum if she could go down to the river on Saturdays as well as on Sundays. It wasn't the right moment to tell Laura all about the little hut of green leaves and bracken by the red-gum. It wasn't the right moment to ask Nico about the gang of boys and Silver-Bike. So she just ate up her scrambled eggs and said nothing.

Dad was back before they'd finished.

'Uncle Norval wants us all to go to afternoon tea with him at the Royal Alexandra on Tuesday,' he announced.

'Oh no!' shrieked Jess. 'Mum, I don't have to go, do I?'

'You certainly do, Jess. We'll *all* be going,' said Mum, looking at Nico and Laura with a wary eye to squash any protest from that quarter. 'All three of you will be there at ten past four sharp on the front steps of the Royal Alexandra.'

'It's not fair,' groaned Nico loudly. Laura was silent. She fiddled with the fork on her plate.

'Laura's the only kind one among the lot of you,' said Dad.

'Goody-goody!' hissed Jess at Laura.

'Off to bed, Jess,' snapped Mum. 'I've had about enough of you for one day.'

So Jess went to bed. She lay there on her back looking up at the stars. The nights were still warm.

'Poor old Uncle Norval,' she thought to herself. 'I suppose I *was* a bit mean.' And she fell asleep.

When Uncle Norval came to tea on Monday evening, Jess was so unbelievably nice to him that the whole family wondered what had come over her. She plied him with questions about Byron's Creek and his garden. She passed him the pepper and salt without waiting to be asked. She filled up his glass with icy water from the best crystal jug. Mum looked at her very suspiciously. She was pretty sure Jess was up to something but she didn't know what. When Uncle Norval had finally departed at about nine o'clock ('Early to bed, you know, Mary. Early to bed. It's the best rule') all became clear.

'Mum,' began Jess as she started assiduously carrying the dirty dishes through to the kitchen, 'I was just wondering if I could go down to the river on Saturdays as well as Sundays.'

'So that's why you were so polite to Uncle Norval!' laughed Mum, as relieved as anyone that he'd gone. 'I *thought* you must be going to ask for something.'

'Well, *can* I, Mum? You see, we've got this lovely little hut and we want to play in it. And on Sundays I want to talk to Old Lizzie.'

'Talk!' broke in Nico scornfully, 'listen, you

110

mean! Your Old Lizzie's just another Uncle Norval. Just talks, on and on about herself.'

'She does not,' retorted Jess in a flare of indignation. Then she thought for a minute. 'Well – she *does* talk a lot. But it's not boring. It's interesting. And she always notices me. She doesn't just look through me the way Uncle Norval does. She knows I'm there!'

'We'll have to see, Jess,' said Mum, putting an end to the argument with Nico. 'It'll depend on how you behave at afternoon tea, of course. Now let's get these dishes out of the way. You wash, Jess, and Nico can dry.'

'Nico,' said Jess casually as she filled the white sink with hot water and beat the soap-saver vigorously around in it to make the froth pile up, 'I met some friends of yours yesterday.'

'Who?' said Nico.

'Seven boys on bikes. One of them has a silver bike. And the one that knows you best has got round glasses.'

'Not Jack Stevens' gang!' exclaimed Nico, looking alarmed. 'They're not *friends* of mine! They used to be in my form at school till they left, that's all. They've been gone about three years now. Jack Stevens has been in trouble with the police. You keep right away from them, Jess.'

'All right,' murmured Jess, hoping her mother hadn't heard any of this. Luckily for Jess, she hadn't. She was in the dining room, carefully sweeping crumbs from her best tablecloth with a little white ivory brush and tray.

'Who's the one with glasses?' Jess asked Nico as the coast was still clear.

'That's Foggy Healey. He's not a bad kid, really. Pity he got mixed up with Jack Stevens' lot.'

Jess had to be content with this. She'd have to wait till Tuesday evening before she could raise the question of Saturdays by the river again. The very thought of afternoon tea at the Royal Alexandra Hotel, with its thick red carpets and its hot stuffy rooms and its waiters who said 'Sir' and 'Madam', made her feel sick in the stomach.

Nico, Laura and Jess all arrived at the Royal Alexandra on Tuesday afternoon at the same moment, all hastily spruced up in the school locker-rooms after the last lesson had ended. Mum was waiting for them on the steps in her best dress and the blue hat with the wide brim. Dad was inside already. He'd only had to come along the main street from his office.

'Now Jess,' said Mum in her warning voice as they pushed open the heavy front door, 'remember what I said.'

'Yes Mum,' said Jess.

Once inside it was all just as bad as Jess had feared. Uncle Norval sat squarely in a large floral armchair; red carpets stretched in all directions around him; waiters glided in and out with silver trays. Jess knew they'd start saying 'Sir' and 'Madam' any minute now.

'Your table is ready now, Sir,' one of them murmured deferentially to Uncle Norval.

All the family trooped after Uncle Norval into the dining room and sat around the window table. It was beautifully spread with a snowy white cloth and heavy with plates of golden scones, silver dishes of jam and cream, two large round sponge-cakes dusted

112

with icing sugar and oozing with lemon butter, and, best of all, in the very centre of the table, a plate piled high with lamingtons, brown with chocolate and thickly encrusted with coconut.

'Lamingtons!' breathed Jess softly to herself, her heart leaping unexpectedly into sudden happiness. The Royal Alexandra was famous for its lamingtons. They were not shop cakes at all but hand-made in the hotel's vast kitchen downstairs. Mr Singleton, the head cook himself, beat up the sponge mixture every morning, baked it in huge, shallow oblong tins, cut the cooked cakes into little squares, dipped each one into runny chocolate icing and then rolled it in a heap of white desiccated coconut. Even in war-time, Mr Singleton somehow managed to find rare supplies of cocoa and coconut. Not even the skilled ladies of the Country Women's Association could produce a better plate of lamingtons than Mr Singleton of the Royal Alexandra.

Jess really behaved herself very well. She did flinch rather too noticeably every time the waiter called her mother 'Madam'; she did giggle whenever she looked at Nico as he tried to eat his lamington without making a mess; she frowned at him far too much when he started picking up bits of coconut from his plate on his licked fore-finger and she did eat far too many lamingtons herself. Apart from that, she was very good. All the same, the afternoon tea was not a great success. The trouble was that they'd already exhausted all Uncle Norval's possible topics of conversation on Sunday and Monday and no one knew what to say. There was a bit more talk about 'poor old Larry'. Drink, it seemed, was his trouble and Mum shook her head sadly. They talked about the weather. Dad asked about the insurance business. But somehow, nothing ever really got going. There were long pauses when you could clearly hear Nico sipping his tea as quietly as he could. The food itself was lovely. There was no doubt about that. Jess made the most of it and said nothing at all apart from 'please' and 'thank-you'. The waiter poured everyone a second cup of tea and then a third cup. At last, it was time to go. There was much hand-shaking with Uncle Norval, much thanking, much sending of regards to Uncle Norval's mother, Mrs Johnson, in Leongatha.

'We'll see you in October then, Norval,' Dad was saying.

'That's right,' said Uncle Norval as he walked slowly across the red carpet to the front door and out on to the broad steps of the Royal Alexandra. 'I'll be back in the spring. Just a couple of days, you know. I hope to manage it twice a year from now on.'

Jess's heart sank. *Twice* a year! Even the lamingtons could not make up for the thought of it.

'Lovely to see you all again,' called Uncle Norval from the steps as Dad and Mum waved to him from the footpath below and Nico, Laura and Jess rode off home on their bikes.

10
War Effort

Linda Betts had not come back to school yet. Away on Monday, away on Tuesday, away again on Wednesday. On Thursday, as Jess rode the long mile to school, she caught a glimpse of Linda's dark head as the bus sailed past with its load of children and teachers. She knew that the awful moment had come. She wanted to get Linda on her own so she hung about in the crowded, noisy locker-room, trying to catch her before the first siren went. But Linda came in at the very last minute, surrounded by a group of sympathizing friends, Jill on one side, Franny on the other and Eileen hovering behind. Jill was holding Linda's arm. Jess didn't see how she could possibly break in on them. All through the first two lessons Jess looked anxiously across the classroom towards Linda, trying to catch her eye, but Linda was bent down over her work, a long floppy bit of hair hiding her face.

Then, halfway through the morning, Jess's chance came but not at all in the way she'd expected. 'Marching' was announced in every form room when the siren went for recess and the whole school poured itself out on to the oval. 'Marching' was an obsession in the school that year. Jess thought it was somehow connected with the war. The headmaster had first introduced it with a speech about being always ready and the idea had caught on like a fever. The stirring military music that blared out over the vast oval from a pair of loud-speakers strung up on a goal-post, the headmaster's enthusiastic insistence on straight lines and good posture – head held high, stomach pulled in tight, shoulders back and down, arms swinging vigorously – made Jess feel that the entire school of six hundred must be preparing to go into battle. Any day now, she thought, the call might come from New Guinea or Borneo and then they'd all be marching together through the jungle, rifles on their shoulders, khaki slouch hats on their heads. So Jess threw herself into the marching with great concentration and energy, trying to keep in step with everyone else, trying to keep dead level with her row of four, trying to keep exactly behind the girl in front without treading on her heels.

The six hundred were assembled in their four Houses – Red, Blue, Yellow and Green. Jess belonged to Red House and always felt faintly sorry for all the poor things who had to make do with pale, uninteresting colours like Blue, Yellow and Green. In each House, the boys, of course, marched in front, starting with the great hulking figures from the Sixth Form and working down to the little boys in Form One with their earnest pink faces and their short grey trousers. Then came the girls. First the tall, amazingly grown-up-looking Sixth-Formers and gradually dwindling down in size to the little eleven-year-olds with their hair ribbons and plaits and bunches.

A whistle blew shrilly. The teacher with the loudest voice bellowed through his megaphone, 'School! Quick march!' and the first familiar bars of military music burst out from the loud-speakers.

Round and round the oval they marched. The teachers stood in a huddle under the peppercorn trees and looked on. Now and then one of them would dash across the grass to march beside a straggling House to shout instructions, encouragement or reproof. No talking was allowed among the marchers. That was a rule. But Jess found herself beside Linda in the Second Form group of Red House. Jill, Franny and Eileen were all well out of the way in Yellow, Green or Blue. Keeping her head unnaturally high and her eyes fixed firmly on the hair of the girl in front, arms swinging well up and back, stomach pulled in, Jess whispered out of the corner of the mouth.

'Linda!'

'Yes.'

'I'm sorry I didn't speak to you in the library last week.' The words fell out in a rush. Linda made no reply.

'Linda!'

'Yes.'

'Really, truly, I am sorry. I just didn't expect to see you there. I didn't know what to say.'

Again no reply.

Red House swung around by the near goal posts and started the long march up the channel side. Jess went on whispering, urgently, quickly.

'And Linda, I'm very sorry about your father dying so suddenly like that.'

Again, silence.

Had Linda even heard her, Jess wondered. Slowly and stiffly she turned her head a few degrees towards Linda. Linda, too, was striding along with head up, shoulders back and down. She gazed straight in

117

front of her. But tears were running down her cheeks.

'Oh Linda!' cried Jess, forgetting all about the marching rules, turning right round to her, putting out one hand and almost stopping in her tracks, 'I'm so sorry. I didn't mean to upset you!'

'S'all right,' mumbled Linda, fishing out a handkerchief to mop up her tears but still keeping her eyes looking straight ahead.

'Red House!' roared the teacher with the megaphone. 'No talking there! How can we win the war when you silly little girls in Form II keep on nattering and chattering? Heads up now! Shoulders back! Swing those arms, Red House! You're a disgrace to the whole school!'

Jess felt tears in her own eyes too. To think that Linda, so calm, so grown-up, so surrounded by admiring friends, could actually *cry* just like anybody else. Jess was amazed. She was more amazed still when, as they came round again to the poplar-tree side of the oval and the music changed with a few hiccups from brass to bagpipes, Linda whispered, 'I'm leaving school at Christmas.'

'But I thought you wanted to stay on! Aren't you going to do hairdressing after Fifth Form?'

'I was going to. But not now. Mum wants me to help the boys in the shop. Don will have to be in charge of the shop now. Mick'll help him but they need me too. I'll be fourteen in December.'

'Do you mind?' whispered Jess.

'No. Don't like school much. It's the best thing to do, Mum says.'

Jess was silent now. She half envied Linda who could be so confident about joining the grown-up world at Christmas. But she was more relieved than envious – relieved that she still had years and years ahead of her in this safe little world of school.

Round and round went the marchers. A solid forty minutes of marching to help win the war. Blue House got the highest marks that day. Red House came last. Jess didn't care. As the final whistle blew, she smiled uncertainly at Linda and Linda smiled back.

A whole period had been lost altogether by the marching. That didn't worry Jess. It was Maths she'd missed. Now she had only English before lunch-time. They were reading *Kidnapped* that term; they read it out loud, one sentence each around the class and then back to the first person once more. Jess tried, as usual, to calculate by a quick count which sentence would be hers. Keeping her finger firmly on the place, she read on faster in the book until she was a few pages ahead of the class reading. As usual, she was caught out. It happened every time. Either she'd counted wrong in the first place or she didn't notice it was her turn to read or the teacher unexpectedly changed the order of the readers. Every time she would hear urgent, whispered warnings from both sides of her, 'Jess! Jess! It's your turn.'

Flustered and confused, she always launched into the wrong sentence. Today it happened again. There was a sudden burst of laughter from the whole class as Jess began to read out a sentence someone else had just read. Jess looked up anxiously to see the teacher's face clouded with annoyance. But Jess was lucky. Before Miss Guthrie could speak and before Jess had even had time to search for the right sentence, Linda Betts suddenly announced, 'Look, Miss Guthrie! It's raining!'

All heads turned to the window. Linda was right. The sky had darkened suddenly and now large, slow drops where splashing down on to the dry concrete outside. It was the first rain in Glencarra for almost five months.

'Can we go out please? Can we go?' shouted some of the boys excitedly, standing up in their places already.

'The third forms are out, Miss Guthrie,' said Eileen.

Miss Guthrie walked to the door. It opened straight on to the quadrangle. From all four sides, shrieking girls and boys were running out of their classrooms and into the rain.

'All right,' said Miss Guthrie wearily, 'you can go.' There was a wild rush to the door and a wild cry of 'Rain!' Once out in the quadrangle, everyone leaped and danced and laughed while the rain, heavier and heavier every minute, poured down all over them. The children bumped into each other in their excitement. Their hair was soaked. Their clothes were dripping. Still the crazy, excited dance and the shouting went on – 'Rain! Rain! Rain!'

Finally the headmaster had a long siren sounded to mark the end of this wild corroboree. Wet and bedraggled, the children trooped reluctantly back into their classrooms to take up again whatever lesson they'd left so suddenly.

'Jess McCallum,' said Miss Guthrie when everyone in Form II was settled at last, 'will you go on reading please. We're at the top of page 94.' Jess quickly found the place and read out her allotted sentence. She considered herself a good reader and one sentence was all too short for her to show off her ability – or so she always thought. Drops of water were falling from her hair all over her copy of *Kidnapped*. Her feet squelched happily inside their warm wet shoes and socks.

In the afternoon of that same Thursday when the whole school had more or less dried off and rain was still falling steadily outside, Jess's form had to divide into two. The boys went to woodwork and the girls to sewing and knitting. Jess always wished she was a boy on Thursday afternoons. She knew she'd love to be wielding a plane or a hammer or a saw instead of fumbling awkwardly with two, thick knitting needles and a ball of khaki wool. Knitting was all a part of the War Effort, just like the marching. Every girl in the school had to make at least one ribbed khaki scarf, five feet long and one foot wide. Two plain, two purl. Some girls had whipped through their first scarf in a matter of weeks and were on to their second or even their third, knitting nonchalantly as they strolled around the playground at lunchtime, a long snake of scarf draped over their shoulders and down their backs. A few had moved on to balaclavas – funny, long khaki hats with a round hole for the face to peep through. Jess could never work out how the knitters managed to make the holes. She made plenty of little holes herself but not on purpose. Mum sewed them up at home with khaki wool in the hope that Miss Tarrant would never notice.

Jess's scarf was still only two feet long and even to get it to two feet she'd pulled it and stretched it a good deal. Aunt Essie, who'd come to stay for a week, had kindly knitted six inches for her. Laura did a bit. Mrs Owen next door could probably be persuaded to add a few more inches while Jess minded her baby for a couple of hours. Jess herself was a painfully slow knitter. She pulled each stitch so tight that she could hardly force the needle in. She paused between every stitch and let go of the wool in her right hand. Then she'd pick it up again carefully to start the next stitch. She would look around in astonishment at Rona, Linda, Franny, Jill, Eileen and most of the others as their hands flew and their needles clicked. They seemed to have found a knack of looping the wool around the needle by just using a finger and without taking the whole hand off the other needle. For Jess that knack was impossible. Her hand had to come right off every time, up and round the needle, yanking the wool tight and hard.

Miss Tarrant wanted no talking and that was Jess's other problem. To knit in silence was a double torture. So when Miss Tarrant was busy at the far end of the room, sorting out someone's tangled balaclava, Jess began in a careful whisper to tell Rona about the hut by the river and Jack Stevens with his silver bike and boring old Uncle Norval and the lamingtons.

'Jess McCallum!' Miss Tarrant's voice was as sharp as a needle. 'Up on your stool, please! Up you get! No! Leave that knitting! I pity the poor soldier who ever has to wear *your* scarf! Here's the Shakespeare,' and she pushed a book into Jess's hands. 'You must learn another sonnet before the siren goes. Rona Fraser, get on with your knitting in *silence*, please, or you'll be up on your stool too.'

Jess was pleased. She'd far rather learn a sonnet by heart than knit, but she did her best to look sulky so that Miss Tarrant would never guess. She'd already had to stand up on her stool with the Shakespeare through many knitting lessons last year and this. She knew about ten sonnets now, off by heart, and was rather pleased with herself. Today she turned the pages to find a new one.

'Hurry up, Jess,' said Miss Tarrant. 'Stop flapping those pages. Any one will do.' So Jess chose the one on the page that happened to be open. While the needles clicked around her and the long khaki scarves trailed over the tables and on to the floor, Jess moved off into a world of her own.

When to the sessions of sweet silent thought
I summon up remembrance of things past,
I sigh the lack of many a thing I sought,
And with old woes new wail my dear time's waste, ...

By the time the siren wailed out to mark the end of school for the afternoon, Jess had learned the sonnet and had recited it to Miss Tarrant. Not for the first time, Miss Tarrant wondered out loud how a girl who knitted so atrociously could learn sonnets so easily.

Jess said the sonnet over to herself as she rode home. The rain had stopped now and the wet road was steaming in the new sunshine. Mum had a pot of tea and a cooling-tray of Anzac biscuits ready on the kitchen table for Nico, Laura and Jess as they came in from school one after the other. She had some good news for Jess too.

'Dad and I have talked over your river plan, Jess,' she said as they all sat around the table drinking their tea. 'We've decided you can go on Saturdays as well as Sundays but only till the end of March. That's when Daylight Saving ends and the evenings will get dark much earlier. It will be getting colder then too

123

as the autumn comes on. You mightn't even want to go to the river in the winter but if you do we'll probably let you go for a couple of hours on Sundays. So make the most of these next few weekends. Perhaps the little boys would like to come and play here sometimes in the winter.'

Jess didn't think they would but she didn't stop to worry about that. She rushed to the missionary calendar over the ice-chest to count the Saturdays till the end of March.

'Three!' she announced with satisfaction. 'There's the 13th, the 20th and the 27th. Thanks Mum. That'll be lovely.'

11
The Tent of Leaves

On Saturday the 13th March, Jess persuaded Mum to have lunch early so she could make a quick getaway to the river. Mum had given her an old, moth-eaten rug for the floor of the bush hut, three chipped enamel mugs and a tin of oatmeal biscuits.

'Are you taking your painting things, Jess?' Mum asked.

'Might as well. There'll probably be no time for painting but you never know. I'll put in a couple of extra brushes for Kenny and Snowy too.'

'Do they really *like* painting?' asked Mum rather doubtfully.

'Don't know. Don't think they've ever tried. They might like to have a go.'

Jess sped away on her long ride to the river, her front basket stuffed full, her sandals flapping against the pedals. The boys were pleased to see her. She propped her bike against the bike tree – a thick red-gum entirely surrounded by the Drury family's collection of five battered bicycles – and produced the rug, the mugs and the biscuits.

'Your Mum's a real good sort, Jess,' said Kenny approvingly.

'Mm,' agreed Snowy. 'Might as well have one straight away.'

'No,' said Jess firmly, 'it's far too soon. Let's get started on our hut.'

Old Lizzie was sitting out on the shady bank in her wicker chair as usual, reading *David Copperfield* (for the seventeenth time, so she said) and flicking away the flies with a switch of young, blue-tinged gum leaves.

'I thought your mother would let you come, Jess,' she said, smiling.

'Ju-st t-ill the e-nd of M-ar-ch,' mouthed Jess.

Lizzie nodded.

'Yes, it will be getting a bit chilly in the late afternoons by then. And darker. Will I keep an eye on those biscuits for you?'

Jess hid the tin under Lizzie's chair and hurried after the boys into the bush. Their tent of leaves was only a stone's throw from the boats but completely hidden by a dense cluster of young saplings and two sturdy, spreading red-gums. Jess dodged in and out among the trees. There was the hut. Kenny and Snowy were inside already and grinning out at her from the doorway.

'Here's the rug,' said Jess; 'let's spread it inside.'

Carefully they stretched the faded tartan rug across the floor, tucking it under the leafy walls, pinning it down here and there with sticks and stones, turning it under at the front door to make a neat edge. They spent an hour or so adding still more leaves and bracken to the hut, weaving them in and out, patting them into place. They played a bout of mothers and fathers and another of doctors and nurses and another of Ned Kelly. This last game suited Jess best of all. She was getting rather tired of being mother and nurse. In Ned Kelly she could be a bushranger along with the boys. When Lizzie called them across for a cup of tea, all three trooped up with straw hats pulled down over their eyes, happy and grubby.

'It's a good hut all right,' said Jess contentedly to Kenny as she bit into her third oatmeal biscuit. 'Pity we can't sleep in it all night. Like a real tent.'

'We could. Why don't we? Lizzie said we could, didn't she?' Kenny turned towards Lizzie and caught her attention. He began his slow, silent speech with mouth stretched wide and lips pushed forward.

'Yes. I suppose so, dear,' answered Lizzie. 'If there's a warm night. But Jess will have to ask her mother. There are a couple of sleeping bags in your boat Kenny, and Jess could bring something from home.'

Jess did have a good sleeping bag at home, made out of a pink eiderdown folded over and machined along the open side and the bottom. Mum had fixed it up for the Guide camp last year. It was stuffed with feathers which made Jess sneeze but she just had to put up with that. She wasn't too sure now how her bright pink eiderdown would look on the tartan rug. Suddenly she remembered something and jumped up.

'We meant to have our cup of tea in the hut! We forgot! Come on!' She ran to get the enamel mugs and Lizzie obligingly filled them up with more tea from the brown pot. Snatching up another biscuit each, Jess and Kenny and Snowy trailed off together, carrying the hot mugs carefully, leaving Lizzie to pick up *David Copperfield* again and to read on in peace.

They squatted down on the rug in the tent of leaves, peering out at the river and sipping slowly at their tea. The mugs were almost too hot to hold. Snowy wrapped a couple of large gum leaves round his to get a cooler grip. The river was grey today and the weather sultry. The full blaze of summer's dry heat was certainly over now. Thursday's sudden rain-storm had left an uncomfortable mugginess behind. A file of diligent black ants picked its way between leaves and twigs in front of the hut and clambered up on to the rug. Magpies were carolling and squawking from their tree across the river.

'Kenny,' said Jess.

'Mm.'

'Why is it I never see you at school?'

'What d'you mean?'

'Well, I know I'm in Form II and you must be in Form I and I know the boys keep over to their side of the playground mostly – but you'd think we'd bump into each other sometimes. In the quadrangle, or somewhere. Have you ever seen me?'

'Nope.'

'Why is it?'

''Cos I don't even go to your school,' laughed Kenny.

'You don't go to the High School! Then where *do* you go? There's nowhere else!'

'Yes there is. I go to St Aidan's. Always gone there. Snowy does too.'

'St Aidan's?' Jess sounded puzzled. 'That little place behind the Catholic church? But it only goes up to Grade 6. Anyway, its only for catholics.'

'Nope. It goes up to Grade 8. And we *are* catholics.'

'Are you really?' Jess was astonished and she stared from Kenny to Snowy and back again. 'You never said so before.'

'You never asked us before,' said Snowy. 'What's it matter, anyway?'

'And do you go to the Catholic church on Sundays, then? The one with all the confetti, down the road from our church?'

'Well, sometimes we do and sometimes we don't,' admitted Kenny candidly. 'When Dad's home he generally makes us go. But he doesn't go himself. Says he's too old for that sort of thing. When he's away prospecting we don't bother. Too far. And Mum's too busy.'

Jess looked rather shocked. Kenny went on quickly. 'Of course we *do* go in and pay a visit sometimes. Pray for Grandma.'

'What's the matter with your Grandma?' asked Jess, looking worried. 'I didn't know she was sick.'

'She's not sick. She's dead.'

'Dead! Well what's the use of praying for her if she's dead already?'

Kenny frowned.

128

'Well, of course we got to pray for her. Snowy does too. We all do. Don't we Snow?' Snowy nodded.

'We've got to help her get to heaven,' Kenny added in a matter-of-fact voice.

'But isn't she in heaven yet?' asked Jess in amazement. 'My Grandma went straight to heaven, right on the day she died.'

'How do you *know* she did?' asked Snowy suspiciously, pushing the stream of ants off the rug.

'Everyone said she did. Mum said it. The Minister said it. Grandpa said it. I kept on crying and everyone kept on saying to me "Well we mustn't be sad, Jess. She's with God now." God's in heaven, isn't He? So she must be there too. Grandpa's always talking about how he's going up there soon too.'

'She must've been a saint then,' said Kenny, looking at Jess with a glint of new respect.

'A saint! No, she wasn't a saint at all! She was quite a nice Grandma but she had a terrible temper. She used to fly right off the handle at poor old Grandpa.'

Kenny and Snowy were silent. They looked at each other.

Finally Kenny spoke in an aggrieved voice, 'It doesn't seem fair really. Your Grandma going straight to heaven like that. Our Grandma didn't have a terrible temper. She was really kind, really lovely. Wasn't she Snowy? Remember?'

Snowy nodded again, very solemnly.

Jess tried to explain: 'But Kenny, *all* the Grandmas in our church go straight to heaven. You don't have to be a *saint*! They *all* go there. It's just the usual thing.'

'*All* the Grandmas!' exclaimed Kenny indignantly. 'That's really not fair! Is it Snowy?'

Snowy slowly shook his head.

'I'll ask Sister Thomas Aquinas about it on Monday,' added Kenny. 'She'll know if it's really true or not.'

'Who's she?' asked Jess sharply, annoyed that her word was being doubted.

'She's just one of our teachers. She teaches me English – and drawing. She teaches Snowy too.'

'Is she a nun?' asked Jess.

'Mm. Nearly all our teachers are nuns. The woodwork bloke isn't a nun, though. And the football bloke.'

'What are they like?' asked Jess.

'Who? The woodwork bloke and the football bloke?'

'No. The nuns.'

'Well – just like any other nuns. They're all right, I s'pose.'

'Don't they hit your fingers with rulers? When you make mistakes in your sums? That's what I've heard, anyway.'

Kenny and Snowy burst out laughing.

'Course they don't!' said Kenny. 'They do shout a bit when they get cross, Old Sister David smacked me on the legs once when I kicked Billy Ryan. But no rulers! We've got to be careful with rulers at our school. 'Cos of the war.'

Snowy broke in now.

'Do *your* teachers hit you with rulers Jess? It must be awful!'

'No, of course they don't, silly! They shout a bit. The boys get the strap sometimes. Not the girls though.'

'Mm. Same with us,' said Kenny.

'Have you got tunnels and passages under your school?' asked Jess, trying a new tack.

'Nope. Have you?'

'Of course we haven't. But everyone says *you* have.'

'What for? What are the tunnels for?'

'I don't know,' admitted Jess.

'Air-raid shelters prob'ly,' said Snowy helpfully. Jess nodded. It seemed the best explanation.

'Pity you haven't got any. They'd be handy in this war,' she said. 'My uncle in Ballarat's got a real air-raid shelter in his back garden. I've been right inside it.'

'What's it like?'

'Dark,' said Jess. 'And it smells a bit funny. Damp.'

As Jess and Kenny and Snowy wandered back to the boats, Lizzie was still deep in *David Copperfield*. She looked up at the three of them. Jess smiled and took the book and turned the pages with curiosity.

'Ever read it, Jess?' asked Lizzie.

Jess shook her head and paused to look at a picture of a boat turned upside down and made into a house.

'Would you like to borrow something to read?' asked Lizzie now, heaving herself up awkwardly from the chair and brushing biscuit crumbs from her dress. 'I've got lots more of Dickens inside. Come in and pick whatever you'd like.' Jess followed her up the gang-plank and into the 'Sally Jane'.

'They're all down here on the bottom shelf,' said Lizzie. It seemed quite dark inside the cabin with the heavy dark furniture crowding out the light from the window. Lizzie lit a candle and put it down on the floor beside the bookshelf.

'There you are, Jess,' she said. 'You look all along there and see what you'd like to start on.'

Jess squatted on the floor and moved the candle slowly along the row of books, reading their names one by one. Some were bound in red, some in black. Some had bright gold lettering, others were so old and worn it was hard to make out any lettering at all.

'*Bleak House*,' said Jess to herself, '*The Old Curiosity Shop*, *Oliver Twist*, *Great Expectations* . . .'

Jess pulled out one or two of them and looked at the pictures in front and put them back. How could she ever choose, she wondered. They all looked rather long and the print was small compared with *Biggles Flies Again* and *Little Women*.

'Try *Great Expectations*,' suggested Lizzie. 'That's a good one. I read it first when I was your age. Take it and see how you get on. If you don't like it, just bring it back next week and we'll try another.'

Jess ran her finger along the backs of the books looking for *Great Expectations*. There it was, near the end. She edged it out carefully from the tightly packed row and opened it up. There was a picture in the front of an old lady, as thin as a skeleton, dressed up as a bride and sitting in a room full of cobwebs with a huge mouldy-looking wedding cake in front of her. She held a shoe in one hand. Jess nodded at Lizzie and smiled.

'Th-anks,' she said and blew out the candle.

As Jess came down the gang-plank with *Great Expectations* in her hand, Kenny and Snowy had her bike all ready.

'What are all your painting things doing in your basket, Jess?' asked Kenny, peering in and poking around to see what was there.

'Oh. I forgot all about them. I thought we could do some painting this afternoon. I brought brushes for you and Snowy too. I'll just leave them in the hut. We could do some tomorrow.'

Snowy picked out one of the brushes and turned it round in his hand, looking at it suspiciously.

'I reckon it's a bit sissy doing painting. For boys, I mean. I s'pose it's all right for girls.'

'No it's not sissy,' said Jess. 'Lots of artists are men. Or they were in the old days. They just about *all* were men. I just like it.'

'Don't know how to do it,' said Snowy grumpily. 'Sister Thomas Aquinas says I'm hopeless. She rubs out my drawings and does them herself.'

'Don't worry, Snowy. I'll show you. If I can paint, you can paint. Just have a look at those tubes of paint in the tin.'

Kenny opened the tin and looked in at the ten little tubes, like baby-toothpastes, with different coloured labels.

'We'll look after these for you, Jess,' he said. 'I'll take them on to the boat. See you tomorrow.'

'Righto,' said Jess. 'See you later.' And she rode away down the track towards home with *Great Expectations* in her bike basket. Near the sandy bend she heard a wild burst of caterwauling, bell-ringing, shouting and laughing. It was coming towards her along the track. Jack Stevens' gang again! She didn't want them to see her this time. Quick as a lizard, she twisted her bike off the track and rocketed through thick bush for twenty yards or so, missing saplings by inches and steering suddenly around a prickly patch of grass. Well out of sight of the track, she jumped off her bike and lay down beside it. She waited. The gang roared along the track, swooping and baying on their way. She heard them but could not see them as they tore past her hiding place. Not even a flash of the silver bike. Bit by bit, the noise faded away and Jess came slowly out again, wheeling her bike back to the track, brushing leaves and dust from her clothes. She gripped tightly on the handlebars. She didn't like those boys. She was glad she'd managed to avoid them. 'If they always makes as much noise as that, I'll be able to keep out of their way every time,' she thought to herself. But she was uneasy as she imagined them hurtling along the track towards Lizzie and Kenny and Snowy and the boats.

At home, Jess kept quiet about Jack Stevens' gang. After all, they hadn't seen her. She hadn't even seen them. No need to get Mum all worried about nothing. She produced Lizzie's *Great Expectations* for Mum and Dad to see.

'You'll enjoy that, Jess. One of his best, I always reckon,' said Dad.

'Have you *read* it?' said Jess in surprise and with an edge of disappointment in her voice. 'I've never even *heard* of it before.'

'Yes, of course we've read it, dear,' said Mum with a laugh. 'In fact we've got a nice copy of it somewhere in the house. In that bookcase in the hall, I think. Up near the top.'

Jess felt more disappointed than ever. She'd thought this Dickens person was her very own new discovery.

'Much better to read Lizzie's copy, though, Jess,' put in Dad quickly. 'Books you find in other people's houses – or in other people's boats for that matter – are always much more exciting than books you find at home. Even if they're the very same books.'

'And who's this old lady in the picture?' asked Jess, showing them the frontispiece of the strange, death-like bride and the dark, cobwebby room.

'Ah, that's Miss Havisham!' said Mum. 'Wait till you read it and then you'll find out all about her. Don't let us spoil it by telling you before you start. Has Lizzie got a lot of Dickens books?'

'Oh, yes,' said Jess. '*All* of them. Well, about ten anyway. She says she reads them over and over again. Doesn't bother with new books now, she says. *David Copperfield*'s her favourite one. She's reading it again now.'

'Yes, I think it's mine, too,' said Dad with a smile.

Back at the river the next afternoon, Jess lay on Lizzie's rug and chewed bits of grass while Lizzie told her about her father's little school in Bamburgh. Then Lizzie's memories would suddenly jump forward another thirty years to her first rough journey to Echuca in Cobb's coach, then back again to Newcastle and her first concert, in a draughty, half-empty hall, then on again to Swan Hill and the family next door in Nettle Street. As Lizzie's mind moved confidently backwards and forwards over a lifetime of seventy years, every memory as vivid as every other, Jess found it hard to keep track of her and was often not quite sure whether she was in England or Australia, the 1890's or the 1920's, a child or a woman.

Meanwhile, Kenny and Snowy, with a few instructions from Jess, had set themselves up to paint pictures. They sat propped against a tree, surrounded

135

by saucepan lids and saucers each swimming with a different colour. Kenny was making a painting of Lizzie's paddle-boat. The 'Sally Jane' was about fifty years old now and looked even older. She must have once had a busy life, plying up and down the Murray with bales of wood and live sheep for market, flour and sugar for the outlying stations, passengers moving on from one new river town to another. Now she lay quietly beside the Drurys' long barge, dilapidated and placid, nothing but the worn-out shell of the beautiful boat she'd once been. But she made a good picture all the same and Kenny set to work, squeezing fresh dollops of yellow and blue and red into his saucers and lids, mixing them patiently, dipping his brush in and out of a jam jar of river water. Jess and Lizzie watched him as he worked, an unfamiliar frown of concentration on his face. Snowy was out of sight, over near the green hut, painting a giant, spreading red-gum and the river beyond it. Every now and then, Jess would hear his frantic bellow from behind the saplings.

'Jess, Jess, come quick! It's all messed up.'

Reluctantly Jess would heave herself to her feet and, with a sign to Lizzie, go across to see what Snowy's trouble was this time. He might need a disastrous red blob covered up or a running sky dried off or his curling paper pinned down again on the back of a wooden tray. Then she'd come back to listen to Lizzie and to lose herself in imagining other times, other places, other worlds.

Lizzie made the cup of tea at four o'clock and the boys came to sit with Jess on the rug.

'I'm allowed to stay the night in the hut on the 27th,' Jess told Kenny and Snowy. 'That's just two

weeks off. My last Saturday down here till spring.'
Kenny at once tapped Lizzie on the knee and passed
the news on to her. Lizzie smiled and nodded at Jess.

'B-ut n-o-t if i-t's w-et,' mouthed Jess carefully and
turned back to the boys.

'I have to be sure to be back in town by ten o'clock
on Sunday morning,' she said to them. 'It's for the
Sunday School Anniversary practice. Mum says I
can't miss it.'

'What *is* a Sunday School Anniversary?' asked
Kenny. 'Is it the same thing as a Sunday School
Picnic?'

'No,' laughed Jess, 'nothing like it! How do you
know about Sunday School Picnics?'

'I went on one once,' he said proudly. 'With
Johnny Barrett. Used to meet him at the footy down
at the Rec. His Mum said I could come with them to
the Metho Picnic. It was real good. In a paddock full
of pine trees. Johnny and me picked lots of sparrow-
grass down by the channel and sold it afterwards.
Sixpence a bunch. And there were sack races and lots
of sandwiches and raspberry vinegar. We all had to
sit on the grass and sing a sort of song before we could
start eating. I didn't know the words so I just
hummed.'

Jess laughed. She'd never heard Kenny say so
much before. His eyes were shining.

'Sounds just like ours,' she said. 'They must all be
the same, I suppose. But a Sunday School Anniversary's quite different. It's in the church. The first
Sunday in May, generally. All the kids have new
clothes. And we sit up on special benches and we sing
songs like "Onward, Upward". Do you know
"Onward, Upward", Kenny?'

Kenny shook his head.

'Well that's just one of the songs. There are lots of others. And the church is *packed* with people. You've never seen so many. My Grandpa even came up from Ballarat one year. And there's flowers everywhere. It's lovely.' Jess paused a minute and then added carelessly, 'This year I'm singing a solo.'

'Aw, Madame Jess!' laughed Kenny.

Jess flushed and Lizzie noticed.

'What is it, Kenny?' she asked.

Kenny explained briefly.

'Oh, good, Jess!' exclaimed Lizzie. 'We'll all come and hear you, won't we, boys?'

The boys didn't look very keen.

'Do we have to clap at the end?' asked Snowy.

Jess was horrified.

'No! You don't clap! It's in church!' She wasn't sure that she wanted Lizzie and the boys to come to the Sunday School Anniversary at all. She couldn't quite imagine those three in a pew at St Cuthbert's.

'There's not much room,' she said to Kenny, hoping he could put Lizzie off the whole idea.

Kenny and Snowy pinned their paintings out on a log to dry. Jess and Lizzie were both delighted.

'They're far better than mine,' Jess said honestly. 'They're really good!'

The boys hardly knew whether to be proud or ashamed of this new-found talent of theirs.

'Don't tell anyone, Jess,' said Kenny anxiously. 'Not even your Mum.'

'Let's keep all the pictures in that empty case under your mother's bunk, Kenny,' said Lizzie. 'Then they won't get torn and dirty. She'll be so pleased to see them all.'

Snowy unpinned the two pictures carefully and carried them up into the barge as if they were pieces of delicate china. Kenny packed up the paints and brushes and washed out the saucers and lids in the river. Jess stacked the mugs and teapot on the tray and carried it back to Lizzie's galley. Five o'clock. The pleasure boat was paddling past. Time to go home.

'See you later,' she called to the boys as her bike bounced over the rough grass to the track.

'See you later, Jess,' they called back. Lizzie waved to Jess and turned again to *David Copperfield*.

12
A Perfect Evening

Two weeks later the Saturday came at last when Jess could stay all night in the leafy hut. She sang the whole way down to the river. With 'Onward, Upward!' she whirled round the last bumpy corner and turned down the sandy side-track to the boats. Her full rucksack banged up and down on her back as her wheels jolted and slithered.

'Kenny! Snowy! I'm here!' she bellowed and there they both were on the bank with Old Lizzie, already looking out for her.

'Madame Melba rides again!' she shouted triumphantly as she jumped off, laughing, and

139

pushed her bike to the tree. Kenny and Snowy looked at her solemnly.

'You're crazy, Jess,' said Kenny.

'That's just what Rona says,' said Jess and she flopped down on the rug, easing off her rucksack and opening it up to find the grapes that Mum had sent for Lizzie.

The boys had some new paintings to show Jess. They had laid them out for her, side by side, along a fallen log, with little pebbles to hold each one in place. There was one of the barge, two of the 'Sally Jane', one of Old Lizzie herself, sitting on her chair in a blaze of sunshine with a line full of clothes flapping in the wind behind her. There was one of the little hut, green and leafy in the shade of the towering trees and two of the long, wide view across the brown river at evening. Jess walked up and down the colourful row, exclaiming and admiring. Old Lizzie was as proud of them all as if she'd done them herself, pointing out little details to Jess, comparing one with another. The boys stood by looking pleased and embarrassed at the same time. Jess was really impressed. She wasn't just putting on a polite act to please the boys. She could see at a glance that both of them had a gift that she'd never have, however hard she worked away at her pictures.

'Let's paint some more today,' she said to Kenny and Snowy. 'But I'd love to have a swim first. I brought my bathers. We could go to our secret place – you know, where I met you first. We haven't been there for ages.'

The two boys dashed into their barge to change. Jess put on her bathers in Lizzie's cabin. All three of them picked their way through the trees, going tiptoe in their bare feet over the rough grass, the stones, the twigs, right down to the smooth half-moon of sand between the big red-gums. Before Jess had had time to dip one toe cautiously into the river, Kenny and Snowy had run past her and plunged head-first into the water. With bold and confident strokes they struck out towards mid-stream. Kenny turned round and called back to the bank.

'Come on, Jess! Dive in!'

'I can't swim like that!' Jess shouted back. 'I'll just muck about here by the edge. Do be careful, Kenny!'

Kenny just laughed. He and Snowy slid through the water like snakes, hardly a splash between them. Up and down they went, keeping parallel to the bank, one behind the other. Then in towards Jess for a few strokes and back again towards the very middle of the river where the strong drag of the current pulled them well downstream. Jess kept a rather anxious eye on them all the time. She was amazed at how agile and strong they were in the water. At the same time she was half terrified that at any minute they might sink from her sight and never come out again.

'Come on, Jess,' Snowy shouted but she just shook her head. She let herself slowly and gently into the water. She stood, shivering a bit, with her feet squelching on the muddy bottom, one hand still on the bank, clutching at sand. She made six, splashy, over-arm strokes, kicking desperately and noisily and always keeping the edge a mere arm's length away from her. She turned awkwardly and made six, splashy strokes back again. She dragged herself up on to the sand, warm now after the chill of the water, and sat there, dripping, to watch the boys. That was her swimming for the day. Getting wet and cool was the main thing for Jess. Now, with a slightly worried frown, she looked out at Kenny and Snowy cavorting about in mid-stream like a pair of platypusses.

'Those little river kids really *can* swim,' she thought to herself, half in envy. She stood up and waved to them.

'Come back now Kenny! Come on Snowy! I'm getting cold sitting here!'

Back came the boys to the bank with the same easy, steady strokes. Not much style but plenty of speed and strength. They pulled themselves up beside her, skinny and wet and brown, fair hair plastered down on one round head, dark hair on the other.

'Let's get dressed,' said Jess and she led the way as the three of them ran whooping back to the boats.

It was still rather early for a cup of tea but Lizzie seemed to know they'd need one straight away and it was all ready for them by the time they'd dried themselves and got dressed again. There was a pile of gingerbread too. Jess was sure that this was the best part of swimming – the moment when it was all over and she felt warm and dry again.

Jess and Kenny and Snowy finished off their mugs of tea and wandered across to their hut to spread out the ground sheet carefully, to lay out the three sleeping bags side by side and to get everything ready for the night.

Jess searched by the water's edge and found a special little place for her toothbrush, her soap and her flannel. She hung her towel over a low branch. The boys stood by and watched these arrangements with some amusement. So much care about washing equipment seemed a bit silly to them but they said nothing. Kenny gave Snowy a wink. Snowy grinned. But when Jess turned round they both managed to look solemn again.

'Now for some painting,' said Jess briskly. 'I wonder if Lizzie would read us a bit out of her book while we paint.'

They sat, all three together, each turned in a different direction, one painting a clump of pale saplings, one the old boats side by side and one the line full of washing in a patch of sunlight. Lizzie seated herself on her wicker chair and read to them in her high cracked voice, now loud, now soft from *Our Mutual Friend* – about Simon Wegg with his wooden leg, the strange arrangements at Boffin's Bower and the 'weal and hammer' pie on the shelf. Snowy and Kenny weren't too sure just what was going on in the story but they liked the sound of Lizzie's funny voice going up and down and the way she paused dramatically now and then before she swooped on again with the tale. Jess was a bit worried that nice Mr Boffin might be taken in by the wily Simon Wegg but she couldn't help being fascinated by Simon Wegg, all the same, as he ate the pie and sipped his gin and water to 'meller the organ'.

When the chapter was ended, the pictures were done. Bright with intense blues and greens, slapdash but cheerful, they took their place on the fallen log to dry off beside the others.

Tonight Lizzie and Jess and the two boys were going to eat a proper bush meal cooked on a camp fire. That heavy fall of rain a few weeks back had left the undergrowth a little damp so it was no longer dangerously tinder-dry as it had been all the summer. The four of them took great care about the fire, all the same, setting it in a ring of stones that Jess and Kenny lugged from the river's edge and digging a good wide ditch all the way around it. Jess even insisted on having a bucket of river water nearby, just in case, but Kenny and Snowy clearly thought that was going too far.

'Dad never bothers with buckets of water,' said Kenny firmly, 'and he's a real bushman.'

Jess was all ready to flare up and have an argument but Lizzie just at that moment asked her to go and get the chops and the flour and the salt from the 'Sally Jane'. She brought them out all packed into Lizzie's shopping basket. Meanwhile Snowy had brought the tea and an old blackened billy from the barge. Kenny and Jess built up the fire itself, starting with tiny twigs and ending with solid logs. They lit the fire and soon it began to crackle and hiss. The smoke had a marvellous smell. Soon the chops were stuck on green sticks to grill and the billy of water planted in the centre of the fire. Now Lizzie mixed flour and water into a quick dough, rolled it between her hands into a long snake and wound it around a peeled green stick in a spiral. This was the damper. Lizzie thrust it right into the heart of the fire among the hot glowing embers.

The billy began to boil, bubbling and spitting, one solitary gum leaf whirling round and round in the water to give it flavour. At just the right moment, Snowy flung in a small handful of tea leaves. Then he grabbed the handle with his hanky and whirled the billy round in huge circles, high above his head and down towards the ground like a ferris wheel at the Show.

'Give me a go, Snowy!' begged Jess. 'I really *do* know how to do it.' Reluctantly, Snowy slowed down the whirling billy and let Jess have her swing too.

'That's enough swinging,' said Lizzie. The damper was so well done it was black on the outside. Lizzie broke it up in her hands and spread butter on every chunk.

The chops were ready, the tea was poured and the feast began. Lizzie sat up on her wicker chair facing the river, her legs stuck out towards the fire. Jess, Kenny and Snowy sat cross-legged on the brown rug beside her, gnawing at their juicy chops, chewing on the tough, delicious damper and sipping at the scalding tea.

The sun was dropping down now and the bright air turned grey and soft. Jess gazed across the river and licked the last traces of butter from her fingers.

'Bliss!' she thought to herself. 'I'll never be so happy again! Not if I live for a hundred years!'

'That was really scrumptious,' announced Snowy and lay on his back to look up at the fading sky.

'Bed now, kids,' said Lizzie at last when the sun had finally set and darkness was almost hiding the far bank of the river. 'It's nearly eight o'clock. I must put my watch back an hour – don't forget to do yours too, Jess. That's the end of the summer.'

Kenny thought it was far too early for bed but Lizzie was firm. Jess could hardly wait to be all tucked up in her sleeping bag under the green, leafy roof. That was the moment she had been longing for. It took quite a while before the boys were cleaned up and in their pyjamas and ready to crawl into the hut. Kenny suddenly remembered, just at the last minute, the paintings spread out on the log and he

145

had to take them on board the barge to stow them away in the 'painting case' under his mother's bunk. He borrowed Lizzie's torch and felt his way up and down the gang-plank in bare feet. So Jess was in bed long before the boys – her teeth shiny, her face washed, socks and jumper for the night-time cold pulled on over her pyjamas, her watch set back an hour and left safely on her wrist so she'd know the time when she woke first thing in the morning. She sneezed a bit as she always did in that eiderdown bag.

When Kenny and Snowy came running and hopping to the tent of leaves they announced that they wanted to sleep with their feet at the door and their heads at the far end. So the light wouldn't wake them up too early in the morning, they said. But Jess wanted to be able to look out the door as she lay in bed to see the stars and the trees and the river. So she lay in the middle with her head by the opening and Kenny and Snowy crawled right down to the end and slid into their sensible khaki bags, one on each side of her floral pink one.

Lizzie came to the doorway, bent down and peered in. By the light of the torch, Jess could see every wrinkle in Lizzie's thick brown stockings and every scratch on her old black shoes.

'Now, off to sleep, all of you!' said Lizzie. 'It's nine o'clock so I don't want to hear any talking. I'm not far away if you need me. And if you feel frightened out here in the night when the bush starts to stir, just come in and sleep on the boats. There should be a good clear moon later on tonight. It's only just past the full. See you all in the morning! Sleep tight!'

Carefully Lizzie picked her way back to the 'Sally

Jane', shining her narrow torch-beam on to fallen logs and tangles of grass and clumps of slender saplings.

'Frightened!' snorted Snowy. 'As if we'd be frightened!'

'I might be frightened,' admitted Jess. 'I'm not sure yet. I haven't ever slept away from home before – except at Grandma's.'

'Don't worry, Jess,' said Kenny kindly in a very grown-up voice, 'I'll look after you. Just wake me up if you feel scared.'

'Thanks Kenny,' said Jess and smiled a bit to herself at the way he spoke. Almost like Nico, she thought.

Silence fell. But not for long.

'Kenny,' moaned Snowy, 'I'm not very comfy.'

'What's the matter, Snow?'

'It hurts my side.'

'I know!' shouted Jess, leaping out of her bag. 'We forget to dig our hip-holes!'

'What are hip-holes?' asked Kenny suspiciously, sitting up.

'I learnt about them at Guide camp. You need a hole in the ground, just where your hip is going to go. Then your hip fits nicely in it and you don't get the slightest bit uncomfy in the night.'

'We don't have to get up and dig them now, do we?' wailed Snowy.

'Yes, we do,' said Jess. 'Come on. It's well worth it. Only take a minute.'

The three sleeping-bags were dumped outside. The ground-sheet was rolled up. Jess and Kenny and Snowy tried to work out, by much lying and wriggling this way and that way on the hard ground, where exactly the hip should go. Then they dug their shallow holes out with sticks and fingers and patted them down smooth and firm. The ground-sheet was rolled back into place again and then the three sleeping-bags. When Jess and Kenny and Snowy were all in their bags once more, it took some time and much more wriggling before each hip had found its hole.

'Here's mine!' shouted Kenny and eased himself into it.

'And here's mine,' said Snowy.

Jess took longer but at last she too had her hip firmly planted in its proper hole.

'Good-night, you two,' she murmured.

'Good-night, Jess,' said Kenny and Snowy together.

The boys were soon asleep. Jess lay listening. The bush was full of noises. Leaves rustled, branches creaked in the light wind, a late bird squawked. She thought she could even hear the soft pulse of the river, beating quietly on and on in the dark, down to the distant sea. Then, at last, she too fell asleep.

13
The Terrible Night

How long Jess slept she didn't know but suddenly she was wide awake. She lifted her head and peered out of the hut. Up above, through the trees, she could see thousands of powdery bright stars. Beyond the trees she could see the river, flooded with moonlight. The air was fresh and sweet.

But something had woken her. What could it be? She put her head down again and lay still, hardly breathing. She listened. No sound. Nothing at all.

'Must've been a dream,' she thought to herself and rolled over on to her left side, pulling the bag up around her shoulders. She closed her eyes.

Then a sudden, sharp sound. Jess's head shot up again. A stick breaking perhaps? Another sound, low and soft. Was it a whistle or just the sighing wind? A clink of metal. Jess strained to hear. She thought she must be imagining things. Were those voices whispering? Feet rushing and running? Or was it the wind again, moving the dry leaves in the moonlight.

Propped up on her elbows, Jess leant further out. She lay rigid and tense, her eyes searching the bush around her. She felt scared, very scared but there was nothing to be seen. Only the still white tree-trunks.

Should she wake the boys? No. They'd think she was silly to get scared in the middle of the night. Should she get up and go and have a good look round, just to prove to herself there was nothing there, not even a possum? No. She felt far too scared to do that. She just stayed still, peering, listening, never moving. Five minutes passed. Not a sound except the faint rustle of leaves above her head. She must have imagined it all. Lucky she hadn't woken the boys. Another five minutes. Then slowly her head dropped down again on to her doll's mattress pillow and she eased her stiff elbows back inside the bag.

A funny smell. Up lurched Jess's head again. She sniffed. Very strange. What was it? She knelt up and thrust her head right outside. She sniffed again. Smoke! She was sure of it. Not the pleasant smell of camp-fire smoke but something acrid and frightening. Smoke – and kerosene!

Jess twisted back into the hut and shook Kenny and Snowy roughly.

'Wake up! Wake up! Quick!' she whispered urgently. 'I can smell smoke! Something's wrong, Kenny! Wake up! Oh *please* wake up!'

The two boys sat bolt upright in one movement.

'What is it?' whispered Snowy.

'Smoke! Can't you smell it? And I heard funny sounds. I'm sure I did. But I was too scared to go and look.'

Kenny was out of his bag like a shot. He knelt by the opening of the hut, his head out in the cold night air.

'Yes, Jess! It *is* smoke! Come on!'

Kenny led the way, running quietly but quickly through the trees. Jess followed him, only a foot behind, gasping with fear and with cold. Snowy came last. All three paused as they reached the edge of the clearing. They could see the moon now. It was almost at the full – a huge, round, white disc with just a thin shaving pared off one side. High above the clearing it hung, lighting up every tree, every blade of grass. The clearing was empty. No one was there at all. But the stench of smoke was strong now and Jess could see a yellowish trail of it pouring into the clearing from the river bank. Where was it coming from? The camp-fire? Jess edged forward to look further in. No. The camp-fire lay black and dead. Not even a glow of hot ashes.

'I can't quite see the boats from here,' whispered Kenny. 'We'll have to leave these trees and go further in. But it's OK. You can see there's no one there, Jess.'

Jess nodded. She put out one hand and held on to Kenny's wrist. Snowy held on to Jess's jumper. The three of them tiptoed into the clearing, slowly and cautiously, their eyes scanning the trees ahead for any flicker of movement. Now the river itself was in full view at last. There was the 'Lucky Strike', lying dark and still at the water's edge.

But Lizzie's boat!

Where was it?

The 'Sally Jane' had gone!

Nothing but a thick cloud of smoke filled the space beside the 'Lucky Strike' where Lizzie's boat should be.

Without a word spoken but clutching each other harder, Jess and Kenny and Snowy ran down the clearing to the river. They looked out across the quiet moonlit water, laced with ragged streamers of smoke.

'*There* she is!' breathed Kenny and all three froze suddenly as they caught sight of the 'Sally Jane'. She was drifting, slowly drifting, well out on the river. A good twenty yards separated them from the paddle-boat and with every minute the gap widened. The 'Sally Jane' turned slowly as she drifted downstream, pulled by the current beneath her. A spouting column of thick white smoke belched up from the galley and more smoke oozed out from the windows and from the cracks between the boards on the deck. In the brilliant moonlight, the 'Sally Jane' floated further and further out, further and further down-stream, still slowly turning, drifting in a cloud of smoke.

Jess and Kenny and Snowy stared. It wasn't real!

None of them could speak. They gazed out in silent horror.

'But *Lizzie*'s in there!' gasped Jess at last.

She broke into a sudden wild shout across the water.

'Lizzie! Lizzie! Wake up! The boat's on fire! Wake up!'

Then she remembered. Lizzie couldn't hear. She couldn't hear Jess's call and she couldn't hear the crackle of flames around her.

'Kenny! What *can* we do?' she said desperately turning her eyes from the smoking river to the two boys who stood stunned and unbelieving beside her.

'It can't be true,' muttered Kenny in a daze.

'Yes, it is! It is!' urged Jess. 'Quick! We've got to save Lizzie! Look, the fire's spreading!'

They could see flames now as well as smoke and the windows of the galley glowed with a dull ominous red.

'We've got to wake her up and get her out,' said Kenny, coming out of his shocked daze at last. 'I could swim out there all right. And climb on and wake her up. If the fire doesn't reach her first. But she'd never swim back that far.'

'*Can* she swim?' asked Snowy. 'I've never seen her even go into the water.'

'I think she can,' said Jess quickly, suddenly remembering Lizzie's stories of Bamburgh. 'She used to swim in the sea. Her father made her do it.'

'Kenny! Why don't you take that rope from our barge. You know, that long, thin green one. It's rolled up on the deck. In case she can't swim. In case you can't get back.' This was Snowy's idea and as he spoke he began to run towards the barge to find the rope. In a minute he was back, the long, green coils hanging from his hands.

Kenny pulled off his pyjamas and wound two turns of the rope loosely around his waist. He tied a firm knot.

'We'll keep a good hold on this end,' said Jess. 'I'll loop it round this tree-stump just to make sure it can't slip away from us. Off you go Kenny! Do be quick. And keep well away from the fire. It's not near her cabin yet but it's moving that way. It could spread before you get there! Easily, it could!'

Kenny hadn't waited to hear all this. He'd dived head-first into the river and already he was swimming out towards the drifting boat. Jess let out the rope quickly, leaving plenty of slack to lie on the water behind him. His little white figure flashed in the water, lit up clearly by the steady moon. As he drew nearer to the burning boat one of the galley windows exploded dully in a shower of red sparks and shattering glass and the smoke that billowed through the jagged hole was turning black.

'Snowy!' said Jess urgently, her eyes still fixed on the swimming Kenny. 'Run to your barge and get some blankets. Get three or four. And a towel. And – can you light the primus?'

'Yes, of course I can!'

'Well, light up the lanterns first. Then the primus. And put on a kettleful of water. We'll need to give Lizzie hot tea – if we ever get her back here, that is,' she added hopelessly. It all seemed impossible. 'And then bring the blankets. Quick, Snowy, quick!' and Snowy dashed up the gang-plank of the 'Lucky Strike'.

Now Jess stood alone on the bank. She still had plenty of green rope in hand. Across the glittering water she could just make out the movements of Kenny's arms as he drew closer to the 'Sally Jane'. He was edging his way towards the stern as it turned into his path. She could hear the fire in the prow, roaring faintly like wind down a long tunnel, as smoke and live flames leapt up towards the stars. She saw Kenny more clearly now as he heaved himself up on to the narrow lower deck and worked his way along towards the huge round paddle-casing. Then he disappeared. Jess dealt out more rope and still more.

She waited.

Nothing happened.

The boat drifted further downstream and Jess eased the rope again as she felt it pull in her hands. It tightened as the boat turned slowly away from her and then fell slack again as the boat swung slowly back. Red shadows of fire burned on the water. The smoke was so thick now that Jess could hardly see the dark hole where Kenny had disappeared in search of Lizzie.

She paid out the last coil of rope, her eyes fixed on the boat. Then came a white flicker on the dark deck. A movement of something or someone. Jess clung to the rope and strained to see through the smoke. There were two blurred figures – one tall, one small. He had found her!

'Lizzie! Lizzie!' called Jess frantically. Then she remembered again and was silent. Snowy came running back, staggering under a load of blankets and towels.

The last coil of rope slipped through Jess's hands.

It pulled taut on the tree stump, where she'd tied it firm.

'There's no more rope, Snowy!' she sobbed, tears suddenly burning in her eyes. 'And I can't see what they're doing out there. Why don't they jump?'

'I can see them,' said Snowy. 'Look, Kenny's fixing the rope to Lizzie. Can't you see? Now he's wrapping it round himself again. Look!'

'I can't see! I can't see. It's the smoke. You're making it all up.'

'I'm not!' said Snowy indignantly. 'Look! They're diving now.'

Now Jess could see. The smoke lifted for an instant and she saw two white figures fly in a long, slow arc from boat to water. Behind them the fire gushed out again and stretched its long red fingers towards the cabin where Lizzie had been sleeping.

'Just in time, Snowy,' Jess gasped and began to pull gently on the slackened rope. Four white arms rose and fell in the water, slowly, rhythmically, as the swimmers pulled away from the burning boat.

'Jeepers!' breathed Snowy in amazement. 'Look at that, Jess! Lizzie really *can* swim.'

Lizzie's long, even strokes were astonishingly powerful. She had learnt well in those rough Northumbrian seas, thought Jess to herself, and now the old skill came back. She was over seventy and hadn't swum for forty years but she moved through the water steadily, Kenny a few yards behind her, the green rope stretched between them. Kenny was floundering and splashing now in the eerie moonlit water. His strength was gone, all of a sudden. His arms moved heavily, slowly and Jess could see his pale, frightened face as his eyes measured the distance to the bank. She leant back and pulled harder on the rope, its rough twine burning and scraping her hands. Snowy dumped the blankets and towels and pulled with her to help Kenny over the last ten yards.

With a last desperate heave of all her strength, Lizzie was at the bank now, her hands clutching at the mud. Grey hair was over her eyes and her white, wrinkled face looked old and exhausted. She turned to stretch out one arm towards Kenny as he wallowed and gasped, straining his head back for air. Snowy slipped into the water, pyjamas and all, and got behind Kenny to push him over that last enormous yard to the bank. He pushed and Jess heaved and between them they managed to haul Kenny up the slithery, muddy edge and on to the bank. Lizzie was harder to move. She was big and heavy, her long flannel nightdress clung to her body and she had no strength left to lift herself.

'Lift her feet, Snowy! Then push!' called Jess as she flung herself backwards again, the rope tight in her hands.

Slowly, slowly, as Snowy pushed and shoved, Jess dragged Lizzie up over the edge. There she lay, smeared with mud and green weed from head to foot, her nightdress bunched around her knees, her face pressed into the ground, her eyes shut. Blood was pouring from a cut on her arm. Kenny lay sobbing beside her.

'The rope!' he whispered to Jess. 'Undo the rope! It's cutting me in half!'

Jess and Snowy fumbled with the water-logged rope. The knot was behind Lizzie's back and they turned her gently over and tore and pulled and picked at it in vain.

'Get a knife, Snowy. We'll have to cut it. I'll try to stop this blood,' muttered Jess and as Snowy ran off she rolled one towel into a long snake and wound it hard round and round Lizzie's limp, bleeding arm. She pulled it tight and tucked in the ends to hold it firm. Snowy was back now and set to work sawing desperately at the rope. Lizzie was free of it first and Jess pulled it carefully away from her as Snowy eased it off Kenny's waist. Kenny groaned with the pain. His brown body was girdled with violent red weals where the rope had rubbed and torn at him.

'Get him dry, Snowy, and I'll dry Lizzie,' said Jess and she snatched up one towel while Snowy grabbed the other. Roughly and quickly they rubbed at the cold, shivering limbs, trying to bring some warmth back into the heavy bodies. With the knife, Jess slashed down the back and sleeves of Lizzie's water-logged night-dress and pulled it out from under her. She rolled Lizzie on to a blanket and wrapped it round her firmly. She rubbed at Lizzie's wet hair. Lizzie moaned but her eyes were still shut. Her breathing was heavy and noisy. Jess felt frightened.

'Will we take them back to the barge, Jess?' asked Snowy, standing up beside the two blanket-swathed bundles and looking doubtfully down at them.

'We can't possibly,' said Jess. 'Lizzie's too heavy. We could drag her a few yards but we'd never get her up the gang-plank. We'll have to leave them here. You make that tea, Snowy, and I'll see if I can get the camp-fire going again.'

The ashes, though black, were still warm to the touch. Jess piled on little twigs for the kindling and built a framework of dry logs around them. She ran for matches to the barge where Snowy was working in the galley by the light of his lantern and pouring boiling water into the teapot.

'Bring sugar, too,' shouted Jess as she ran back to put a match to the fire. It caught on straight away. She hurried to the tent of leaves and dragged out the three sleeping bags. She arranged two of them at one side of the camp-fire for Lizzie and one for Kenny.

But Kenny was sitting up. His thin face peered out at Jess from the folds of pink blanket.

'Get me some clothes, Jess,' he whispered. 'I've got nothing on.'

'You've got a blanket,' said Jess.

'I know. I want clothes.'

'But you should rest, Kenny.'

'I'm all right. All I want is some decent clothes.'

'All right,' and Jess was off to the barge yet again to get Snowy to bring the lantern into the boys' cabin and help her find Kenny's shorts and socks and jumper and shoes. Snowy took them out to Kenny and Jess followed behind with tea and mugs and sugar, feeling her way slowly down the gang-plank in the moonlight.

Snowy peeled the blanket off Kenny and helped him pull his clothes on. Kenny could hardly move. He flopped back on the blanket exhausted. Snowy and Jess dragged him along the bank towards the camp-fire and rolled him on to the sleeping-bag. Then they went back to drag Lizzie. Still she shivered and groaned, her cold hands clawing and clutching at the blanket's edge. Inch by slow inch, they moved her to the warmth of the fire, one sleeping-bag beneath her and one piled on top.

158

Jess poured out four mugs of tea and put heaped spoonfuls of sugar in them all.

'Lizzie doesn't take sugar,' objected Snowy.

'She needs it now,' said Jess. 'We all need it. You give Kenny his, Snowy. Help him drink it.'

Kenny sat half upright, propped against Snowy's knee, and took the mug in both hands.

'Can you drink it all right Kenny?' asked Snowy anxiously, letting himself look properly into Kenny's face for the first time.

Kenny nodded and sipped.

Jess had more trouble with Lizzie. Was she conscious or not? Jess couldn't tell. No use trying to give her tea if she wasn't conscious. She put one arm right under Lizzie's neck and managed to lift her head a few inches towards the tilted mug. Lizzie opened her eyes. Her lips went out hungrily towards the tea and she gulped at it noisily. She sank back again and her eyes closed once more.

'I'd better do something about Lizzie's arm, Snowy. That towel's too tight. I can't leave it like that. Have you got any bandages?'

Snowy looked vague but Kenny answered for him.

'Yes, we have. They're in that First Aid box of Mum's. You know, Snowy, it's in her cabin. Just behind the door.'

Snowy ran off yet again. When he brought the First Aid box and a lantern out to Jess he knelt down close beside her and whispered so Kenny couldn't hear him.

'Jess. There's a terrible mess in Mum's cabin. All the clothes are pulled out of the drawers. Everything's piled up on the floor.'

'What's that Snowy?' asked Kenny.

159

'Nothing. Nothing,' mumbled Snowy. Jess noticed that he was starting to cry. His hands were shaking as he took bandages and Dettol out of the box.

'Snowy, you have your tea now,' said Jess to him gently. 'I'll have mine too. I forgot all about us. The shock is starting to hit us too.'

Snowy rubbed his fists in his eyes and gulped down the hot sweet tea, turning well away from Kenny so his tears couldn't be seen.

'We need more clothes on, Snowy. We're crazy to be still running round in pyjamas and socks and jumpers. Could you go and get properly dressed and bring me out some of your mother's things for me? My clothes have gone off in Lizzie's boat.'

For the first time since Lizzie and Kenny had left the boat, Jess thought to look out for it. But by now it had floated well out of sight down the mid-stream current. The river was empty apart from some wisps of smoke. The bright moon still poured its light across water and bush, slowly slipping lower now in the sky.

Jess set to work on Lizzie's arm. First she pulled back the blanket so she could get at it and then she unwound the tight towel bit by bit. The towel was drenched with blood but once Jess had unwrapped the arm she could see that the bleeding had almost stopped. There were two deep cuts just above Lizzie's elbow and from each one a slow trickle of blood oozed out. Jess dabbed the cuts with Dettol, covered them with lint and wound the thin gauze bandage round and round Lizzie's arm, firmly but not too tight. There were even safety pins on a card in the First Aid box so Jess was able to fix the bandage in place neatly. Then she pulled the blanket up

160

round Lizzie's neck again. All this while Lizzie had not stirred or spoken. Her eyes were still shut and her breathing rasped in and out noisily.

'We must get help,' thought Jess to herself and looked round for Snowy. Kenny lay quietly on the other side of the camp-fire. He seemed to be asleep. Jess could see Snowy emerging from the barge. He beckoned to her. Jess took the lantern from beside the fire and went across to him.

'Jess,' he whispered urgently, pulling on her sleeve. He was dressed now and looked warmer. 'Come in and see Mum's cabin. I want you to see it. I've found you some clothes.'

Jess followed him on board and into his mother's cabin. It was dark inside except for the shaft of moonlight that came through one window. Jess held the lantern high above her head and looked around her. The cabin was in absolute chaos. All the drawers were pulled out. Clothes lay all over the floor. The door of the oak wardrobe swung wide open. Nothing was left hanging inside. Even the blankets were pulled off the bunks. And from under the bunk the suitcase of paintings had been tipped out on top of everything else. Jess gazed at it all in amazement that turned to sick fear.

'Snowy,' she whispered. 'What on earth has happened?'

Snowy said nothing. He simply stared. Suddenly he dropped down on his knees and shouted, 'I know! I know!'

He dived under his father's bunk on one side and then under his mother's bunk on the other, ferreting about noisily among the empty cases, pushing them this way and that.

'Hold the lantern lower down, Jess. I can't see a thing.'

Jess put the lantern on the floor and Snowy reached out and pulled it in under the bunk with him.

'Jess! It's gone! It's gone! Mum's brooch – the gold-nugget brooch! It's not here! The whole box has gone!' Snowy was crying now, sobbing desperately as he pushed and pulled at the cases.

Jess got down on her knees and peered in under the bed.

'Let's pull out all the cases, Snowy. We'd better make sure.'

They pulled them out, one by one, and stacked them up on the bunks on each side. Four cases and a round hat box. All empty. But no locked black box with the gold-nugget brooch inside. Snowy was right. The brooch was gone.

'Don't tell Kenny yet,' said Jess. 'Let's hope he stays asleep. Snowy, I'll have to go and get help. Or you'll have to go. Lizzie needs a doctor.'

'I don't want to go, Jess,' said Snowy, standing up and holding the lantern high again as he looked around the devastated cabin. 'I'd be too scared in the dark on that track. Please, please, *you* go! I'll look after Lizzie and Kenny. I'll sit right beside them. I won't go to sleep, truly I won't.'

'But won't you be scared here, all alone in the bush?'

'Yes. I will be scared,' admitted Snowy, 'but it's beter than riding on the dark track. Kenny's not too bad. I can wake him up if I'm scared. Here are the clothes.'

Snowy presented Jess with an oddly assorted

bundle of his mother's clothes. A long warm winter singlet of the sensible kind that Jess's mother was always trying to persuade Jess to wear, a pair of enormous brown bloomers, a skirt that was too big, a red jumper, thick socks and a pair of old white sand shoes.

Snowy went to get Jess a couple of safety pins from the First Aid box while Jess put on the clothes. With the pins she was able to fix the gaping skirt firmly round her waist. Then she hunted through the pile of clothes and blankets on the cabin floor for a coat of some sort. She found a short khaki one of Snowy's Dad's and pulled it on.

'You do look funny, Jess,' said Snowy solemnly as he surveyed her new rig-out, peering at her by the dim lantern light.

'I know,' said Jess, 'but it doesn't matter. I'm warm. That's the main thing. Now Snowy, keep watching them both, won't you? Make more hot tea if they wake up. Keep the fire going, too. And keep warm yourself.'

'Do be quick, Jess. I don't like it out here on my own. What if the burglar comes back? The one that took Mum's brooch?'

'He won't. Burglars never come back,' said Jess firmly. She wasn't at all sure if this was true but she didn't want Snowy to be worried. She suddenly gave him a quick hug, rather to his surprise, and ran off to get her bike from the big tree.

14
A Ride In The Dark

Jess had no time to light up her carbide lamp. In any case, she hated the stink of it. She'd just have to ride without lights and trust to what was left of the moonlight to see her way.

Jess pushed her bike to the main track, jumped on and pedalled for dear life towards home. The sandy track lay clear and silver before her, bending and twisting this way and that, dark shadowy trees on either side. Her bike rattled and bumped as she sped along. The back mud-guard was loose and made a dreadful clatter as she tore over ruts and corrugations. Jess had no time to be afraid though each time she glanced into the darkness on left or right, her heart gave a lurch of panic. Who might be hiding there, watching and waiting? She turned her eyes back to the track ahead and set her mind on home, on Dad. He'd know what to do. Would they need a doctor? an ambulance? the police? the fire-brigade? How had the fire started? How had Lizzie's boat broken loose? Who had taken the gold-nugget brooch? Why was Lizzie breathing so noisily and why didn't she open her eyes? Had Jess done the right thing about those deep cuts on Lizzie's arm? How had they got there, anyway? Jess had no idea how to answer any of her questions but she felt sure that Dad would know.

She was over the wide irrigation ditch now and

past the sleeping green blocks with their quiet rows of vines. Into the town at last and through the dark, deserted streets. The only sound was the howling of a dog cooped up in someone's backyard. The town-hall clock struck six. Was that the 'old' six or the 'new' six, Jess wondered. She looked at her watch for the first time. Five o'clock. More than another hour till sunrise. What an unbelievably long night.

Orange Avenue, Lemon Avenue – she passed them all one by one under the familiar pines of Eleventh Street and turned into her own street at last. Dropping her bike inside the gate, she ran to the front door and rang again and again on the bell.

'Dad! Dad!' she called, banging with her fist on the door as she pressed hard with her other hand on the bell. 'Dad! Mum! Please come quick! It's me! It's Jess! Oh *please* wake up, all of you!'

There was a rush of feet and voices inside the house. A blaze of lights shone out of every window. The front door flew open. There was Dad and there was Mum. Jess leapt into Dad's arms with a sob of relief. Laura was there now and Nico too, all of them pressing around Jess with alarmed eyes and half-formed questions.

'Jess, Jess! What on earth's the matter?' asked Dad, holding her tight.

'It's Lizzie!' gasped out Jess, hardly knowing where to begin. 'It's Lizzie – and Kenny. Lizzie's boat floated away in the night! And it was all on fire! And Kenny swam out to wake her up! And they swam back! And Lizzie's hurt her arm! And she's breathing a funny way! And we need a doctor! And, Dad, the brooch is gone – the gold-nugget brooch!'

And Jess burst into wild, uncontrolled tears of exhaustion.

Mum and Dad looked at each other over Jess's head.

'Police,' said Dad, 'and an ambulance. Jess, I'm afraid you'll have to come back with us. I'd never find the right turn off the track in the dark. Mary dear, give her a hot drink while I get on the phone.'

'*And* some proper clothes,' said Mum as she led Jess to the bedroom. 'Laura, you heat some milk please. Come on Jess. We'll soon have you feeling better.'

So Dad got on the phone to the police station and then to the ambulance depot at the hospital. Laura made lots of hot sweet cocoa and Mum washed Jess's face and helped her get dressed again in fresh clothes of her own. Warm and comforted, her tears all gone, Jess felt she could face the river again after all. The police car was at the door and an ambulance close behind it.

The two policemen came into the hall and seemed to Jess to fill it with their bulk. She gazed up at them, rather over-awed by this unusual sight in her own house. Constable Lithgow seemed to be the one in charge.

'I'll go with you, Mr McCallum,' he said, 'and then I can ask Jess a few questions on the way down. Constable Hayes here will drive our car. I'll just go and have a word with the lads in the ambulance.'

'Righto, Jess,' said Dad briskly. 'Off we go. You come too, Nico. Mary, we'll be bringing the boys back here, or Snowy at least, so perhaps you'd get a spare bed ready.'

A little cavalcade set off through the still, sleeping

town. Dad's car went first, Constable Lithgow sitting in the back seat with Jess. Then came the black police car with Constable Hayes at the wheel and finally the white ambulance. There were no sirens blaring or bells ringing. The streets were empty and there was no need to announce their approach. Dad drove fast and the others followed suit. With tyres screeching and springs bouncing, they were soon out of the town and jolting, shaking, shuddering down the rough track to the river.

'How did the boat get loose, Jess?' asked Constable Lithgow.

'I don't know. It was always chained to an iron stake on the bank. And there was a thick rope that tied it to the barge as well. I don't think it could possibly have come undone by itself.'

'No, I don't think so either,' he said grimly.

'I did hear some funny noises,' remembered Jess. 'That's what woke me up in the first place. Shuffling sounds. A whistle. A chain clinking. But I thought I must have been imagining it all. There are so many peculiar sounds in the bush at night.'

'Perhaps you didn't imagine it. Tell me about the brooch. Who knew it was there?'

'Only Lizzie and the boys . . . and me, of course. And the boys' mother and father. No one else.'

'Would their Dad have told anyone else, do you think?'

'No. I don't think so. Unless . . .' Jess paused as a new idea struck her.

'Unless what?' asked the constable.

'I was just wondering about that old swaggie who called in. He seemed to know everything about the boys and the barge and Lizzie. He said he was a

167

friend of the boys' father. He'd met him up the Ovens valley, he said. But he didn't mention the brooch at all. So I don't suppose he'd have anything to do with it.'

'Mmm,' said the constable, 'what did he look like and when was he there?'

Jess described the old swaggie as best she could. 'I didn't much like him,' she added lamely, 'but I don't know why. He seemed too smooth, somehow.'

'Sounds like Tiger Hawkins,' said Constable Lithgow. 'I heard he was passing through this way a few weeks back. Harmless old coot really. Still, we'll have to look into it. Might have something to do with this business.'

'Here's the turn,' shouted Jess suddenly. 'Stop, Dad!' She'd only just recognized it in time as Dad was about to roar past it.

Dad pumped his brakes to warn the police car behind. Both cars and the ambulance pulled up sharply. Everyone leapt out and Jess led the way down the little side track to the water. The moon was lower in the sky now, yellowish and not silver. In the east were the first faint streaks of morning. The stars were fading. Up in the gum-trees, against the vast grey sky, magpies were carolling and calling, liquid sounds rising and falling. The river looked quiet and still. A faint night-mist still clung to the surface of the water. The camp-fire was burning brightly and beside it sat the small hunched form of Snowy, still keeping guard over the two blanket-wrapped bodies beside him.

'Snowy!' called Jess as she ran towards him. 'We're back!'

Snowy's head shot up and a grin of relief and

welcome came over his face as he saw Jess and Mr McCallum and Nico and two policemen and two ambulance-men all pounding down the pathway towards him. Suddenly this whole adventure seemed exciting instead of only frightening and lonely.

'How are they?' panted Jess, peering into Lizzie's blanket.

'Kenny's O.K.,' said Snowy. 'He's been talking to me on and off. But Lizzie doesn't look too good.'

The two ambulance-men took a careful look at Lizzie, feeling her pulse and her forehead, looking at her banaged arm with a quick nod of approval, listening closely to her noisy breathing.

'She'll be all right,' said one of the men. 'You kids have done a darn good job. I want to get her off to hospital straight away. Let's have a look at the other one.'

Kenny was sitting up by now, swathed in a blue blanket, his face alive with interest in this sudden dramatic invasion.

'Nothing much wrong with him, I'd say,' said the oher ambulance-man. 'Looks as fit as a fiddle. But we'd better take him too. Just for a check-up. Probably let him out by lunch time.'

'Am I going in an *ambulance*?' asked Kenny in delight.

Dad picked him up, blanket and all, and carried him through the trees to the ambulance while the two men lifted Lizzie carefully on to a stretcher and followed Dad more slowly and gently. Lizzie said nothing at all. Her eyes were still closed. Was she asleep? Jess wasn't sure. The strange, rasping breathing still went on, in and out, in and out. Jess couldn't work out if that was a hopeful sign or a dangerous one.

Once Lizzie and Kenny were installed in the ambulance, it backed and turned and set off steadily towards the town. Meanwhile Constable Lithgow and Constable Hayes had set to work with torches to search along the bank where the 'Sally Jane' used to lie. As the light became a little stronger, they peered at faint footsteps in the mud and found the place where the iron stake, chain and all, had been wrenched from the ground. There was no sign of it now. Only a jagged hole where it had once been. The thick double rope that had tied the 'Sally Jane' to the 'Lucky Strike' lay cut and frayed, trailing in the water beside the barge. Constable Lithgow went on board and inspected the wrecked cabin while Snowy gave him a running commentary on what his mother would say when she saw the mess. Dad collected together a few clothes for the boys.

'Snowy,' he said. 'Do you know your auntie's address in Melbourne? The auntie where your mother's staying? We'll need to get in touch with her.'

'She lives in Sunshine,' said Snowy. 'Mum keeps all her letters in the dresser drawer. I'll have a look.'

Jess followed Snowy into the galley on the barge and helped him go through the untidy bundle of letters from the drawer.

'They're mainly from Dad but there's sure to be a couple from Auntie Vi,' he said, flipping them over on the bench in the faint light that came through the window.

'Here's one!' he cried and ran out to Dad with it.

'Mm,' said Dad. 'That's from your Auntie Vi all

170

right. Fourteen Crampton Road, Sunshine. Now what's her other name, Snowy? Auntie Vi who?'

Snowy thought for a minute and then he remembered.

'Black!' he announced. 'Auntie Vi Black! That's her name. She's not on the phone though but the lady next door is. Mum sometimes rings her and leaves a message. Mrs Levitt, she's called. Auntie Vi says she's a real good sort.'

'Right,' said Dad as he led Snowy and Nico and Jess off to the car. 'We'll get on the phone to Mrs Levitt and see if we can have a word with your mother. Bring that letter with you, Snowy. We'll need the address to track down Mrs Levitt's number.'

All four climbed wearily into the old Ford, leaving the two policemen to continue their search. They didn't seem to have found much, thought Jess to herself. She wasn't even sure what they were looking for. Dad turned the car and took it right off the track to pass the police-car and then steered back on to the track again. He drove slowly home. The sun was just pushing its thin red rim above the horizon and the bush was alive with birds calling and screeching. Jess hardly heard them. She lay back in the car, half awake and half asleep, remembering weakly that the groundsheet had been left out in the tent of leaves and her good toothbrush and orange flannel left abandoned on their special twigs by the river. Would she ever see them again, she wondered. It didn't seem to matter.

By the time they got home, it was almost seven. Mum had breakfast ready but Jess couldn't eat it. All she wanted was sleep. So Laura plied Snowy with

171

bacon and eggs and heard his lurid account of the night's adventures while Mum tucked Jess up in her safe, familiar bed in the sleep-out.

'What a night, Mary!' said Dad and as Jess fell asleep, the last sound she heard was the steady swish of the shoe brush as Dad set to work to clean all the family's shoes for Sunday.

15
Hospital Visit

Jess slept all day that Sunday. Mum stayed home from church and tiptoed to Jess's room every half hour or so just to watch her breathing gently and evenly in her sleep. Snowy was more restless. He'd sleep an hour or two and then jump out of bed and come through to the kitchen in his bare feet, white hair ruffled up around his face.

'I'm hungry,' he'd say each time.

So Jess's mother would cut still more bread or fry more eggs or quarter more apples. His hunger satisfied, Snowy would drift back to bed and fall asleep once more. Dad came in from church with Nico and Laura soon after twelve and went straight to look at both the sleeping children, first Jess, then Snowy.

'They're absolutely exhausted. And shocked of course,' he said to Jess's mother when he came back into the kitchen. 'But don't worry, Mary. They'll both be right as rain in the morning.'

Then Dad rang the hospital. Kenny was doing

well. There was nothing the matter with him but they wanted to keep him in until Monday morning, just to make quite sure. Miss Forrester? Yes, she was conscious now but still very weak. There was a danger of pneumonia setting in. No visitors yet, the sister said. Ring again tomorrow.

Rona came round on her bike that afternoon. She sang out for Jess at the gate as usual though she'd heard wild rumours of the night's accident at Sunday School and knew very well that Jess couldn't come running out to see her. Laura went out and told her the whole story. Rona stayed propped on her bike and holding firmly to the gate-post as she listened, her eyes opening wider in horror. Then she rode slowly home.

Now the whole house was quiet. Mum and Dad snoozed in their chairs. Laura and Nico read on their beds. Jess and Snowy slept. It was what Mum always called 'the blessed Sabbath'.

At five o'clock, Jess sat up, wide awake and ravenously hungry. Mum set to work to make a marvellous tea. There was bubble and squeak with bacon, hot scones with butter and jam oozing out of them, Ovaltine frothing in the mugs and crisp, sharp apples to finish it all off. Dad lit a fire too. It wasn't really quite cold enough, still only March, but the late afternoon air was cool and a warm fire was comforting. Jess and Snowy sat nearest to the blaze, slippers on their feet and a blanket well wrapped round each of them. Mum and Dad, Laura and Nico made up the circle. Snowy looked very much at home as if he'd been sitting by that particular fireside for years. The wood crackled and spat; sparks from the knobbly mallee roots leapt up the chimney and even

173

out on to the hearth rug. Nico stamped them out without a pause in his eating.

Then they sat and talked and talked. Jess told the night's adventures all through again with every little detail she could remember. Snowy butted in now and then with the bits she'd left out. Over and over the whole story they went again and again. Questions and answers; puzzles and problems; guesses and theories; worries and fears. Jess always came back again to Lizzie. Again and again she asked Mum the same question,

'But will Lizzie really be all right?'

'Yes, dear,' Mum said in reply every time. 'I'm sure she'll be all right. The cuts on her arm aren't very bad. She's suffering from the cold and the shock – and exhaustion too. Perhaps all that smoke as well. But there's no sign of pneumonia yet. The doctors at the hospital will take good care of her. She's an old lady, you know, Jess. Old enough to be your Grandma. Older, in fact. So she's bound to be knocked out after a terrible night like that.'

'Jeepers, Mrs McCallum,' said Snowy through a mouthful of scone, 'you should have seen her swim! I never seen nothing like it!'

'Mary,' said Dad suddenly. 'I think we better try to ring the boys' parents. I should have done it sooner really. I don't seem to be thinking straight today. Now, Snowy, your mother's Mrs Drury, is that right?'

Snowy nodded.

'And what did you say the name of the lady next door to Auntie Vi in Sunshine is?'

'It's Levitt. Mrs Levitt.'

'So she must live at 16 – or 12 – Crampton Street.'

'Mmmm, I s'pose so,' agreed Snowy.

'I'll try the operator. We'll see if we can get through to them.'

Dad went into the next room and there was much dialling and talking to the operator and waiting and trying again. At last he was through to Mrs Levitt. Some talking and then another long pause.

'She must've gone in next door to get Mum,' said Snowy.

'Ah, Mrs Drury!' bellowed Dad in the next room. He always spoke far too loudly on long distance calls as if he had to make his voice travel all those hundreds of miles down south. 'This is Arthur McCallum speaking, from Glencarra. I'm ringing about Kenny and Snowy. No, No! It's all right. There *has* been a spot of trouble up here on the river but they're both safe and sound. No, no. There's no need to worry. Let me just tell you what has happened.'

Mum got up and quietly shut the door between Dad on the phone and the family round the fire. She could not bear to hear it all again especially now she was imagining just what Mrs Drury must be feeling. They could hear Dad's voice rising and falling, explaining and reassuring. Then suddenly he called out.

'Snowy! Would you like to come and have a talk with your mother?'

Snowy jumped up, his face very pink, and ran into the next room. Dad came back and shut the door. Jess could barely hear Snowy's little voice talking softly to his mother. He didn't talk for long. When he came back he was crying.

'Soon as I said "Hullo" to Mum she went and

burst out howling!' he explained crossly to Jess. 'And then that set me off too. It's nothing!' He wrapped himself up in his blanket again and sat down in his chair by the fire.

'Mum's coming back!' he announced a couple of minutes later, all tears now gone. 'Tuesday night she's catching the train. And Dad's coming too! They'll be here on Wednesday morning!'

'Oh Snowy, that's good news! Then you'll all be together again,' said Jess.

'Not Annie, though. She's got to stop on a bit longer with Auntie Vi, Mum says.'

'Time for bed,' said Dad. 'No school for you two tomorrow. We'll see how things are on Tuesday. You both need another good long lie in.'

On Monday the hospital said Kenny could come home. Dad went to collect him at lunch time. Kenny was full of energy, bouncing all over the house, peering into every room, talking about the lovely kind nurses at the hospital and about the horrible pink junket he'd had to eat.

'They said it'd just slip down easy,' he said indignantly, 'but I couldn't swallow the stuff!'

Snowy had to tell Kenny now about the missing brooch. Kenny was horrified.

'Whatever'll Mum say, Snowy? And Dad'll go crook at us when he hears. Mum told us to be *sure* to look after it, didn't she?'

Snowy nodded. They looked at each other with worried frowns. Jess was worried too. She didn't think the police had a chance of finding the thief. The gold-nugget brooch was gone for good and the boys' father could go as crook as he liked – that wasn't going to bring it back.

But news of Lizzie was better. She seemed to be picking up well and could have her first visitors on Tuesday.

'And,' said the doctor from the hospital on the phone to Dad, 'when we do let her out in a few weeks' time, she mustn't go back to live on that boat! Or on any other boat for that matter. She's far too old to be stuck down there on the river bank like that. It's just asking for trouble. She'll have to move into the town. We'll hang on to her here as long as we can to give you people time to fix up something for her.'

Dad now looked worried. Where *could* she live in the town? And who was going to find a place? And would she agree to leave the river bank anyway? And what had happened to the old 'Sally Jane'? Was it just a burnt-out shell or could Lizzie live in it again? He decided to ring Constable Lithgow at the police station.

'No luck with Tiger Hawkins yet,' said the constable. 'We've had our blokes out looking for him. Not a sign! No one seems to have seen him for a couple of weeks. But don't worry. We'll get on his trail soon enough. He can't get far on foot. Everyone along this river knows old Tiger Hawkins.'

'And what about the boat?' asked Dad.

'Yep. We've got the boat all right. She'd drifted three miles downstream and right over to the other side. Stuck in the sand and mud she was and listing badly. We're going to pull her off the mud tomorrow sometime. Then we'll tow her up to the town jetty.'

'But what state is she in?' asked Dad. 'What about the fire?'

'Well, that little kitchen place – or whatever you call it – that's burnt right out. It's just a black hole with a black saucepan or two at the bottom. But the hull's iron and there was a thick sheet of tin nailed to the door into the next cabin so the fire didn't get much further. Lucky that door was shut, Mr McCallum, or the whole thing would have gone up in smoke. The old lady's stuff's OK though it stinks of fire and there are black stains all over her books and furniture.'

'Does she know?' asked Dad.

'Well, we rang through to the hospital. They said they'd let her know when she's feeling better. They seem to be having a bit of trouble getting through to her.'

'Yes,' said Dad, 'she's deaf. Well, thanks, Constable. I'm glad we'll be able to salvage most of her things for her anyway.'

On Tuesday afternoon, Mum and Jess went to the hospital to visit Lizzie. Jess had a bunch of late yellow roses from the garden all wrapped up in a sheet of smooth, greaseproof paper. The hospital was white – a long, low building full of large windows. Mum asked at the desk inside the front door. The nurse on duty looked up her list.

'Miss Forrester? Yes, she's in E 12. Just go through this door on the right and take the third corridor on the left.'

Jess had never been inside a hospital before – except when she was born, of course, and she couldn't remember that. The whole place had a very strange smell. Through the open doors as they passed she could see alarming pulleys and tubes slung up over the beds, and nurses in white veils gliding silently over the polished floors. The long brown and green corridors seemed to go on forever.

Mum and Jess took the wrong turning and lost their way but at last, after asking again, they found the right door. 'E 12' it said in large red letters outside the ward. They peered in through the glass pane in the door. It looked a huge ward to Jess. Eight beds down one side, eight beds down the other, and two bright, square windows at the far end. Every bed was covered with a neat, white bedspread and in every bed there was a lady propped up on the pillows. Pink bed-jackets, blue bed-jackets. Where was Lizzie? Jess's eyes travelled along the two rows of beds searching for her. There she was! The third from the end on the right-hand-side. But there, too, sitting beside her, was a man all in black – a small, dark, nuggetty-looking man that Jess had never seen before.

'Oh dear,' said Mum in disappointment. 'There's someone with her. Who is it, Jess?'

'I don't know,' said Jess. 'Never seen him before.'

'Can I help you?' said a cheerful, brisk voice right behind them. It was the ward sister. Mum looked a bit embarrassed at being caught staring through the glass in the door like that.

'Thank you, Sister. We've just come to see Miss Forrester. But there's someone with her already. I don't know if we should go in.'

'Oh yes. Come in. Come in. She *will* be pleased to see you. You must be Mrs McCallum. That's just Father Byrne with her now. He's been there quite long enough. I'll hurry him along.'

The sister bustled into the ward and descended on Father Byrne who got quickly to his feet.

Mum and Jess looked at each other, still outside the door.

'Father Byrne?' whispered Mum to Jess. 'That must be the catholic priest, Jess. You didn't ever say that Lizzie was a catholic.'

'I didn't know she was,' Jess whispered back.

'Come on. We'd better go in,' said Mum.

As they walked down the long ward to the third bed from the end, all the ladies and all their visitors watched them. Father Byrne came towards them smiling, his hand held out.

'Ah, Mrs McCallum. And this must be Jess! Miss Forrester's been telling me all about you, Jess. And about how you and those two little Drury rascals saved her life the other night.'

Jess turned pink.

'I don't think we've met before, Mrs McCallum, have we? Perhaps you're new to the town.'

'No. Not really,' said Mum, 'we've been here fifteen years now. We come from down south.'

'Fifteen years! Well, well! So have I! Exactly fifteen years on Easter Day! And to think our paths have never crossed in all that time!'

'We go to church at St Cuthbert's, you see,' explained Mum with a touch of pride, 'so I suppose it's not so surprising we've never met.'

'St Cuthbert's? Ah yes! I always call those dear people "our friends down the road". Well now, Jess will be wanting to talk to Miss Forrester. Perhaps I could have a word with you outside the door, Mrs McCallum. Just a quick word,' and Father Byrne shepherded Mum back down the ward again.

Jess had been hopping impatiently from one foot to the other. She could see Lizzie there, smiling towards her, but she couldn't break free to hurry across to her. At last Mum and Father Byrne walked away down the ward. He was smiling and nodding and waving to all the ladies in their beds as he passed them. Jess rushed to Lizzie and gave her a hug.

'Oh Lizzie!'

'There now, Jess,' said Lizzie comfortably, her high voice a note or two higher than usual. 'Sit down beside me and tell me how you are.'

'I-'m all-right. H-ow a-re y-ou?' Jess mouthed slowly.

The other fifteen ladies and their visitors watched Jess in fascination as she stretched her mouth open and shut, silently making each word.

'Much better, Jess. Much better!' The whole ward could hear Lizzie's loud voice. 'All that smoke and all that cold water were a bit much for me, I'm afraid, but the doctor says there's no harm done. I'm so stiff from that swim, Jess, I can hardly move. It must be nearly forty years since I last swam. Isn't it funny how it comes back to you? And Jess. Have you heard about the boat? The "Sally Jane"? All my things are safe. The books aren't burnt. It's only the galley that's gone. Sister just told me today. She wrote it all down for me on this pad.'

Jess nodded.

'So I'll soon be able to get back there. Jim'll fix up the galley for me. He can turn his hand to anything. It won't be long now, Jess.' Lizzie smiled happily.

Jess looked doubtful.

'Th-e doc-tor s-ays n-o.'

'The doctor!' exclaimed Lizzie crossly and still as loud as ever. 'The doctor! He's as bad as the priest! They both think I'm too old for the boat. Want me to live in a *house*! Lot of nonsense, isn't it, Jess?'

Jess wasn't too sure. She half agreed with the

181

doctor and the priest but she didn't want to upset Lizze so she changed the subject.

'Wh-y w-as the pr-iest h-ere?'

'That's Father Byrne. He came to see me. This morning I had to fill in one of those blue forms – you know the sort of thing, Jess. Name, place and date of birth, any other illnesses, religion. I'm a catholic, you see. So after lunch the Sister rang Father Byrne and he was here an hour later. I was quite glad to see him, as a matter of fact, Jess. Though I've never seen him before!' and Lizzie laughed her odd cracked laugh.

'I did-n't kn-ow y-ou w-ere a cath-o-lic,' said Jess, rather embarrassed.

'Didn't you? I suppose it never came up, did it? Anyway, I wasn't always one, Jess. I grew up in the Church of England just like anyone else.'

Lizzie paused. Jess waited.

'I became a catholic to marry Brendan Meath.'

'B-ut y-ou d-id-n't m-arry-y h-im!'

'No, I didn't. But there was no point in changing back again, was there?'

Jess felt shocked but she tried to smile so Lizzie wouldn't know. She stared hard at the white bed-spread. Lizzie went on talking.

'When I moved up to Echuca I never went near any church and none of them came near me either. But down in Swan Hill, Christine's mother dragged me along to midnight mass one Christmas. She didn't like to think I'd just given it all up. She was strict all right! She'd come in every Sunday morning after that to make sure I was getting ready to go with them. But somehow or other, since I moved down here to the boat, I've lapsed all over again. It's too far to get into mass from our river bend. I couldn't walk it – well, perhaps I could but I've never tried. Christine goes in on her bike now and then. Jim makes the boys go when he's there but he never bothers himself. So that's why I've never set eyes on Father Byrne till this afternoon!'

Jess's mother came back down the ward at that moment and the conversation changed. Lizzie was delighted with the roses. A nurse put them into water for her while Mrs McCallum wrote on a pad the good news that Kenny and Snowy were full of life and the even better news that their parents would be back in Glencarra tomorrow morning.

'Thank goodness,' breathed Lizzie with relief. 'I'll be glad to see Christine take over those two boys again. It's been more of a responsibility than I'd bargained for.'

She lay back on her pillows with her eyes closed and her tired, brown face relaxed. She looked ready for sleep so Jess and her mother sneaked quietly away down the ward. Jess only paused to scribble on the pad, 'See you later!'

On the way home, Jess asked Mum about Father Byrne.

'What on earth did he want to talk to you about, Mum?'

'It was just about Lizzie,' she explained. 'He doesn't think she should go back to the boat. The doctor doesn't think so either. He wanted to know what we thought.'

'And what *do* you think?'

'I'm not sure, really. I don't think she should go back. It's very isolated down there. And she can't even hear any danger coming. It's not safe. And Jim Drury's only there for half the year to keep an eye on things. All the same, Jess, she's very independent. I can't see her settling into an old folks' home. I told Father Byrne that.'

'What did he say?'

'He agreed with me. He says he's got an idea. There's some lady at his church who's just divided her house in two. I forget her name. Her son's a plumber and he's put in an extra bathroom and an extra kitchen so each half is quite separate. It seems she's looking for a good tenant to live in the other half. Father Byrne is off to see her now. He'll be in touch with us tonight, he says.'

'Lizzie won't be too pleased,' said Jess. 'She's determined to go back to the boat.'

'Yes, dear, I know.' Mum sounded worried.

'Mum, are Kenny and Snowy going back to their barge tomorrow? When their mother and father come?'

'I suppose so, dear. They'll want to get back. We can't fit them all into our house, can we?'

'No. I suppose not. But I wish Kenny and Snowy could stay. They love our house. They love playing hide-and-seek in all the wardrobes.'

'Yes, I know. But they do love their own mother and father more than our wardrobes, don't they?' And Mum laughed.

'I *suppose* they do,' said Jess doubtfully.

'You can still go down to the river and see them sometimes on Sundays, Jess, though there's going to be no more staying the night. It's not the absolute end, you know.'

Jess wasn't sure. Somehow, to her, it did feel like the end.

16
New Plans

When Mum and Jess got back from the hospital, there was Rona waiting for them on the front verandah with an enormous bunch of bronze chrysanthemums.

'They're for you!' she said to Jess, holding the bunch of flowers out stiffly in front of her at arm's length. 'They're from the whole form. Even the boys! Everyone had to bring threepence. You know, just like that time when we got the wreath for Linda's father's funeral.'

Jess laughed.

'Yes, I remember,' she said, 'but I'm not dead!'

'No, I know,' said Rona solemnly. 'That's why it's a bunch and not a wreath. Wreaths are just for funerals. This is because you were brave, rescuing that old lady from the fire.'

'Kenny was really the brave one,' said Jess honestly, 'I only helped. But the flowers are lovely. Thanks so much Rona,' and she put her arms right round the bunch and sniffed up their delicious strong scent.

'And I'm coming back to school tomorrow, aren't I Mum?' she added.

'Yes, dear. I think so.'

The overnight train from Melbourne was due in at the Glencarra station at 7 o'clock the next morning.

Jess went down to the station with Dad and the two boys to meet Mr and Mrs Drury – or Jim and Christine as Jess found she'd begun to call them in her own mind, simply because Lizzie did. The great steam engine roared in right on the stroke of seven. Doors flew open all along the train and everyone waiting on the platform rushed forward, waving and calling, to greet their friends and relations. There were a good few young soldiers in khaki running into their mothers' arms and a carriage full of singing airmen who didn't seem to want to get off. Jess and Dad stood well back against the paling fence while Kenny and Snowy darted in and out among the crowd, looking everywhere for their parents. At last Jess could see that they'd found them, a fair way down the platform. She saw Christine bend down to hug and kiss the boys and she saw Jim lifting Snowy right up into the air and holding him there. Snowy was kicking wildly with delight high above his father's head. Christine and Jim didn't look at all the way Jess had expected them to look. She'd imagined Christine to be round and jolly and plump. She thought Jim would be skinny and tall with fair hair like Snowy's. She couldn't have been more wrong. Christine was neat and smart and small. She wore a closely-fitting grey coat and had a pretty blue scarf on her head. *She* was the fair one. Little wisps of blonde hair crept out of the scarf at each side. On her feet were a pair of pointed, shiny black shoes. Jim was tall all right but not skinny. He was older than Jess had expected, older even than Dad. His skin was olive, like Kenny's, and his face was brown and wrinkled from the sun. He was a big man, stout and strong and cheerful with a hat pushed back on his head. His mouth was wide and smiling. Happy-go-lucky, thought Jess.

'How odd,' she said to herself, reluctantly putting aside the very solid pictures of Christine and Jim that she'd made up for herself over the past few weeks. But she had no more time to wonder. Kenny and Snowy were dragging their mother and father by the hand along the platform towards Jess and Dad.

'And this is Jess,' Snowy was saying, 'and this is Mr McCallum and at home they've got Laura and Nico and Mrs McCallum as well.' His excited little voice burbled on and on as he pulled all the time on his mother's hand.

Dad shook hands with both the Drurys and Jess shook hands too, feeling very grown-up.

'Hullo, there!' said Dad.

'Pleased to meet you,' said Jim.

'Pleased to meet you,' said Christine.

'How about breakfast?' said Dad.

They all piled into the Ford and drove home through the quiet morning streets. The four Drurys were crammed together in the back seat, laughing and talking and hugging all the way home. Jess sat in the front with Dad, feeling a bit left out of it all. She wasn't too sure if she really was glad the Drurys were back after all.

But Mum was certainly delighted to meet the boys' mother at last. They liked each other straight away. Round the breakfast table Jess and Kenny and Snowy told the whole story all over again. Christine's face went white when Jess got to the bit about Kenny swimming out alone to the burning boat to wake Lizzie.

'Oh Kenny! Kenny!' she said anxiously. 'If only

187

I'd been there!'

'What could you have done, Mum? You can't even swim!' laughed Kenny.

'That's true. I can't. Well, if only your Dad had been there then. If only we'd all been together.'

Jim Drury looked uncomfortable.

'I don't know how we're ever going to thank you people,' he said awkwardly, 'all you've done for them two kids. Christine's right, really. I *should've* been there. It was putting too much on poor old Lizzie.'

'And how's Annie?' asked Mum, who didn't really want to be thanked.

'She's fine. Really fine,' said Jim more happily. 'She's got this iron thing on her leg now. The left leg. The other's OK. She gets along with her crutches now so fast we can hardly keep up with her. She's lost a good bit of weight, though. She's real thin, isn't she Chrissy?' He turned to Christine.

'Yes, she is. But that nice lady doctor says she can come back up here next month. She'll have to go on doing special exercises every day though. Auntie Vi really spoils her, doesn't she, Jim?'

Jim nodded. 'Poor little devil,' he said, 'she needs spoiling, I reckon. She'll always have that iron, you know.'

There was a silence around the table. Then Mum looked at the clock.

'Time you were off to school, Jess, and you too Laura, and Nico. It's almost half past eight.'

Reluctantly Jess packed her school bag, put in her lunch in its brown paper bag, said goodbye to the cheerful ring of Drurys round the table and set off slowly for school. It was the first time she'd been back on her bike since the night of her desperate ride home in the dark. Only four nights ago. It seemed like another world!

At school, Jess found herself the centre of attention. Everyone crowded around her in the bicycle shed and then in the locker rooms with questions and exclamations. The headmaster even made a little speech in Assembly, just before the National Anthem, to welcome Jess back to school and to say how brave she'd been. Everyone clapped and cheered. Jess looked down at her knees. Her eyes began to prick again in that funny way they sometimes did. Rona nudged her.

'Stand up, Jess,' she whispered. 'Mr Simmonds wants you to stand up.'

Jess stood up, very red in the face, looked round at the six hundred smiling faces and sat down again as quickly as she could.

'Now, girls and boys,' said Mr Simmonds, 'shall we all stand for the National Anthem?' That was what he said every day at the end of Assembly and Jess was never more glad to hear the familiar words. With much shuffling, coughing and banging of seats, the six hundred stood up to sing.

While Jess was working her way through her usual Wednesday timetable, Jim and Christine Drury were having a busy day. Kenny and Snowy trailed everywhere with them and told Jess all about it after school. First they had to go to the Glencarra police station. Constable Hayes drove them down to the river bend and the 'Lucky Strike'. Together they went through all the piles of clothes, all the drawers and cupboards, to see if anything else was missing.

'No. Everything's there,' said Christine at last.

'Looks to me as if the bloke was only after that gold brooch. He must've known it was here. Once he'd found it, he pushed off. Didn't take another thing. Not even a pair of boots. Left a terrible mess though, didn't he?' Jim looked around at it all and scratched the back of his head.

Christine was folding the clothes and putting them away in the drawers. She swept out the galley and pushed and pulled the carpet-sweeper over the rag rug on the floor of the main cabin.

'This place needs a real good going over, Jim,' she said wearily.

'Don't do it now, Chrissy,' said Jim, taking the carpet-sweeper from her. 'We've got to get back to town. Just leave it till tomorrow.'

So back to town they went in the police car again and on to the McCallums' for a quick bite of lunch.

'Now, I do want to see Lizzie,' said Christine. 'Kenny, you and Snowy stay here. We won't be long.'

Jim rode Dad's old bicycle and Christine borrowed Mrs McCallum's and they set off for the hospital, less than a mile across town. Then after they'd seen Lizzie, on to Father Byrne's house to talk about Lizzie and where she was going to live. Then on to the shops to buy provisions. They filled Christine's four string bags and rode back to the McCallums' house with a bulging bag swinging dangerously from each handle-bar. Meanwhile Kenny and Snowy had been playing happily all afternoon with Jess's toys, reading Jess's books, climbing in and out of Jess's wardrobe and swinging on the tyre that hung from a peppercorn tree out in the back-yard. Jess herself was just in from school as

Christine and Jim wobbled up the front path and lifted off the string bags.

Another cup of tea in the kitchen and then it was time for the boys to gather up their things and go back to the boat. It was after five now and Dad was home from work. He was going to drive them all down to the river bend.

'Kenny,' said Christine suddenly from the back seat just as Dad was putting the one case and the string bags in the boot, 'I found lots of paintings scattered around the cabin this morning. Can I throw them out? I want to have a good clear up tomorrow.'

'No, Mum, no!' wailed Kenny.

'They're *our* paintings, Mum,' explained Snowy, 'and Jess's too. Please don't chuck them out. We want them, don't we Jess?' He stuck his head out of the car window to appeal to Jess.

Jess nodded and looked worried.

'It's all right,' said Christine quickly, much to Jess's relief. 'I don't mind them. I didn't know the boys liked painting, that's all. They never used to. I won't throw them out, don't worry, Jess.'

'Goodbye! goodbye!' called Jess and Mum and Laura and Nico as the Ford backed down the drive and swung out into the road.

'Goodbye! goodbye!' called Kenny and Snowy, waving out of the car windows.

'See you later!' called Jess as the car drove off.

'Toorooloo!' called Jim and settled back in his seat. He started yarning away with Dad as if they'd been old cobbers for twenty years.

Father Byrne came in that night as he'd said he would. He had good news. Mum and Dad thought it was good, anyway. Jess wasn't so sure. He'd been along to see Mrs O'Malley in Lime Avenue. She was very willing to let half her house, unfurnished, to Lizzie. Father Byrne had been taken all over the half-house by Mrs O'Malley who was only too glad to show it off. It was very nice, he said. An old weatherboard house in good order. Two separate front gates and two front doors. The only thing Lizzie'd have to share was the wash-house out the back.

'Mrs O'Malley thought that'd be no trouble at all,' added Father Byrne. 'She always washes on a Monday. If Miss Forrester doesn't mind doing her bit of washing on some other day of the week, then all will be well. There's even a spare patch for vegetables out the back too if she'd like to do some gardening of her own.'

'I'm sure she won't mind not washing on a Monday,' said Mum, 'I'm only worried that she might not want to go there at all. *I* think it sounds perfect. But Lizzie's so used to her boat and she does love to be near the Drurys, especially Mrs Drury, Christine that is. Lizzie's known her for nearly thirty years. It seems a pity to separate them, doesn't it?'

'Yes. I know. That worries me too,' said Father Byrne. 'I've had a talk to Jim and Christine this afternoon. Jim sees he's got to give up this prospecting craze of his. He ought to be here all the year round, looking after his family, and I told him so. He's going to see Mr Reardon tomorrow to ask if there's a permanent job on the block. I think Christine would easily be able to ride in to see Miss Forrester once or twice a week.'

'How's Annie going to get to school?' asked Jess.

'With crutches and a lame leg, she can't ride a bike in the way the boys do.'

Everyone was silent. No one could think how Annie could possibly get to school from the barge down on the river bend.

'I wonder if Jim would agree to moving his boat nearer the town,' said Dad. 'There are two or three houseboats already tied up near the town jetty and there's plenty of room for more. Then Annie could catch the school bus from town and Christine would be much nearer to Miss Forrester.'

'And the boys might have some other kids to play with,' put in Jess.

'But Jim doesn't like the town,' said Mum. 'He likes the bush.'

'Yes, but he can't have just what he likes – not when he thinks of Annie,' said Father Byrne firmly. 'That's a good idea, Mr McCallum. I'll put it to him. Just leave it to me!'

Father Byrne got up.

'Jess, I think you're the best one to have a word with Miss Forrester about the house,' he said. 'You know her well and you're the only one of us who can talk to her properly so she can understand. Will you have a try?'

'Yes. I will,' agreed Jess, 'but there's one thing I don't like. Has the front door got a bell?'

'Yes, of course it has. There's a bell and a knocker, too, I think,' said Father Byrne.

'But Lizzie can't hear knockers and bells! How will she know if anyone's there at the front door?'

Silence again. Everyone was stumped this time.

'We'll have to think about that, Jess,' said Dad. 'There must be a solution.'

'Yes. There must be,' said Father Byrne. 'You do your best with Miss Forrester at the hospital, Jess, and I'll see what we can do about the front door bell.'

They all walked down the front path to the gate with Father Byrne.

'God bless you, my dears!' he said with a smile and a wave of his hand and he set off walking briskly along the street.

'Well!' exclaimed Mum as soon as they were back inside the house, 'he certainly does tell his flock what to do, doesn't he! I can't see Mr Adam bossing us around like that, can you, Arthur?'

'No. And I can't see us putting up with it either! But he is right about Jim Drury, isn't he, dear?' said Dad mildly. 'That man ought to look after his family instead of wandering around the State looking for gold! It's a problem our Mr Adam hasn't ever had to face at St Cuthbert's, now has he?'

'No,' laughed Mum. 'That's true enough. And I mut say I'm glad Father Byrne told Jim straight. Christine should have told him years ago! Well, Jess, I don't know about you but I'm worn out!' said Mum.

'Let's all go to bed,' said Jess wearily.

The next afternoon, straight after school, Jess went to the hospital to see Lizzie. Lizzie certainly looked much better. There was fresh colour in her cheeks now. Her eyes had their old, cheerful glint again.

'Jess,' she said, leaning over towards Jess the minute she sat down on the straight chair beside the bed, 'what I need is something to read. There's nothing here except a pile of last year's *Women's Weeklies*. I'm nearly going mad! Do you think your mother could lend me some decent books?'

Jess nodded with a smile.

'Wh-at b-ooks?' she asked.

'Dickens,' said Lizzie firmly.

'Wh-ich o-ne?'

Lizzie thought for a minute and then she said, 'Bring me *David Copperfield*, Jess.'

'To-morr-ow,' promised Jess.

Now she had to get the conversation away from *David Copperfield* and on to the awkward matter of Mrs O'Malley's house in Lime Avenue. She was very much afraid that Lizzie would dig her heels in. She tried to think of a tactful way to begin but the more she thought, the more blank her mind seemed to be. Lizzie looked at her curiously.

'What's up, Jess? You look worried.'

Jess smiled a worried smile.

'What is it?' asked Lizzie. 'Write it down if it's too complicated.' She pushed the pad and pencil over to Jess.

Jess was glad to write. That made it much easier. She could only manage short sentences when she spoke so Lizzie could lip-read her. Short and simple they had to be but this question of Mrs O'Malley's house wasn't simple at all. So she leant Lizzie's writing pad on the edge of the bed and began. It wasn't only Lizzie who was watching and waiting. Most of the other fifteen ladies had their eye on Jess's moving pencil, too.

'We would all like you to move into town,' wrote Jess. 'River-boat far too dangerous. Mrs O'Malley in Lime Avenue has half her house to let. Quite cheap. Near us. Christine can easily visit you. Boys too. Jim may move his boat to town jetty. Then we'd all be close. Please agree, Lizzie.'

Jess tore off the sheet and held it out to Lizzie who got her round tortoiseshell glasses out and put them on. Slowly she read through the message. Jess watched her face anxiously. There seemed to be a trace of a wrinkled frown on Lizzie's forehead.

'Oh dear,' thought Jess, 'that looks bad!'

Lizzie leant back on her pillows and took off her glasses. Then to Jess's astonishment, she said,

'Yes, Jess. That's a good idea. I like it. When can I move in?'

Jess hardly knew what to say. No battles at all! It was all over! Lizzie had agreed. She pulled her thoughts together.

'A-s s-oon a-s y-ou l-eave hosp-ital.' ,

'Good,' said Lizzie She lowered her voice a little but she still spoke louder than she knew and Jess wasn't the only one who could hear perfectly well.

'You see, Jess, I'm quite enjoying myself in here. All these ladies in the other beds – I can't hear what they say to me, of course, and they speak too fast for me to read them. But they're all so friendly. So kind. They lend me their magazines and they share their chocolates and grapes with me and they show me photos of their children and grandchildren. I've been far too cut off from people down there by the river. Deafness cuts me off a lot anyway. If I live down there, miles from town, I'm still more cut off. When people *think* I'm odd, I'm sure I begin to *get* a bit odd. But here where everyone's so friendly, I'm beginning to feel quite normal. Just like anyone else! It's a good feeling, Jess. I don't want to lose it. Now if I moved into the town and lived in an ordinary street with friendly people all around, I wouldn't feel so cut off, would I? I'd like to keep this nice normal feeling.'

'Y-ou s-eem norm-al to m-e an-y-w-ay!' said Jess indignantly.

'Yes, but that's because you know me. If you didn't know me and just saw me one day pottering around on the river bank, wouldn't you think I was a bit odd?'

Jess grinned. She had to admit that she probably would. Lizzie *had* looked such a sight with her childishly-short grey hair, her baggy clothes and her wrinkled stockings.

'Well, that's why I'd love a house – or even half a house – right in the town. I could do a bit of gardening. Perhaps I could even keep a few chooks out the back. But I do want to be sure I can still see Christine and the children. And you, too, Jess. You'll be much nearer. You'll be able to pop in any day after school to borrow my books and to have a talk. There's that book of ballads I want you to read. Have you ever read any of the old ballads, Jess?'

Jess thought hard. Then she remembered one and wrote *Sir Patrick Spens*??? on Lizzie's pad.

'Yes, yes,' said Lizzie enthusiastically. 'That's one of the best.' And to Jess's embarrassment she actually began to recite the first verse, so loudly and in so broad an accent that every lady in the ward turned to look at them.

> The king sits in Dunfermline town,
> Drinking the blude-red wine,
> 'O whare will I get a skeely skipper
> To sail this new ship o'mine?'

There was a burst of applause from all the beds around. Lizzie saw it rather than heard it. To Jess's intense relief she went no further but started, instead, to tell her of other good ballads in the book.

'There's *Tam Lin* and *The Wife of Ussher's Well* and *Thomas the Rhymer* and *Edward, Edward* and a host of others, Jess,' she said. 'We'll have a grand time reading them when you come round to visit me in Lime Avenue.'

Jess was glad to hear Lizzie talking about Lime Avenue now as if it were all a settled thing. Suddenly she remembered something more she'd meant to say. It called for paper. She wrote quickly.

'Father Byrne is going to fix up something instead of a front-door bell so you'll know when someone is at the front door.'

Lizzie smiled.

'That's kind of him. I had a little light in the Swan Hill house. It went on when anyone pressed the bell-push. It worked very well. I must tell him about it when he comes in to see me tonight.'

Jess got up to go and heaved her brown school-bag full of books on to her shoulder.

'The doctor says I can't leave hospital for at least another two weeks, Jess. I think it's ridiculous. There's nothing the matter with me really. But he says he wants me to rest. He doesn't like the sound of my chest, he says!' and Lizzie laughed, quite unperturbed.

Jess looked disappointed. Two weeks seemed a long time.

'Never mind,' said Lizzie, 'I'm enjoying myself in here. It's giving me a new lease of life. When I finally move into Lime Avenue, we'll have to have a house-warming party, won't we?'

Jess hadn't even heard of such a thing as a house-warming party but she thought it sounded nice. She gave Lizzie a hug, smiled at the other fifteen ladies in their beds, walked down the long ward and rode home to bring the good news. Lizzie would live in the town! Better than that! She actually *wanted* to live in the town!

17
Tiger Hawkins

On Friday morning, just after eight o'clock, the phone rang in the McCallums' house. It was Dad who went to answer it.

'Oh, good, good!' Jess could hear him saying. There was quite a long conversation. Jess couldn't make much of it.

'Yes, we'll let her know,' said Dad at last. 'No trouble at all. Thanks for ringing. Yes. Goodbye.'

Dad came back into the kitchen when all the family was having breakfast round the table.

'What is it, Dad?' asked Nico.

'They've got him!' said Dad.

'Got who?' asked Jess.

'Tiger Hawkins. You know – that old swaggie you saw down by the river. Jim Drury's mate. They tracked him down at Rosella Bend. He'd certainly got a long way from Glencarra.'

'And what did he say, dear?' asked Mum.

'Said he knew nothing about the brooch. Nothing about the fire. Nothing about ropes being cut or a boat drifting out into the middle of the river. Then, of course, they searched him. And sure enough, there was the missing brooch – wrapped up in pink newspaper and stuffed right down at the bottom of his billy! So he's been arrested and charged with theft. He's in the lock-up down at the police station now. I suppose he'll plead guilty. Not much else he *can* do, is there, now they've found the brooch in his billy?'

'Do the Drurys know yet? That it's found, I mean,' asked Jess excitedly. 'They will be pleased.'

'Not yet, Jess. But Constable Lithgow says he's going to go down the river himself this morning to tell them. He wants us to let Lizzie know. I think those policemen down at the station aren't too sure how to handle Old Lizzie. Bit scared to talk to her!' Dad laughed. 'So now it's just a matter of time,' he went on. 'Old Tiger's safely under lock and key and they reckon he'll soon come clean about the boat and the fire. That gold brooch in his billy pretty well proves it. Constable Lithgow's got a Detective Sergeant to give him a bit of a hand on all this now but he's still in charge of the case himself. He seems to be enjoying it as a matter of fact. He'll soon have it all sewn up. Jess, I'm afraid he wants you to go in this morning to identify Tiger Hawkins. Just to make sure it is the same old codger who called in at the boats that day when you were there. It seems a bit pointless, really, since they've found the brooch on him but they have to check up on his story.'

So Dad took Jess into the police station an hour later. She'd just have to be late for school. It couldn't be helped. The constable took them along a narrow, brown corridor to the cells at the back. With much rattling and jangling of keys, he unlocked the second cell down on the left and all three of them crowded in.

There wasn't much room for them. Jess held on tight to her father's hand and felt suddenly much younger than thirteen. The little room stank. It was bare except for an iron bed and two grey blankets on the mattress. Bars guarded the high window. Names and messages were scratched and scrawled all over the walls. Tiger Hawkins sat neatly, almost primly, at one end of the bed, his hands joined together on his lap. He looked up as Jess and her father came into the cell with the constable.

Anyone less like a tiger, Jess had never seen. All the smooth and cheery over-confidence that Jess hadn't liked in him had drained away now. He looked simply crushed and defeated. His grey beard, once so jaunty, now drooped. Jess felt suddenly sorry for him.

'I never done it,' said Tiger Hawkins in a flat, wooden voice. 'All I done was nicked that damn gold brooch.'

'OK, Tiger, OK,' said the constable mildly, 'never mind about that now. Well, Jess?'

'Yes, that's the same man,' she said, embarrassed. She couldn't look Tiger Hawkins in the eye.

'I remember *you*, too, girlie,' said Tiger to Jess. 'You got real wild with me that day, didn't you? Just because I went and said something you didn't like about that old girl! And now they reckon I fired her boat. I never did! *And* I don't like the stink in this cell. I've never been in a place like this in all my life!'

'Righto, Tiger. That'll do. Come on, Jess,' and Constable Lithgow shepherded her out.

'Poor Old Tiger!' said Jess sadly to her father as soon as they were outside the door. 'I don't think he set fire to the boat, do you? He looks all out of place in there, Dad. He belongs out in the bush. I don't think he even cut the rope.'

'Well, we'll have to see,' said the constable. 'There's no evidence one way or the other yet. He's got his lawyer coming in to see him this morning. So you don't need to worry about Tiger, Jess. He'll get a fair go.'

'But that cell!' said Jess indignantly. 'It's horrible!'

'Well, I can't do much about that, lassie. We've had lots of customers in and out of there. He'll just have to put up with it, I'm afraid. Don't forget we *did* find the brooch tucked up in his billy! He does look a sad case, all right, but you mustn't let your feelings run away with you.'

'Come on, Jess. Off to school now,' put in Dad quickly before Jess could launch into another speech. 'The constable will soon sort it all out.'

But it didn't work out quite as easily as Dad had expected. A week later, Tiger Hawkins was still insisting that he knew nothing at all about the fire or the drifting boat. His story – and he stuck to it down to the smallest detail – was this. He did know about the gold-nugget brooch, he said. He'd met Jim Drury and a few of his mates down the Ovens some months back. Never knew Jim before but got talking to him over a few beers in the pub. Heard Jim skiting about this bonzer gold-nugget brooch that he had on his barge up on the big river. He'd thought no more of it, he said, till that day when he was passing through Glencarra, looking for odd jobs of work on the blocks. Thought he'd just call in to say hello to Jim Drury's missus. He wanted to get a look at that brooch. When he got to the boats, she wasn't home. Gone down south. No one there except the two little kids and the 'mad old deafo' next door. That's when temptation seized him, he said. He decided he'd hang around the district for a bit and take his chance. All he wanted to do was *look* at the brooch. He didn't ever mean to go and pinch it off them!

So he'd moved on to Wentworth, over on the other side. Stayed there about three weeks doing a job on the channels for a blockie he knew. Then he'd made his way back to the river bend and the two old boats. On Thursday, the 25th March (or so he reckoned, when faced with a calendar and asked to count back the days exactly) he'd slept rough a mile or so down the river and early on Friday morning he'd crept up closer to keep a watch on the boats.

He'd seen the two boys ride off to school on their bikes that morning and the 'old woman' waving to them as they went. There was no sign of the mother so Tiger guessed she was still away. So long as the old woman stayed inside her boat, she'd never know he was anywhere round the place. He'd kept his eyes open, seized his chance, nipped up the gang-plank of the 'Lucky Strike', torn the cabin to bits looking for the 'blasted brooch' and at last he'd found the locked box under the bunk, right down at the far end. He knew that must be it. He couldn't force the box open there and that's when he suddenly shoved it under his coat. When he came out of the barge, the coast was still clear. So he'd dashed down the plank and off into the bush again with the box still stuffed under his coat. He'd picked up his swag from the place where he'd left it under a tree. For quite a few miles he'd kept hold of the box. Then he'd bust the lock open with his knife, taken out the brooch (a 'real beauty' he said it was) and chucked the empty box out into the river. It sank straight away. He was well clear of the place by Friday midday and he'd never been back since. He'd kept on the move every day and hadn't let up till he got to Rosella Bend a week later. He'd thought he was safe. And then the police had tracked him down and found the brooch on him. He wished he'd never heard of the blinking brooch!

Jess and Mr McCallum heard this whole long story of Tiger's from Constable Lithgow when he came in on Tuesday to ask them still more questions. He'd barely finished giving them Tiger's tale when Jess burst out, 'But that can't possibly be true! He *couldn't* have taken it on the Friday morning?'

'Why not, lassie?' asked the constable.

'Well – because the boys would have found all that mess in the cabin when they got back from school on Friday afternoon. They couldn't have missed it. The door into that cabin was always open. And anyway, *I* was there on the Saturday and I saw the boys going backwards and forwards to their barge. I know Kenny went right into that cabin. He put the pictures in a case under his mother's bunk. Nothing was messed up then.'

'Mm. You're quite right, Jess,' said Mr McCallum. The constable nodded slowly.

'So Tiger's been spinning us a yarn again,' he said with a sigh and with half a smile of admiration for Tiger. 'We'll have to start with him all over again. Now, Jess,' he went on, 'I want you to remember all the events of that night again. I know you've told me the whole thing before and I've got a good note of it but I'd like you to go through it again. We might have missed some little detail that could give us a clue. You said . . .' and here Constable Lithgow got out his notebook and found the right page, 'you fell asleep at about ten o'clock by summer time and suddenly woke up some hours later. Now what exactly was it that woke you? What did you hear?'

Jess tried to remember.

'The trouble is that at the time I thought I must be imagining all the funny sounds. They didn't seem real. First of all there was a sharp sound like a biggish stick breaking. Then a whistle. Short and soft. I thought it was a bird perhaps. Then a sort of clank or clink. Metal, I think. I listened hard in case it came again but it didn't. Only the once. Then I wondered if I could hear voices whispering but I wasn't sure. It could have just been leaves rustling but it seemed quicker than leaves. That's what scared me worst of all. Then at the end there was a soft, rushing sound. A whoosh! Like bare feet running. But when I listened harder it had gone.'

Jess stopped.

'That's all,' she said. 'I began to smell the smoke about a quarter of an hour later.'

Constable Lithgow had added just a note or two to Jess's earlier account.

'Thanks, lassie. That's very clear. I'll have to have another talk with Tiger Hawkins. He's certainly telling one lie and he might well be telling more.'

Within two hours, apparently, Tiger had changed his story. The constable was on the phone to Dad with the new version later in the morning and Jess heard it from Dad at tea that night. Tiger had now entirely given up his tale about coming to the boats and taking the brooch on the Friday. He said he'd only made all that up so they wouldn't connect him with the fire on the boat on Saturday night. He still swore he'd had nothing to do with all that and didn't even know about it till the police caught up with him and questioned him. It was, in fact, on the Saturday night, at about eleven o'clock, that he'd pinched the brooch. Not a soul stirring, he said. He knew the three kids were camping out in their little humpy. He'd been watching them carefully from the bush just a few yards away while they had their camp-fire meal, thinking he'd have to sneak on to the barge while the kids were asleep inside. A tricky job, it would've been. Then he saw them making for their hut in their pyjamas so he knew he'd have no trouble at all. He just waited a good couple of hours after they'd all gone to bed and then crept up to the barge and went on board. All the rest of the story was true, cross his heart and hope to die, it was. There was no fire on the old girl's boat while he was there. The camp-fire was still glowing but that's all. The rope wasn't cut and the stake wasn't pulled up and the boat wasn't drifting. He made his getaway at about half past eleven and didn't see another soul all night. The bush was as quiet as the grave apart from a touch of wind and the odd squawk from a waking bird. This was Tiger's story now and he stuck to it even more firmly than he'd stuck to the first one. The police could get no further. They were stumped – at least for the time being.

Meanwhile, Father Byrne had been busy. He'd got Vic O'Malley to fix up a new kind of electric bell on Lizzie's front door. It wasn't really a bell at all. When you pressed a white button by the front door four small red lights lit up inside the house. There was one light over the kitchen sink, one over the fireplace in the living-room, one in the bathroom and one in the bedroom. Whichever room Lizzie might be in, she'd always see a little red light flash on and know there was someone to visit her at the front door.

The next day Father Byrne drove down the track to the river to see Jim. They had a long talk, sitting on a log by the water's edge while Christine kept the two boys out of the way.

'Chrissy,' Jim called out after an hour or so, 'come here a sec, could you?'

Christine joined him and Father Byrne on the log. The boys followed.

'Father here's been saying he thinks we'd do well to move the barge up near the town. So Annie can get the bus to school. What d'you think Chris?'

Christine smiled.

'I'd like it,' she said simply. 'I'd be nearer Lizzie and I could get to mass on Sundays – and the boys would have some other kids to play with. It's really too lonely down here, Jim. But what about you?'

'I like it here, Chrissy. You know that. But I see what Father means. And if *you'd* like it, that settles it. I'll get a lift up to town with Father now and fix up with Bruce to give us a tow tomorrow sometime.'

And by Friday, sure enough, the 'Lucky Strike' was tied up snugly between two other house-boats by the town jetty. Kenny and Snowy were soon running in and out of the other boats, making friends with a whole new mob of boys and Christine was getting to know young Mrs Davey on the boat next door.

Mr Reardon was glad to give Jim a job. He needed a permanent man and he knew that Jim could turn his hand to anything. Mrs Reardon wanted

Christine to help her out in the house every Tuesday and Thursday from now on.

Jess heard all this good news from Father Byrne himself when he called in on the McCallums on Wednesday to talk over the next problem – what to do about Lizzie's boat.

The old 'Sally Jane' herself was far too dilapidated now for anyone ever to live in again. The galley was completely burnt out and the rest was badly worn and corroded. She'd probably have to be sold for scrap. Lizzie wouldn't get much for her but then she hadn't paid much for her in the first place. The police had had the boat towed right down to the town jetty and boarded her up so no one could break in. Father Byrne's idea was to organize a working-bee of five or six men from St Aidan's on Saturday afternoon.

'We'll soon shift all her stuff out of the boat and up to Lime Avenue. We'll take the whole lot, lock, stock and barrel. We can use Vic O'Malley's van.'

'I'll come and give you a hand, Father,' said Dad.

'Can't I come too?' asked Jess.

'Good idea, Jess,' said Father Byrne. 'The more the merrier!'

It was lucky that Jess joined the working-bee. Up at Lime Avenue she had a good idea where Lizzie would like things to go so she directed the unpacking operations as the men hauled everything off the van and carried it all into the house. The books and furniture were badly stained with black smears of smoke and a strange unpleasant smell still clung around them.

When the van was completely unloaded, only the kitchen was empty. While the men opened a few bottles of beer, Jess stood and looked around the little room that was bare except for the fire stove in one corner.

'What can we do about this, Dad?'

'I'm sure we can lend her a few pots and pans and crockery to tide her over. But I don't know what we can do about a table.'

'I think I can rustle up a table and a couple of chairs,' said Father Byrne, a bottle opener in his hand. 'The Farrells are moving south. They've got a few things they want to get rid of. Just leave it to me, Jess, and you see what your mother can do in the way of plates and saucepans. We'll soon have it all as right as rain.'

So by Tuesday the half-house in Lime Avenue was almost ready.

'Christine and I are going in there tomorrow to give Lizzie's furniture and books a good clean up,' said Mum at tea time. 'We'll take a picnic lunch with us and stay all day.'

On Wednesday after school, Jess tore down to Lime Avenue in all the heat of a very warm afternoon to see if Mum and Christine were still at work. They'd just finished and were having their cup of tea out on the prickly back lawn. Jess walked from room to room. The whole place had been transformed. The furniture had been cleaned with Mum's special mixture of vinegar and water and then polished with beeswax. The acrid stink of smoke had gone. Lizzie's huge picture of Bamburgh Castle was hanging on the living-room wall and all her books were arranged along the shelves. The bed was even made up with clean sheets; the crockery and cutlery had been put away in a kitchen cupboard that the departing Farrells had left behind. They'd even given Lizzie their old ice-chest. Everything was ready! Jess felt sure that Lizzie could come home now.

Luckily, the doctor thought so too.

'Friday afternoon,' he said to Mum on the phone that night. 'She'll be right by then.'

Friday afternoon came at last. Mum had stocked up Lizzie's cupboard with food for the weekend and straight after school she and Jess drove to the hospital. Lizzie was sitting on the chair by the bed, her old brown coat buttoned on and her bag packed. Round the ward she walked, moving from bed to bed, shaking hands with all the ladies.

'Do come and see me,' she said to them in turn, '29A Lime Avenue.'

The ladies nodded and smiled in reply and waved to Jess as she and Mum followed Lizzie down the ward, carrying her bag between them.

When the three of them arrived at Lime Avenue, Jess gave Lizzie the key to her front door. Lizzie turned the key in the lock and into the new house they went, Lizzie first, then Mum and Jess last. Lizzie walked around it all in amazement, admiring everything, opening every cupboard, peering into the ice-chest, patting all her old books lovingly, looking up at the castle on the wall. She tried out the bell-push and said it was far better than the one she'd had in Swan Hill. Jess hopped and danced along after her, just as delighted with it all as Lizzie herself.

'Now, how about a cup of tea?' said Lizzie.

Jess filled up the brown electric jug, Mum got out the cups and saucers, and Lizzie found the tea, the milk and a tin full of Anzac biscuits that Christine had made for her homecoming.

'A place for everything and everything in its place!'

murmured Lizzie as she surveyed the kitchen. Mum smiled with satisfaction. That was one thing she and Lizzie were sure to agree about.

'Well, Jess,' said Mum as they drove off home at five o'clock, leaving Lizzie waving happily to them from her front door, 'that's a happy ending, isn't it?'

Was it an ending, Jess wondered, or a new beginning? Would she really enjoy her visits to Lizzie so much now that she lived in an ordinary house in an ordinary street? Had it really been Lizzie herself who had drawn her down to the river every Sunday or was it the two boys and the wide river itself and the battered old 'Sally Jane', riding quietly at the water's edge?

18
An Anzac Easter

On Saturday morning, before breakfast was finished, Jess was already asking Mum if she could go to see Lizzie today.

'Just to see how she's settling in. *Please* can I, Mum?'

'No, dear, you certainly can't. It's not good manners to go and call on someone so soon after they've moved in. Anyway, you saw her yesterday, Jess. She won't want to be bothered with you again today. You can go sometime next week. On Wednesday or Thursday. That will be quite time enough.'

Jess stumped off noisily to the bedroom and made

her bed in as rough and as slap-dash way as she could. Well, she'd go and see Kenny and Snowy, anyway, she thought to herself. And she wouldn't ask Mum about it. Mum might say no again. She'd just slip down to the river when she was doing the Saturday's shopping in town. Mum wouldn't even know she'd gone.

Mum might have had her suspicions all the same. Jess was so unusually keen to be given the shopping list and the money and the meat coupons at nine o'clock, a good hour before her normal time. She raced from one shop to the next and had her string bags full to overflowing by ten o'clock. Her heavily-weighted bike kept a firm and steady balance as she rode down the steep road past the swimming baths to the river. Near the jetty were three newish house-boats and the Drurys' barge. Lizzie's old paddler had been towed away already to the scrap-yard. Jim had given the 'Lucky Strike' a fresh coat of paint so she did not look too disgraceful beside the more splendid boats. Some children were playing on the deck of one of these but Jess couldn't see any sign of Kenny or Snowy among them. She left her bike and its heavy load against a tree and ran up the plank to knock on the Drurys' cabin door. There was no reply! Jess called out,

'Kenny! Snowy! Where are you? It's me – Jess!'

Still no answer.

One of the children on the boat next door called across to her.

'Are you looking for them Drury kids?'

Jess nodded.

'They've gone up town. So's their Mum and Dad.

Going to visit someone in Lime Avenue, Snowy said. They won't be back all day.'

Jess turned slowly away. So Kenny and Snowy were allowed to visit Lizzie but she wasn't. It wasn't fair. All she could do now was to wander off home again, walking with her heavy bike up the road past the baths, and riding listlessly along Orange Avenue. Lizzie and Kenny and Snowy would all be sitting around in Lizzie's new house, laughing and talking and looking in all the cupboards and pressing the front-door bell while she had no one to play with and no one to talk to. It wasn't fair.

Jess had to wait until Wednesday before her mother would let her go and see Lizzie. Three more whole days! Jess was sure Lizzie would be wondering why she hadn't come sooner.

On Wednesday, at last, Jess sped down Lime Avenue after school and pressed hard on Lizzie's bell. A slight pause and then the door opened wide. There was Lizzie herself, looking strong and well again, her grey hair neatly combed, her old creased face smiling, her forefinger beckoning Jess inside.

'I'm so glad to see you, Jess. How kind of you to give me a few days to get my bearings. Now I'm all ready for visitors. You couldn't have come at a better time.'

Lizzie led Jess into the kitchen. It reeked of onions. A large saucepan was bubbling away hard on the stove. Jess went and peered in but she soon jumped back, her eyes stinging. She looked at Lizzie in a questioning way, and pointed to the saucepan.

'It's eggs, Jess. Easter eggs. I'm making them for you and Kenny and Snowy. And I've popped in a

213

couple more for your brother and sister. Next Sunday's Easter Day, you know.'

Jess took another look at the bubbling pan. She held her nose and kept well back. All she could see was tumbling yellow water. She couldn't see any Easter eggs at all. It was the last place she'd look for them, anyway. The only Easter eggs Jess knew were made of chocolate and had lovely square patterns on them like the shell of a tortoise. They always came wrapped up in pretty coloured foil. Only a madman would plunge them in boiling yellow water. Jess turned back to Lizzie.

'Ea-ster e-ggs?' she mouthed slowly.

'These are *real* Easter eggs,' said Lizzie. 'You take real eggs and you wrap each one up in a little jacket of onion-skins. Then you tie it round and round with cotton to hold the onion-skins in place. You put them into a saucepan of cold water, bring them to the boil and keep them on the boil for a good ten minutes. Then you leave them to dry. When you take off the onion jackets the eggs are a lovely yellow colour with scribbly, mottled patterns all over them.'

'D-o y-ou ea-t th-em?' asked Jess.

Lizzie laughed.

'In the end you do. But the main thing is to roll them. When I was a girl we'd all go out to a sloping green field near Bamburgh on Easter morning. We'd line up at the top of the field and roll our eggs right down to the bottom. It wasn't exactly a race. The shells got rather crushed and bashed as the eggs rolled downhill. The winner was the one whose shell survived the best. Then we sat around on the beach

214

and ate our eggs. We just buried the yellow shells in the sand.'

The eggs were done. Lizzie lifted them out and left them to dry on her kitchen window-sill.

'Come in here, Jess,' said Lizzie, smiling as she led the way into her living-room. 'I've something even better than Easter eggs to show you.'

Jess gasped. One whole wall, from floor to ceiling, was papered with the pictures she and the boys had painted down by the river. Trees and boats and water and sky crowded together in a medley of greens and blues and browns.

'They're all there,' said Lizzie, 'every single one of them. Mrs O'Malley said she didn't mind a bit so I got Christine to bring the whole caseful here on Saturday. Kenny and Snowy climbed up on chairs and pasted them on the wall for me. I wanted to keep a bit of the river here in my new house. I don't want to forget the river, Jess.'

Jess felt sad she hadn't had a hand in the pasting. Still, she was happy to see all her own pictures in their places among Kenny's and Snowy's. They didn't look too bad at all, she thought. The Murray River would never be forgotten here any more than the old stones of Bamburgh Castle or the wild North Sea. Jess was sure of that.

The 'real' Easter eggs did not please Laura and Nico as much as Jess had hoped when she presented them very early on Easter morning.

'Poor little English kids!' groaned Nico. 'Is this all they can get over there? Now let me have another half-hour's sleep, Jess.'

At breakfast, when everyone was properly awake, and when Jess had rolled her yellow egg down a sloping plank from the wood-shed roof, Dad reminded them all that this was not only Easter Sunday – it was Anzac Day as well!

'Yes, the 25th of April. Now *there's* a challenge for the minister this morning!' he said with satisfaction.

'How on earth is he going to combine them?' asked Mum. 'We won't know whether to laugh or cry!'

'Mr Adam will find a way, dear, don't worry. I bet he's enjoying himself, stitching the two things together. It's the chance of a lifetime!'

Dad was right. Mr Adam found a way. He had the entire congregation assembled outside the church by eleven o'clock, instead of inside. Everyone looked puzzled and a bit ill at ease out there in the garden and leaning against the wall of the church. Mum had to hold her hat on her head as a cool south wind blew through the crowd. Suddenly, everyone stiffened. Every head was lifted. Every ear was listening. From inside the church came the stirring sound of the bagpipes.

'It's "The Flowers of the Forest", Jess,' whispered Dad, bending down to her.

'What's that?'

'It's a Scottish song about the men killed in battle.'

'In the Great War,' whispered Jess.

'No, no. Long before that.'

Andrew Sutherland, the piper, dressed in his splendid kilt, was now at the church door. He stood on the top step beside the minister and faced the crowd. His pipes poured out their strange, sad melody. He was the only piper left in Glencarra now. All the others were prisoners on the Burma railway with Rona's father but Andrew Sutherland was blind. When he'd tried to enlist in 1940, he'd been turned away.

216

The grown-ups seemed to know the old tune well. Jess could hear people humming softly all around her. A few were even singing the words. Now old Mrs Urquhart, dressed in black as she had been ever since her son was killed at Gallipoli twenty-eight years ago, made her way through the crowd to lay a wreath of white chrysanthemums on the war-memorial by the church gate. Everyone stood in silence for two long minutes.

Suddenly the piper struck up a new tune. It was the Easter hymn! On a tide of Hallelujahs, the people surged into the church behind the piper who was being guided up the aisle by his son. The mood had switched from Anzac to Easter. Everyone was smiling. By the time the triumphant music had finished, Mr Adam was up in his pulpit and the members of St Cuthbert's congregation had simmered down again to their more usual serious state of mind. Jess settled back into her old familiar seat and let the service take its old familiar course.

'He did very well, I thought,' said Dad to Mum as he sharpened up his carving knife at dinner time.

'Who, Dad? The piper, do you mean?' asked Jess.

'No dear,' said Mum with a smile. 'Dad means the minister. He had a hard job putting Anzac and Easter together. He did it splendidly.'

'I wish we could have the pipes *every* Sunday,' said Nico.

That Monday was a public holiday, because of Easter, and so was Tuesday, because of Anzac. Jess had to wait till Wednesday before the shops would be open again and she could meet Lizzie in town. They'd arranged to meet at Maitland's to buy all the

217

things Lizzie needed for her house. It was easily the biggest shop in town and stood squarely on the central corner, not far from the Town Hall and the library. Jess arrived, breathless and rushed, a bit later than Lizzie. She liked Maitland's. It was a shop that sold everything and Jess loved to wander from one department to the next, looking at hair ribbons, armchairs, step-ladders, carpets, writing-paper, tea-cups. Best of all, she liked to watch the little cages attached to wires overhead, as they whirled on their way from counter to office with the money and back again with the change and the receipt. Buying and selling in Maitlands was always accompanied by this merry sound of flying money-carriers.

First Jess and Lizzie went to the department that sold curtain materials. Jess was amazed at how quickly Lizzie could make up her mind. *She* would have dithered all day trying to choose between the pink and the blue, the checked or the flowery. Lizzie was very definite. Within ten minutes, she had made all her decisions, referring to a scrap of paper with the measurements of every window listed.

'I'll have this green and white gingham for the kitchen and bathroom, Jess. That'll be eight yards. And that pretty floral pattern over there – the pink and blue one – for the living room. I'll need ten yards of that. Now, the bedroom. Look! There it is! See that yellow and white stripe, Jess? That will be just the thing. Six of that. There we are! That was easy! And I'd better get four dozen curtain rings too. What a job it's going to be, sewing on all those rings!'

'I'll he-lp,' offered Jess nobly. Her sewing was not much better than her knitting but she thought she could probably manage to sew on some curtain rings.

Lizzie paid for the material and handed over her ration book. Not one coupon had ever been cut from it before! The assistant pulled a cord to send the money whirling on its way to the office and then carefully cut ten coupons from the book. Lizzie stuffed the parcels in her string bags.

In the crockery department, Lizzie chose six of everything – cups, saucers, dishes and plates, all in a blue willow pattern. And then, in the next department, knives, forks and spoons. Jess gave Lizzie's name and address to the nice, black-dressed saleswoman and explained that she wanted them sent.

'They'll be there tomorrow dear,' said the woman to Jess as she wrote '29A Lime Avenue' clearly on the docket.

'Now, Jess, hardware. It must be down in the basement, I think,' and Lizzie led the way downstairs. It was quiet down there. They were the only customers. The one salesman (or, rather, salesboy as he seemed to be) was high up a ladder arranging tins of paint on a shelf.

Lizzie scuttled about choosing saucepans and brooms and bringing them back, one by one, to the counter. Jess felt she wasn't really much help. Lizzie knew exactly what she wanted. So Jess waited by the counter and stacked up the things as Lizzie brought them.

The salesboy, in his grey overall, backed slowly down his ladder and came across to Jess.

'Can I help you?' he asked.

Jess looked up at him, startled. He had round glasses. She knew him at once. It was Foggy Healey!

'*You're* the boy in Jack Stevens' gang!' she blurted out loudly. '*You're* the friend of Silver-Bike!'

219

Foggy went white. He looked back nervously over his shoulder.

'Shsh!' he whispered anxiously. 'I was lucky to get this job. Don't let on that I was in Jack's gang.' Foggy lowered his voice still further and spoke urgently, gripping Jess's wrist hard.

'I know Jack'll split on me in the end. He always does. But it *was* an accident! I never meant to do it! Can't you tell your Dad it was an accident? He might stick up for me. Can't you give me a chance?'

Jess was puzzled. She tried to pull her arm away but Foggy still held it tight.

'*What* was an accident?' she whispered back to Foggy.

'The fire. The fire on the boat. Jack made me run up into the boat. He said it was a test – or he'd chuck me out of the gang. I had to get a spoon – a spoon or a fork – and bring it right back to him. To show I wasn't scared. But I was scared. Jack was cutting through the ropes.'

'And did you go right on to the boat?' asked Jess, still in a whisper. Light was beginning to dawn. She could hardly speak for excitement and fear. She desperately hoped Lizzie wouldn't come back yet with another saucepan.

Foggy nodded.

'I *had* to,' he said. 'They were all standing round watching. And Jack kept sawing at the rope with his knife. It was dark inside. I felt my way through that room with all the furniture. Then into that kitchen-place. There was a bit of moonlight in there. But I couldn't see any spoons. I lit a match. It was just so I could see. Then I heard Jack whistle. They were going to give the boat a push. I was scared. I thought I'd

220

never get off in time. I saw the spoons and made a grab. I knocked over the bottle of kerosene. It smashed all over the floor. I dropped the match and ran. The boat was moving. I had to jump into the water to get back. Then we *all* ran. Back to our bikes by the track. I never knew about the fire till it was all in the paper. It must have been the match. But I never meant it. Jack's gone. I don't know where he is. If they catch him he's bound to put it all on to me.'

Foggy stopped suddenly and let go of Jess's wrist. Lizzie was coming back. Jess was now as white as he was.

'Here we are, Jess,' said Lizzie cheerfully. 'This is the best one. That's the lot now.'

'I'll tell Dad,' whispered Jess to Foggy, turning away so Lizzie wouldn't see her lips move. 'He might be able to help.'

'Thanks,' muttered Foggy and reached for his pencil to write down Lizzie's name and address and to add up all her purchases.

'Is it your Grandma?' Foggy asked Jess, nodding towards Lizzie.

'No,' said Jess. 'Just a friend. *She* was the one in the boat. The night of the fire. She's deaf.'

Foggy gripped the counter.

'But Jack said it was just some old looney! A mad old witch, he said it was!'

Jess said nothing. Lizzie paid Foggy and they waited in silence for the change. Then Jess and Lizzie walked to the lift, leaving Foggy staring blankly after them.

'Thanks, Jess,' said Lizzie, patting her on the arm. 'You were such a help.'

Jess felt she'd been no help at all but perhaps

Lizzie liked to have her there. She found her bike propped against the verandah-post outside the shop and, with a wave to Lizzie, she rode off home, burning with news.

'Jack Stevens' gang!' she said to herself. 'Old Silver-Bike!'

Jess told Dad the minute he got in from work. Dad rang Constable Lithgow and asked him if he could drop in. The constable was at the front door ten minutes later. Jess told him Foggy's story.

'Jack Stevens!' he exclaimed. 'Yes, I know that lad. He's been in trouble before. *And* his gang. Never anything serious, mind. They're just a lot of larrikins really but this time they've gone too far. Thanks, Jess. I'd better get back to the station straight away. We'll be after Jack Stevens tonight.'

But it took the police rather longer to find Jack Stevens than they thought it would. All the rest of the gang were lying low, not even getting in touch with each other but keeping on at work as if nothing had happened. Jack Stevens himself had disappeared. Even his mother and father had no idea where he was. The police eventually ran him to earth right down at Tempy, working on a mallee farm. Once they'd brought him back to Glencarra, they soon found all the other boys at home, one by one Constable Lithgow began his questions and soon had their story pieced together.

'Why on earth did Foggy *tell* me, Dad?' Jess asked her father over tea later that week. 'He didn't have to. I'd never have guessed. He just gave it all away.'

'I expect he thought you knew already. He probably thought the police knew too – or that they soon would know. He wanted to be sure you knew that he

222

hadn't lit the fire on purpose. He didn't realize he was giving the whole thing away.'

'*Was* the fire an accident, do you think?'

'Yes. I think it probably was. Nico knows Foggy quite well. He says he's not the sort of boy to start a fire on purpose. Anyway, his account of what happened has the ring of truth about it.'

'But why did Silver-Bike and his gang go down there to the boats in the first place? They must have been up to something.'

Jess had to wait for the constable's next visit for an answer. Then, at last, everything began to become clearer.

'You see, Mr McCallum,' said Constable Lithgow, loosening his collar and stretching out his legs under the kitchen table where Mum was setting out the cups of tea, 'it turns out that Tiger Hawkins was behind it after all – though he had nothing to do with the fire or with cutting the ropes. He's told us the truth – but not the *whole* truth. The boys all say that a couple of months back, when old Tiger was passing through the district, they chased him along the track and threatened him and generally got his wind up. That's where those boys are a blessed nuisance. They can make people scared and that leads to trouble. Anyway, Tiger promised to tell them about something really worth pinching if they'd only leave him alone. So he told them all about the gold-nugget brooch and how it was kept on the barge and how there was no one there to guard it except a couple of little kids and a deaf old lady. He even said he knew exactly where it was – though, in fact, he didn't. A few weeks later he saw the boys again and agreed to meet them near the barge at one o'clock on the

Sunday morning. He reckoned they could easily creep on board and he'd show them where the brooch was. Jack Stevens and his mates turned up at one all right but no sign of Tiger. They waited around for an hour or so. Still no Tiger. Then they got tired of waiting and Jack went on board the barge while the others kept on the look-out. He had a torch with him and he took a good look into every cabin. There was no one there at all. No kids. The bunks were empty. And in one cabin there was the most terrible mess. Clothes, blankets, everything thrown all over the floor. Then Jack knew that Tiger must have beaten them to it. He'd come early and pinched the brooch himself. Jack came racing out to the others in a fury. He said he was going to cut the ropes and pull up the chain on the "old girl's" boat. But first he made Foggy go on board to test him. And you know what that led to.'

'What will happen to them?' asked Jess. 'And what about Tiger Hawkins?'

'He's never been in trouble before so I think he'll probably get off with a suspended sentence. Most likely he'll be "bound over" for eighteen months or so. That means he won't have to go to prison. But he *will* have to be sure to be of "good behaviour" as we say. Old Tiger's often done odd jobs for various blockies around here so he won't have any trouble finding work. He likes to camp out but with the winter coming on he'd be better under cover. We'll see if we can find him a job that gives him a bed too. That'd be the best thing. In a couple of years he'll be on the move again, I'd say. These old swaggies get restless if they have to stay in one place for too long.'

'And what about the boys?' Jess asked again,

feeling oddly relieved that Tiger wouldn't have to stay in prison.

'Well, lassie,' said the constable, 'that fire is a very serious matter. Even if it *was* an accident, it's still a serious matter. I reckon the magistrate'll be pretty firm. He'll probably send Jack to the Castlemaine Reformatory for three months or so and Foggy down to Rupertswood in Sunbury. Best to keep them apart. The other boys might get off with a warning. They've all had a nasty shock and they're not likely to bother us again. That farmer down in Tempy really stuck up for Jack Stevens. Said he'd never had a better worker. He's even willing to take him back on the farm when his sentence is over. So Jack's a lucky lad. Let's hope Maitland's will take Foggy back too.'

'Dad,' said Jess, 'how was it that Tiger Hawkins didn't know it was Jack's gang that untied Lizzie's boat and set off the fire? He must have guessed they did it. He knew they were all coming there to meet him at one in the morning. Why didn't he tell the police about them – especially when the police thought *he'd* done it himself?'

'I'm not sure, Jess. What do you think, Constable?'

'Perhaps there's "honour among thieves" as they say. Or at least among old-timers like Tiger,' said the constable. 'Or perhaps he was scared that the gang would get after him if he gave them away. So he just stuck to his story that he took the brooch and ran off but didn't touch the ropes or the chain and didn't see any fire. It was all true enough though it left out a lot.'

The constable paused. Everyone round the table was silent. Dad was frowning.

'It's lucky Kenny and Snowy weren't on that

barge,' he said. 'They might have come off badly if they'd come face to face with Jack. I'm glad Jack had no idea they were sleeping in your humpy near by. And, of course, Jack knew nothing about *you*, Jess. He'd never set eyes on you, had he?'

Jess turned rather red and stared into her tea-cup.

'Well, yes, he had,' she admitted. 'I met the whole gang one Sunday on the track. They all crowded round me and told me to keep right away from that bit of the river. And on another Sunday, I saw them again but I hid in the bush so they didn't see me. I was really scared of them, Dad.'

'Why on earth didn't you tell us, girl?' said Dad sharply. 'You might have prevented all this trouble.'

'I thought you wouldn't let me go to the river if I told you. So I just kept quiet. I wish I hadn't now.'

'Well, let it be a lesson to you,' said Dad. He still sounded annoyed, even angry.

19
Anniversary

The next Sunday, the day of the Anniversary, Jess was up very early, practising the 23rd Psalm under her hot shower. 'It's funny,' she thought, 'how I always sing so much better in the bathroom.'

'Mary,' she heard Dad say to Mum out in the kitchen, 'I'm getting sick and tired of that 23rd Psalm.'

'Oh Arthur! What a thing to say! And we had it at our wedding too!'

226

'Did we dear?' said Dad mildly.

'You know, Jess,' said Mum over breakfast, 'I'm so glad Lizzie's coming to dinner today but I'm not sure that you should have invited her and the boys to the Anniversary. They're not supposed to come into our church. Father Byrne won't like it. He's very strict.'

'I asked Lizzie about that,' said Jess. 'She said she wouldn't worry him by even mentioning it to him. She said what the eye doesn't see the heart doesn't grieve over.'

Mum looked rather doubtful about this view but she let it pass.

Jess had her new blue dress on by ten o'clock. It had been hanging in her wardrobe for a month now, all ready for this great day. Often she'd opened the wardrobe to look at it and to run her hand up and down the pleats to enjoy the feel of soft material. At last she was able to wear it. She put on her new white socks and her best black shoes, polished by Dad to a brilliant shine. She picked up her new white gloves.

'Mum, I *do* wish I had long plaits like Rona's,' she said sadly as she gazed at herself in the mirror, looking with dissatisfaction at her short ginger hair.

'Your hair is very nice as it is dear,' said Mum in her comforting voice. 'Now off you go or they'll think you're never coming.'

At St Cuthbert's, all the Sunday School children in their fresh new clothes were milling excitedly up and down the aisles. Four long rows of benches stretched right across the church beneath the pulpit, from the organ to the vestry door. They were banked in tiers with high benches at the back and low ones in front. The whole church was overflowing with flowers.

There were flowers tumbling in cascades from the window ledges and flowers hanging from the pulpit and flowers in the entrance porch and flowers tied with white ribbons to every pew. Their heavy, sweet smell filled the church. Their rich colours transformed St Cuthbert's from its usual plain, sensible, Sunday appearance to an exotic garden. Jess gasped in amazement.

The children rushed to clamber up on to the benches, jostling and pushing and talking in whispers until they found their right places. The girls were banked on one side, the boys on the other. All of them faced the empty pews of the church and waited for the congregation to arrive. At about half-past-ten, people began to trickle in. Those who came early could be sure of a good seat near the front.

Jess looked out for her family. Not here yet. Dad had been going to pick up Kenny and Snowy from the barge first, and then Lizzie. They wouldn't be long. Mum and Laura and Nico would be walking.

'There's Mum now,' whispered Jess to Rona, her heart giving a thump of excitement. 'And Laura and Nico. And there's Dad! And look, there's Lizzie behind him. Doesn't she look nice? And here comes Kenny and there's Snowy. Rona! Look at that!' Jess was pointing up the aisle.

Rona whispered 'Shh' but Jess took no notice. She was staring and staring, half standing in her place, her eyes stretched wide open. Down the aisle they came – Mum and Dad, Nico and Laura, Lizzie and Kenny and Snowy. And there, right behind them, was a little figure swinging confidently along on two crutches, a little girl with straight black hair and a round, smiling face.

'It's Annie!' gasped Jess softly. 'It must be Annie! She's back!'

Kenny waved to Jess and pointed excitedly to Annie. Jess nodded. Mum hustled them all into a pew, telling Kenny firmly not to wave in church. The two boys were spruced up as Jess had never seen them before in pressed grey shorts, long grey socks and dark grey jumpers. They had startlingly new white sand shoes on their feet. Even Lizzie looked different. In place of her old loose 'missionary dress', as Jess called it, she wore a navy-blue suit. Still no hat, of course, no gloves, no hand-bag, but, all the same, Lizzie didn't look so very different now from all the other neat, navy-blue-clad ladies in the church. Jess didn't know whether to feel glad or sorry.

No sooner were Kenny and Snowy in their pew than Jess saw them both go down on their knees on the bare boards of the floor. She blushed with embarrassment. Oh dear, she thought miserably, I forgot to tell them we don't do that sort of thing here. Everyone will notice. But most people were so busy looking intently along the rows of children to find their own that they didn't seem to notice Kenny and Snowy kneeling. Annie didn't try to kneel. She put her crutches down on the floor and wriggled herself up on to the seat, gazing around at the memorial tablets on the walls. Mum smiled up at Jess.

The church was full. There were even chairs in the aisles now. Eleven o'clock. Time to begin. Mr Adam, in his long black gown with two neat white bands at the neck, walked slowly into the church and up to his pulpit.

'Let us worship God!' he said in his rich Scottish

voice that still had a faint tinge of sadness even on this happy festival day.

They were off! 'Onward, upward!' sang the children triumphantly. Every mother and father had their eyes fixed on their own children. Then came 'The Saviour of Galilee' and a rousing chorus, so utterly different from St Cuthbert's usual hymns, 'Will your anchor hold in the storms of life?' Jess knew Mum would like that one. She'd sung it herself at her own Sunday School Anniversary, all those years ago in Ballarat, and Jess had often heard her humming it to herself while she did the dusting. Mum was smiling now as she listened.

'And now,' said Mr Adam, 'Jessica McCallum is going to sing for us the 23rd Psalm to that fine old tune Wiltshire!'

Jess stood up. All the faces in front of her went blurry. The organist played over the first line very softly and then gave her the note. Jess took a deep breath. She began to sing.

> The Lord's my shepherd, I'll not want,
> He makes me down to lie
> In pastures green, he leadeth me
> The quiet waters by.

Jess's voice rang out through the packed church as clear as a bell. She certainly wasn't the world's greatest singer as she'd sometimes fondly hoped. No second Madame Melba! But at least she sang in tune and, as Mum always said proudly, you could hear the words. Not that anyone really needed to hear the words of that psalm. Most people there knew them off by heart. And Jess needed no book to remind her which verse came next. As she sang she could see

230

several people in the congregation silently making the old familiar words with their lips. There was Mum wiping her eyes and there was Lizzie doing the same even though she couldn't hear a word Jess sang. Kenny and Snowy and Annie simply gazed up at Jess in open admiration and astonishment.

Jess was at the last verse already. The middle verses seemed to have flown past almost without her noticing them.

> Goodness and mercy all my life
> Shall surely follow me
> And in God's house for evermore
> My dwelling place shall be.

There was a hush of absolute silence in the church. It seemed as if no one even breathed. Jess sat down. Mr Adam stood up.

'Thank you, Jessica,' he said seriously. 'And now,' he went on, 'you will find my next text for this morning in St John's gospel, chapter 21, at verse 6.

> And He said unto them, Cast
> the net on the right side of
> the ship, and ye shall find.
> They cast therefore, and now
> they were not able to draw it
> for the multitude of fishes.

Jess turned her head and looked up instinctively at the window whose tiny coloured panes she had counted on so many other Sundays. Suddenly her window made sense! The green sea, the red and gold fish, the disciples heaving on the nets, a white figure waving from the yellow sandy shore. So *that's* what it was all about! Mr Adam's kind, sad voice droned on but Jess didn't hear another word of his sermon.

While the collection was being taken up, the children romped through 'Violets and Daisies' with new gusto. Then came a prayer. Last of all was 'Fling wide the gate of the temple!' and Mr Adam gave the benediction. It was over. Jess was relieved to have her solo safely past but the wonderful event was finished all too soon and now there'd be a whole long year of ordinary Sundays until the next Anniversary came round. She hurried out of the vestry door with all the other children and raced round to the front to meet her family as they came out. She pulled off her white gloves now. Mum surely wouldn't expect her to keep them on any longer. There they all came, down the front steps together. There was lots of hugging and kissing.

'You were splendid, Jess!' said Dad.

'You were real good, Jess!' said Kenny.

'But I don't think you'd better be a famous singer,' added Snowy.

'Why not?' Jess felt nettled.

'You do go a bit red in the face,' he explained kindly.

'And this is Annie!' said Lizzie to Jess, her hand on the shoulder of the little girl with crutches.

'Hullo Annie,' said Jess, smiling.

'Hullo Jess. I thought your song was beautiful.'

Kenny explained how Annie had arrived on the train that very morning.

'We knew she was coming, Jess, but we didn't tell you. We wanted you to get a big surprise.'

'Well, I certainly did!' said Jess. 'I could hardly

believe my eyes when I saw her coming down the aisle with you.'

'Funny church you've got, Jess,' said Snowy in a confidential whisper.

'Funny!' exclaimed Jess indignantly. 'What's so funny about it?'

'I didn't mean to be rude or anything. It's just that you haven't got any statues or candles or things like that,' he explained candidly. 'We've got lots.'

Dad took the boys and Annie back to the barge. Lizzie walked home with the rest of them for Sunday dinner. Jess walked too, pushing her bike beside her on the footpath by the ragged palm trees.

Mum had put the leaf into the dining-room table. Six for Sunday dinner! That's what Mum loved to see – a good table full of people and a good leg of mutton for Dad to carve. And all the Drurys were coming in for afternoon tea. She'd just have time to knock up a quick batch of scones after dinner while the oven was still nice and hot.

'Well, Jess,' said Dad as he began to carve. 'You did very well this morning. Your mother and I were proud of you. I wish your Grandfather McCallum had been alive to hear you. He loved that psalm best of all. Do you remember how he gave you a shilling for learning it off by heart? You were only about five or six then, I think. It wasn't long before he died.'

When everyone was served and Dad had said grace, suddenly the phone rang, shattering the peace of Sunday dinner. He went to answer it while all the others went on eating as quietly as they could.

'Silly time for anyone to ring!' muttered Mum under her breath.

'Long distance!' called Dad to Mum with his hand over the mouthpiece.

Everyone listened. Dad's voice sounded puzzled.

'Yes. Yes. This is Arthur McCallum speaking. From Glencarra, yes. Sorry. I can't quite hear you. Who? Mrs Johnson? Oh yes, of course! I know! Oh, Mrs Johnson! I'm so sorry! On Thursday, you say? ... What a terrible shock for you, Mrs Johnson. . . . What's that? . . . Sorry, I can't quite hear. . . . To us? At Byron's Creek? Good heavens! . . . *what* was it he said? . . .' There was a long pause while Dad listened. 'Well, thank you again for ringing, Mrs Johnson.' Jess thought Dad's voice sounded rather odd now. Very wobbly. Not like him at all. He was speaking again. 'Please accept my deepest sympathy, Mrs Johnson. Goodbye.'

Dad put down the phone. He turned back to the table. Everyone had stopped eating. They all waited for him to speak.

'Uncle Norval's dead!' he said. 'He died of a sudden heart attack on Thursday. The funeral's on Wednesday down at Leongatha. Poor old Norval! I've known him all my life!' Dad turned towards Mum.

'But Mary,' he said, 'he's left us his house! His house at Byron's Creek! For our holidays, Norval said. And Mary, do you know what he said to his mother? That we'd always made him feel so welcome in our family circle!'

Dad sat down heavily in his chair. There was a stunned silence. Lizzie was looking from face to face, trying to fathom what was going on. At last Jess burst out, 'But Dad! We didn't! We didn't! We didn't make him welcome at all! We thought he was so boring. The only thing we liked was the lamingtons! Oh Dad! Isn't it awful! I wish I'd been kinder to him!' Jess was nearly crying now.

'Well Jess,' said Mum, putting her arm around her, 'you did all complain about poor old Uncle Norval rather a lot but we *tried* to make him feel at home. It was hard going sometimes, I have to admit, but we did our best. Perhaps it all meant much more to him than we ever knew. Perhaps that's all he wanted – someone to ask him about his health and his house and his mother. Someone to listen. We all certainly did that now, didn't we Jess?'

'A holiday house!' cried Nico, excitedly. 'When can we go, Dad?'

'Not till Christmas, I'm afraid. We'll have to save up our petrol coupons till then,' said Dad.

Jess wrote down for Lizzie what had been going on.

'I'm very sorry to hear about your friend's death, Mr McCallum,' Lizzie said at once to Dad. 'You were at school together?'

Dad nodded and Laura went to get the photo of the cricket team in 1915 to show her. Everyone felt sad. No one could talk. Nico and Laura and Jess felt sorry they'd moaned and complained so much about Uncle Norval on every one of his annual visits.

'Poor old Norval!' said Dad again and they finished their dinner in silence. Mum's trifle, delicious as ever, was eaten without the usual words of praise.

By half past three, the dishes were done, the

golden-brown scones were cooling on a wire rack on the kitchen table and the Drurys were arriving at the front door with Father Byrne. He'd driven them up from the barge – Annie couldn't walk so far with her crutches – so Mum asked him in for afternoon tea too.

'Twelve!' murmured Mum happily to herself. She was really in her element. With Jess and Laura to help her, she dashed briskly back and forth from the kitchen to the front room, bringing the best cups and saucers, the scones, the jam and cream, the chocolate cake made with Grandma's recipe, the silver tea-pot, the milk and sugar and teaspoons. Mum just had everyone settled with a cup of tea and a scone with jam and cream when the front-door bell peeled loudly. Everyone jumped except Lizzie who went on calmly sipping her tea.

Jess put down her cup and went to the front door. It was Rona! And not just Rona but Iona, Eriskay and Sandray as well! They stood there together on the verandah, their long smooth plaits hanging down in front of their shoulders.

'I've come to see your mother,' said Rona importantly, 'just to show her something.' She had a blue envelope in her hand.

'Come in! Come in!' cried Jess, 'but where's James?'

'He didn't want to come,' said Iona softly. 'He's too shy.'

'Mum!' called Jess as she led the girls into the sitting room. 'Here's Rona and Iona and Eriskay and Sandray! They've got something to show you!'

The four girls came into the room and stood silently in a row, gazing at all the people.

'What is it, Rona dear?' asked Mum, smiling at her. 'Do sit down, girls. You must have some scones and tea.'

The girls sat down promptly on the carpet. There was nowhere else to sit. Rona held out the blue envelope to Mum.

'We've had a letter from Dad!' she said. 'A real letter! Six pages! And he's all right! He's still a prisoner-of-war but he says he's all right! And Mum said, would you like to look at it! She said please don't read it, but you can take it out and have a look.'

Mum had tears in her eyes as she took the letter out of the blue envelope. The paper was blue too – thin, pale-blue paper, covered with small black writing. Mum turned the pages over, one by one.

'Oh Rona!' she said at last. 'That's wonderful! I'm so thankful he's safe and well. Let's hope this war will soon be over and then he'll be back home with you all again!'

Jess had tears pricking in her eyes too and she blinked hard so no one would see.

'Can I have a look, Mum?' she said.

The pale-blue letter passed from hand to hand. Everyone wanted to feel it and see it. Everyone was careful not to read it. 'Dear Lil' was all they saw.

Then Mum folded the letter carefully up again and put it in the envelope and gave it back to Rona.

'There you are, dear. And please thank your mother very much. It was really kind of her to let us see it. I know how happy she must be. Now girls, how about some scones?'

Jess darted to the kitchen for four more plates and four mugs as the cups had run out. Laura made another pot of tea. Dad and Nico passed the scones and jam and cream. Rona, Iona, Eriskay and Sandray bit into their jammy, creamy scones, their faces shining with happiness. One day, when this war was over, their father would be coming home.

DEEP WATER

Set in Australia during the First World War, the story is told through 14-year-old Char. When her older brother enlists in the army, Char finds herself helping to run the farm. Drought, persecution and the horrifying massacre at Gallipoli affect Char and the entire community. But, throughout it all, Char remains determined that the settlers will survive . . . .

STRINGYBARK SUMMER

Sophie didn't want to spend the holidays miles away from home at Stringybark Mill. She wanted to stay at the farm and help her mother with the new baby when it came. But Sophie soon became absorbed in the busy daily life of the little township in the bush and grew to love Stringybark Mill. Through Grandpa she learned to love the horses too, especially old Clinker . . .

A Selected List of Fiction from Mammoth

While every effort is made to keep prices low, it is sometimes necessary to increase prices at short notice. Mammoth Books reserves the right to show new retail prices on covers which may differ from those previously advertised in the text or elsewhere.

The prices shown below were correct at the time of going to press.

☐	416 13972 8	**Why the Whales Came**	Michael Murpurgo	£2.50
☐	7497 0034 3	**My Friend Walter**	Michael Murpurgo	£2.50
☐	7497 0035 1	**The Animals of Farthing Wood**	Colin Dann	£2.99
☐	7497 0136 6	**I Am David**	Anne Holm	£2.50
☐	7497 0139 0	**Snow Spider**	Jenny Nimmo	£2.50
☐	7497 0140 4	**Emlyn's Moon**	Jenny Nimmo	£2.25
☐	7497 0344 X	**The Haunting**	Margaret Mahy	£2.25
☐	416 96850 3	**Catalogue of the Universe**	Margaret Mahy	£1.95
☐	7497 0051 3	**My Friend Flicka**	Mary O'Hara	£2.99
☐	7497 0079 3	**Thunderhead**	Mary O'Hara	£2.99
☐	7497 0219 2	**Green Grass of Wyoming**	Mary O'Hara	£2.99
☐	416 13722 9	**Rival Games**	Michael Hardcastle	£1.99
☐	416 13212 X	**Mascot**	Michael Hardcastle	£1.99
☐	7497 0126 9	**Half a Team**	Michael Hardcastle	£1.99
☐	416 08812 0	**The Whipping Boy**	Sid Fleischman	£1.99
☐	7497 0033 5	**The Lives of Christopher Chant**	Diana Wynne-Jones	£2.50
☐	7497 0164 1	**A Visit to Folly Castle**	Nina Beechcroft	£2.25

All these books are available at your bookshop or newsagent, or can be ordered direct from the publisher. Just tick the titles you want and fill in the form below.

Mandarin Paperbacks, Cash Sales Department, PO Box 11, Falmouth, Cornwall TR10 9EN.

Please send cheque or postal order, no currency, for purchase price quoted and allow the following for postage and packing:

UK	80p for the first book, 20p for each additional book ordered to a maximum charge of £2.00.
BFPO	80p for the first book, 20p for each additional book.
Overseas including Eire	£1.50 for the first book, £1.00 for the second and 30p for each additional book thereafter.

NAME (Block letters) ....

ADDRESS ....

....

....